A DECENT
RANSOM

A DECENT
RANSOM

A story of a kidnapping gone right

IVANA HRUBÁ

LARGO, USA

A D e c e n t R a n s o m
Copyright © 2008 by Ivana Hrubá.

For information, contact Kunati Inc., Book Publishers in both USA and Canada.
In USA: 6901 Bryan Dairy Road, Suite 150, Largo, FL 33777 USA
In Canada: 75 First Street, Suite 128, Orangeville, ON L9W 5B6 CANADA,
or e-mail to info@kunati.com.

FIRST EDITION

Designed by Kam Wai Yu
Persona Corp. | www.personaco.com

ISBN-13: 978-1-60164-162-5   EAN 9781601641625
FIC000000 FICTION/General

Published by Kunati Inc. (USA) and Kunati Inc. (Canada).
Provocative. Bold. Controversial.™

h t t p : / / w w w . k u n a t i . c o m

TM — Kunati and Kunati Trailer are trademarks
owned by Kunati Inc. Persona is a trademark owned by Persona Corp.
All other trademarks are the property of their respective owners.

Library of Congress Cataloging-in-Publication Data

Hrubá, Ivana.
    A decent ransom : a story of a kidnapping gone right / Ivana Hrubá.
-- 1st ed.
        p. cm.
    Summary: "A psychological drama involving kidnapping that explores
themes of betrayal, redemption and forgiveness"--Provided by publisher.
    ISBN 978-1-60164-162-5 (alk. paper)
    1. Brothers and sisters--Fiction. 2. Kidnapping--Fiction. 3. Poor--
Fiction. 4. Australia--Fiction. 5. Psychological fiction. I. Title.
    PR9619.4.H78D43 2008
    823'.92--dc22
                            2008024742

ACKNOWLEDGEMENTS

I am grateful and indebted to every single person at
Kunati Publishing.

I particularly want to thank my publisher Derek Armstrong for having
faith in this story, Kam Wai Yu for his wonderful artwork and
James McKinnon for liking the manuscript in the first place.

On a personal level I would like to thank my friends
Kylie Clark and Jane Panetta for taking the time to read
the very first draft and for the discussions that followed.

My special thanks go to my friend
James Kable who graciously donated his time to read the first,
the second, the third and the fourth draft.

Thank you Jamie for your insight and kindness.

A big thank you to Lynne Bradley,
Helen Kable and Gina Jeffery—thank you guys
for your support and enthusiasm.

My heartfelt thanks go to my editor,
the very patient and meticulous James McKinnon who misses
nothing—thank you James for your sharp eye, foresight and guidance.

Finally, my biggest thank you goes to Michael and to our boys
Eamon and Kian for being there.

I love you.

PART I

Dear God,

Please make Kenny change his mind. Please make him forget his plan. I have tried but he won't listen to me. I don't want him to kidnap that lady and I don't want to help him, but if you don't do something, he's going to make me. Please, God, help me just this once and I will never ask you for anything again. This time I promise.

Phoebus

1

It began with a perfect plan. Shape-wise we had a circle, a simple uncomplicated curve to guide us comfortably from one thing to another, an easy predictable ride promising a natural progression from A to B, C and D, and so on until we reached our destination. But somewhere down that smooth line, I think around F, it all went pear-shaped.

I had warned Kenny before it all started but he wouldn't listen.

You'll n—never pull it off, I told him. Kenny's only response was to burp.

Shirtless, he lounged on the sofa, drinking rum. In between swallows he grinned and pulled at his chest hair; to show how relaxed he felt, he drummed a beat on his stomach with his fingers.

What are you worried about? Kenny laughed, seeing I stood there with an anxious frown on my face. I've thought this thing through.

This statement did nothing to alleviate my fears. Indeed, excepting Uncle Clem, there was nothing I ever really feared more than Kenny's way of thinking things through.

You can't just k—kidnap people, I said, trying to sound firm. Of course, it didn't work. In those days, whenever I was upset, my stutter just became worse. Y—you just c—can't.

Kenny frowned. Suspending the beat, he clicked his spurs and flicked back his sombrero. Fixing me with a stare, he raised his eyebrow and held it there until I apologized. Then he slapped me on the shoulder and went back to drinking. A brief silence followed during which I corresponded with God while Kenny lay there contemplating his favorite tree just visible out of the kitchen window. The moment passed when Kenny cackled, the shrill sound reminding me of our mum, who also had liked to laze about in her underwear.

Indeed, looking at Kenny sprawled across the sofa, I really saw her tipping the bottle, her toothless mouth gaping wide and her cackle ringing in my ears.

Mum left us a long time ago. For a while, I missed her. I wrote to her a lot, always signing Kenny's name next to mine until one day he sprung me. He punched me in the face, and when I reeled backwards, he punched me in the stomach. As I lay on the lino, choking on the blood gushing out of my nose, the consequences of my subterfuge became painfully clear: Kenny was seriously pissed off. He stood over me a while looking grim, looking as if he couldn't decide what to do next, but eventually he bent to my ear and whispered, his words appearing in front of my eyes like skywriting. If you ever sign my name again, I will do to you things Uncle Clem wouldn't dream about. The words faded and I promised myself I would never mention mum again. Still, I thought about her from time to time, especially on days like today when Kenny hogged the sofa, drinking and cackling and looking like a bloated toad.

What are you staring at, you turd? Kenny suddenly asked, noticing that I hadn't cleared the table. Snapping out of my reverie, I jumped to it. Meanwhile, Kenny continued drinking and when he was done, he threw the empty bottle out the window. It hit the roof of the crapper and broke into pieces. At the sound, Kenny snapped his fingers. Seeing his mood was darkening, I quickly dropped to my knees and gently, carefully eased off his boots. Feeling more comfortable, Kenny stretched out and soon fell asleep.

I sat quietly by his side, watching over him. As he lay there sleeping, my brother looked to me as innocent as a newborn babe dreaming of good things to come. Relaxed, his face looked peaceful, the scars, the dents and the bumps barely visible; it was as if his real face came out of hiding, showing Kenny the way he was on the inside, a kind, generous and big-hearted man. Seeing him like this, I wished everybody could. However, deep down I knew people would always see Kenny only from the outside.

Of course, on the outside things are always a bit complicated. I had known from the beginning I should have handled everything differently. I should have talked to someone other than God, but the thing is, there truly was no one else. As far as I can remember, we had always lived alone. And I mean alone, with no other people around.

Pristine Mountain, population three, we used to joke, but it was true. Nobody ever came to see us. When I was little, I thought that people didn't come because they couldn't find our cottage hidden in the woods, but as I grew older I realized that people didn't come because they didn't want to know us. And who could blame them? After all, we were dirt poor, our mother was a drunk, and Kenny a dangerous psychotic beast best left alone. Accordingly, people avoided us like the plague. Even the cops let us be. Only once, when mum was still around, they came to make enquiries after the truck stop down the road from us burned down, but they were dead wrong. Still, they accused Kenny and they wanted to take him away, but Kenny barricaded us in the house and there was a bit of a siege. At first, the cops spoke to him through a funnel; however, as Kenny wouldn't budge, eventually they took out their weapons.

Kenny stood his ground. Sixteen years old and just four feet two inches high, he looked to me as powerful as God. The very image of brute force, Kenny faced the enemy in all his compact glory, standing motionless under the window. Of course, he had meant to fill the frame with his menacing pose, but being bootless, he had just managed to show the top of his sombrero. Nevertheless, he was terrifying to behold. His trusty sling in one hand and a full beer bottle in the other, Kenny roared at the fat cop who was in charge: come get me, Shorty! All hell broke loose.

When the cops charged, mum and I hid behind the kitchen sofa. Kenny, however, remained at the window, dodging bullets and giving as good as he got. From behind the couch we watched his every move, feeling very proud. Mum especially was deeply stirred. She fell into reminiscing about Kenny's dad, alleging Kenny had the same irresistible charisma, the kind of animal allure that made women swoon. She also claimed that she really missed him. This I strictly did not believe because when sober, mum maintained that Kenny's dad had been nothing but a loser. During the siege, though, mum kept drinking.

Takes after his dad, she slobbered, watching her firstborn slinging bottles through the window, and you could see just how pleased she was. Although I shared in her happiness, I hoped her claims weren't true because Kenny's dad had left us two weeks after coming out of jail, taking our television and the car. Mum had tried to stop him. She jumped on the bonnet and aimed her shotgun at him telling him to leave our things alone, but he just grabbed the gun by the barrel and knocked her out. Then he left and we never saw him again. Still, mum had a soft spot for Kenny all those years.

Anyway, all this happened a long time ago. The siege ended after the cops had busted every window in the house. Just as they were about to storm, new evidence surfaced implicating the owner of the shop, and the cops redirected their investigation, leaving us to sift through the debris in peace.

For a while our life went on quite as we were used to. Kenny kept his job in town, collecting garbage for the council, and mum stayed home looking after the house. Well, she was supposed to but she could never manage it, so it fell to me to do the housework after school. Still, we were happy until my dad came to live with us. Not long after he came, Kenny left. I didn't blame him; it was for the best, seeing father never took to him. He could just tolerate me, father said, but this tolerance did not extend to Kenny who got the strap fairly regularly. After Kenny left, I copped it because father said I was an ugly bastard and he was sick of looking at me. But then one night he broke my arm, accidentally, and by the time the cops brought me back from the hospital, he was gone. Then mum started corresponding with Noah. They fell in love and she moved out of town to be closer to him because he still had a couple of years before parole. So then I was truly alone and I was scared because Uncle Clem kept coming over. After a while I couldn't stand it anymore, so I tracked Kenny down and he came back to take care of me. Of course, when Kenny returned Uncle Clem stopped coming and nobody's seen him since.

From then on we lived very well. I mean, we weren't rich or anything, but we enjoyed being together and doing whatever we wanted. Well, Kenny did what he wanted, and I did whatever he wanted me to do. This was a perfect arrangement for us. Of course, at times Kenny could be harsh, even unreasonable, but to tell the truth, I wouldn't have had it any other way. I always knew that whatever decisions Kenny made, he made with good intentions, wanting only the best for me, and for that I was grateful.

After he got rid of Uncle Clem, Kenny got a job at the truck stop which by then had been revamped and put under new management. Kenny's job was to put petrol into people's cars. He also cleaned their windshields and pumped their tires, but only if they asked, and this suited him fine. Turning on the charm, Kenny told everyone there were waterfalls in the mountains. Pleased they'd cottoned onto something that was not in the brochure, the tourists always left a couple of bucks, especially after Kenny told them the waterfalls were pristine, like really clear water which nobody was allowed to see, and he gave directions. Sometimes people came back to complain because, of course, they never found them waterfalls, but Kenny never gave any money back. At any rate, nobody ever asked. I guess they could see it would have been pointless.

Four years went by in this fashion, each year much the same as the last. Then, just before last summer when I turned fourteen, Kenny took me out of school and got me a job at the truck stop too. I didn't like it at first, chiefly because I missed the library, but as the months went by, I changed my mind. After all, my leaving school had always been only a matter of time.

I had never been any good at school work. During lessons I preferred to do my own thing, either staring out the window or reading novels under my desk. Initially, reading hadn't been frowned upon, but when it came out that I only read paperbacks about the wild wild west, it was agreed my needs would be better served in Special Ed. Things did not get any better there. I tried to pay attention, but somehow I could never get Uncle Clem out of my head. I kept thinking about how much I hated him and what it would take to kill him. Yes, every day when I sat at my desk gazing into the sunshine, I imagined his death.

The manner of his demise varied, depending on what I was reading at the time. One day he would be hanged, another time he'd die from a gunshot to the heart or lie wounded in the middle of the prairie, bleeding to death like a stuck pig. I liked him to suffer. Some days I felt so inspired I had to kill him three or four times throughout the day, even at lunch, which I spent alone in the library. But Uncle Clem aside, school for me had always been a trial. My teachers considered me feeble-minded and my peers a weirdo to be avoided at all costs. Whenever I approached people, they scurried away like squirrels, or else I was shooed away as if I were a mangy dog. In class I sat alone and as I never said a word, what with my reading under the desk and not being asked an opinion, eventually people forgot I was there and stopped seeing me altogether. Given the situation, Kenny's decision to terminate my painful existence there was a blessing. The fact was, I never liked anybody from town and they plainly didn't like me because nobody ever questioned why I stopped coming.

From the first day I started work at the truck stop, I felt happier. I was in the kitchen mainly, washing dishes, but sometimes I was allowed behind the counter and this I liked because I could see Kenny outside, working the tourists over. It was there the idea first occurred to him.

That day I was out front selling pies. We were busy and Kenny was in good form bamboozling the tourists; at the end of our shift, he had cleared twenty-five bucks. We used the money to buy a box of wine and some beef jerky on the way home. We were really happy; it wasn't often we could afford treats. Kenny especially was feeling on top of the world. In the truck, he kept talking footy and slapping me on the back good-naturedly all the way up the mountain. He asked me about my day and even listened to my replies, wearing such an interested expression that I got suspicious and began to wonder a bit; the last time Kenny had shown such spirits, he finished up in the watch house. He had thrashed Uncle Clem, and although that had been a good thing, there was some unpleasantness. Kenny got arrested and it looked likely he was going to jail, but Uncle Clem couldn't be persuaded to press charges so the cops had had no choice but to let Kenny go. Of course Kenny gloated, lording it over me, laughing at my fears of losing him and saying he had always known he'd come up trumps. Seeing him so happy, I had gone along with it, pretending I agreed, but deep down I felt wretched, being certain he had just had a lucky escape. And now I was getting the same sinking feeling, that dreaded knot in the stomach telling me that something wasn't right.

When we got home, Kenny's good mood continued. Feeling exhilarated, he decided to have a soak; he sat in the bath with the door open, farting under water and cracking jokes while I prepared dinner. Everything was going well, I had the food ready by the time Kenny called me in to dry his back. I fetched his robe and his slippers, and then we sat down to our regular Sunday feed: beans and sausages and creamy potato mash. It was then Kenny made his announcement.

We're going to kidnap a rich woman, Kenny announced as I carefully ladled the hot beans into his bowl. We'll clean up! He banged his spoon triumphantly on the table, grinning from ear to ear.

Truly, at first I didn't know what to say. Having heard a lot of crap from Kenny in my life, I only sighed, keeping my face devoid of all expression. But then as Kenny persevered with the grin, beaming at me expectantly, I ventured to express my doubt.

You'll never pull it off.

In response Kenny cuffed me, telling me to shut up and listen.

It'll be a piece of cake, Kenny proclaimed confidently, tucking into his mash. She's home alone all day. He began to talk about his plan, speaking and eating at the same time, and I had trouble keeping up; he certainly wasn't making much sense to me. Indeed, Kenny was very much on edge. He tore at his sausages and shoveled the beans into his mouth at an extraordinary speed, shouting and gesticulating, and all the while he never took his eyes off me, gauging my reaction. I tried to look happy but on the inside I felt only dread, which I hoped to keep contained, but eventually some of that dread showed on the surface because all of a sudden Kenny stopped dead in his tracks and rolled his eyes. Clearly he was frustrated with me because he sighed and banged his fist on the table so hard that the dishes shook, and then he ordered me to get him a pencil. I quickly fetched it while Kenny snorted at me to show his contempt, but I knew the worst was over because he began drawing the plan on the tablecloth which, luckily for me, happened to be the paper the butcher used to wrap our sausages in.

He drew the house fairly accurately, I must say. I knew the place from way back when I had a job delivering real estate pamphlets, and I thought Kenny's sketch was very lifelike. One got the feeling of space and light and fresh air through all those big floor-length windows and the wide porch. I told Kenny they had a pool at the back but he cuffed me again, growling that he wasn't going to get bogged down in details. He gestured for me to sit down so I quickly cleared the dishes and put a bottle of rum on the table.

Kenny took a swig and tapped the end of his spoon on the butcher paper right in the middle of the driveway on our blueprint, thus indicating that he was ready for dessert. I served the sweets which, as usual, were the leftover cheesecake I got from work on Sundays because they didn't like to keep it past seven days.

I carved the pie, outwardly keeping calm but on the inside I was growing seriously worried because I could see that Kenny had his mind made up. I knew I didn't want to do it, but I also knew that no matter what, I would always stand by him. He was the only family I had left and he had always done the right thing by me.

I asked him if the woman was wealthy.

The husband's loaded, Kenny replied, chewing furiously.

How do you know?

Kenny frowned. I knew he was displeased that I had the nerve to question him, but I was too anxious to think clearly.

They're worth a bundle, that's all you need to know, Kenny eventually mumbled, making a sudden movement towards me. Thinking a cuff was coming, I ducked, and when Kenny saw me ducking, he laughed. He had only wanted a toothpick. I scurried off to get one. While Kenny picked his teeth, I opened the box of wine and then we sat around talking. Kenny was in good humor. Several times he playfully tweaked my ear, saying that I was an ugly bastard but even so he was going to make me rich, and I should stop worrying about not having a girlfriend.

I didn't say a word. I never liked to talk about that. Kenny, however, mentioned it every time he brought a girl home, so a long time ago I developed a strategy, which was to turn a deaf ear. Usually Kenny never noticed my discomfort, and the night he came up with the plan was no exception. Ignoring my pensive mood, he offered to play cards with me and left me some of the cheesecake, and even though things did not progress like we planned, I remember that night fondly.

2

Kenny spent a week checking it out. He told me he wanted to make sure everything went smoothly because our future was at stake. I knew he meant it because Kenny was determined we wouldn't end up in jail like our dads, whom he hated and blamed for everything bad that's ever happened to us. Consequently, we preferred not to talk about them. The most we ever said was when their obituaries arrived.

There goes a stupid fuck, Kenny said, squinting at the notice announcing my father's death. Heart failure, the note said, alleging a quick and merciful expiry. Kenny, although pleased with the end result, was somewhat disappointed. He would have preferred more pain, some drawn out illness requiring torturous treatment accompanied by slow, unstoppable deterioration of the senses; in short, he would have liked father to suffer.

To cheer him up, I ventured an opinion.

Yeah, a stupid f–f–fuck, I repeated, feeling a curious mixture of relief and regret. Having uttered the word that Kenny had forbidden me to use, I regretted the breach of conduct; nevertheless, I felt the occasion permitted such a lapse. Kenny must have sensed how I felt because he didn't say a word, just raised his eyebrow and slapped me on the back in a gesture of well done. Still, I knew this was a special treat. Normally, I wouldn't have dared to swear simply because Kenny couldn't stand it when I got bogged down in the stutter; what with it being so bad it was ever present, even in my thoughts. Anyway, I didn't blame Kenny for getting irate; I myself knew that swearing did not agree with me. No matter how hard I tried, everything always came out wrong so one day Kenny banged down his fist and laid down the law, and I was forbidden to ever swear.

At any rate, I got away with it when our dads died. It was uncanny how they pegged out within days of each other, uncanny because they had never had anything to do with each other, or us for that matter, having left our mother before her pregnancies became known even to her. Sure, they came to visit mum from time to time after we were born, but it was mostly to get a good feed or to lie low. They certainly didn't bother with us; we were good enough to fetch beer but that was about it. That and a kick up the backside was as close to fatherly affection as we ever got.

When, a couple of days later, another obituary arrived, we were stunned. It wasn't so much the news this time; it was the timing, the apparently coincidental nature of our dads' deaths coming so close one after the other that had us perplexed. Kenny was the first one to recover his spirits.

There goes the other stupid fuck, Kenny guffawed, squinting closely at the paper to find out the details of his dad's passing. It appeared the poor sod had died in mysterious circumstances in the communal latrines when a knife had been plunged into his belly while he was doing business. Kenny found it a fitting end.

Indeed, I cautiously agreed, wisely resisting the temptation to swear, being certain it wouldn't be tolerated a second time. But I was wrong. Kenny felt the occasion deserved to be properly commemorated and pegged the notice to his favorite tree. Then he climbed into the hammock and rocked to and fro, cackling quietly to himself.

Eventually Kenny put both notices in my cookbook, so that I could have our dads' bad example on my mind. Indeed, as he made me cook all the time, our dads were never too far from my thoughts.

By all accounts, our dads had been losers. Perpetually incarcerated for offenses too pathetic to recount, our dads were the joke of the underworld, perceived as dumb, hapless bunglers given to haphazard executions of opportunistic crimes. This lack of respect weighed heavily upon Kenny, who vowed never to follow in their footsteps.

It's all in the planning, he declared to me passionately whenever he was drunk, and I never for one second doubted his good intentions. I knew that he desperately wanted to be a hero, a champion of the poor, a real man capable of pulling off the most ambitious, grandest scheme. Yes, my Kenny dreamed of infamy on a large scale, desiring to come up with a tremendous plan, something really special, so utterly monumental, that it would make people's eyeballs spin. Of course, up to now I had fully supported his dream, thinking it would always be just that. I truly never thought we'd get involved in a kidnapping.

Our fathers' deaths had put Kenny in a peculiar mood. It was as if he had realized that time was of the essence and if he didn't act soon, nothing would ever happen. He brooded, full of nervous energy, one minute pacing up and down the room, and the next lying in the hammock, staring into space. This went on for weeks and I worried about him, not knowing how to help, until the day he told me about the plan. As soon as he told me I got that hopeless feeling, the sense of foreboding that I always carried within me intensified, and I knew we were heading for disaster. However, I also realized that resistance would be futile; the wheels were in motion and there was nothing I could do to stop them, so I resigned myself to my fate.

It took him a week of surveillance to decide what the next step would be. Apparently, the woman, our intended victim, lived a predictable life full of routine tasks. A regular housewife, she went out to shop, visit the library and the gym; at home, she spent her time in the garden. The husband was hardly ever there, working at his pool shop or going off on business. There were no children and no neighbors; in fact, the whole thing was set up so beautifully, Kenny was convinced the kidnap was meant to be.

The following Sunday, right after I served the cheesecake, Kenny announced that he was ready for action.

The husband's away, Kenny grinned into my face, tapping his watch. She'll be getting home from yoga just about now.

For a moment, I could not think and I swear my knees were buckling under me. I never really thought … aah … I kinda hoped … Christ …

Seeing the look on my face, Kenny laughed and blew his nose into the butcher paper. Then he scrunched the whole thing into a ball and threw it at me, saying, here, have a swig, you little turd, and then he forced me to drink out of his bottle. The rum burned my throat but didn't stop my knees shaking.

We got in the truck. Straightaway I saw that Kenny wasn't joking.

He showed me a length of rope, a reel of cello tape, and a ski cap to pull over her eyes. He also had a rag to stuff in her mouth. I felt sick to my stomach at the sight of it. It was the same rag he used to clean out the exhaust pipe. Nevertheless, we set out directly after Kenny found the cricket bat he planned to show in case she had any funny ideas.

Down the mountain we went. Below us the town slumbered; even at this hour there was hardly a light to be seen. Indeed, it seemed to me we were the only people alive and I wondered what the world would be like if we were the only ones left. Plunged into these pleasant thoughts I drove, carefully spiraling through the darkness. It wasn't until we were near our destination that it suddenly occurred to me that we never made any preparations for her stay. I slowed down.

Where are we going to put her? I asked Kenny, catching him unawares.

What? He mumbled, contracting his eyebrow as if he did not understand what I was saying. I swerved to pull over, but Kenny grabbed the wheel, making me stay on the road. I drove on. From time to time, I glanced at him but he stared straight ahead without saying a word.

She'll stay in your room, Kenny eventually replied. The way he looked at me clearly showed that he was dead serious so I resigned myself to having her in my room.

When the house came into view, Kenny made me turn off the lights. We parked the truck close to the fence. It was a good thing, Kenny pointed out when he was taking off his shoes, that there was a lot of front yard because she wouldn't have heard. Keeping close to the ground, we sneaked up to the house undetected. For a moment we stood stock still, hidden under the thick branches of an enormous oak, looking at the house and listening for signs of life from within.

Everything was quiet. The house, a two-story brick building built in the old federation style, loomed over me like a dark cavernous fortress, a forbidding sight indeed, with all the doors and windows shut and not a streak of light anywhere. Looking at it, I remembered the windows being open and the white curtains flapping in the wind as I went past the gate on my bike, back in the days when I had my paper run. I remembered admiring the house, so white and neat and proper, and how I had wondered who lived there, and sometimes I even stopped at the gate, hoping I would see them. I remembered how different the house looked to me then; how, on warm summer days, the drapes in the bay window were drawn back and music, strings and piano, wafted across the lawn all the way down to the gate. Then one day I discovered they had hung a wicker rocking chair from the roof on the front porch, but I never saw anybody sit in it, except once a big blue cat lay on the tartan cushion they had there. Another time the cat had stretched out on the wide front steps which lead down from the porch to the gravel driveway, and yet another day I saw it under the railing next to the flower pots full of brightly colored flowers. I am not a flower person so I never knew their names, but the flowers were big and pretty. Looking at the house now, I remembered how I used to wish that I lived there, and I began to wonder what would happen if I told Kenny I didn't want to do this anymore. I turned to speak to him but he didn't give me a chance.

Here, hold this, Kenny whispered as he thrust the rope, the tape, the rag and the hat at me, and I caught everything except for the tape. It fell onto the pavers and made an eency-weency sound. Of course, Kenny automatically cuffed me but remained silent as he crouched to retrieve the tape.

Huddling close, we inched towards the back door, which, Kenny had observed during his stakeout, was never locked until the occupants went to bed. Carefully, quiet as a mouse, Kenny tried the handle. As expected, the door opened and we peered inside into a rather large hallway with an old-fashioned wooden staircase leading to the first floor. Behind the stairs on the right were two sets of doors illuminated by a stained glass lantern mounted on the wall in between them. On the left side of the hallway another door, half-opened, revealed a kitchen bench. The hallway floor was carpeted and there were lots of pictures on the walls; however, it was too dark to see details. The house was quiet except for a low, indistinct sound, like that of a television humming, coming from somewhere upstairs.

We stood in the entrance for a second or two and then Kenny stepped inside, motioning for me to follow. As I tiptoed towards the staircase, Kenny placed his shoes on top of everything I held in my arms and very, very quietly closed the door behind me, and then we got such a fright when a cat appeared at the top of the stairs. Looking straight at us, the cat meowed. I froze. Kenny, too, stood there gob-smacked; it was only when we heard the voice of our intended victim that we were able to move, bolting to the kitchen.

Kleopatra? The woman called from upstairs. In my mind's eye, I saw her leaning over the banister. Kleopatra? Where are you, my love? The woman called, her voice growing stronger with every syllable. I knew then that she was coming down the stairs because the wood creaked under her weight.

In the kitchen, we stood waiting flush against the wall. Kenny's head was right next to the doorknob. I stood behind him, feeling such tension I was certain I was going to faint, and, as the moments ticked by and the tension mounted, I began to pray. I didn't get far. The woman stepped over the threshold and then everything happened all at once.

Quick as a flash, Kenny pounced on her. He hit her on the head with the bat and she went down like a sack of potatoes. As she lay in the doorway, the hallway light showed her features, and it didn't look like she was pretty, but Kenny had already stuffed the rag into her mouth so I wasn't able to tell because her cheeks were bulging. Besides, her hair was all messed up, obscuring her face, and Kenny too was in the way, bending down to fasten the tape over her mouth. That done, he pulled the hat over her face.

The rope! The rope, you turd! Kenny hissed up at me and it was then this weird feeling first came over me. In my hands, the rope changed into a serpent. Swaying majestically from side to side it slowly rose, its diamond-patterned skin glistening, and its red, glowing eyes flashing like giant headlights. All of a sudden, its tongue darted out, hitting Kenny on the neck. Wake up, turd! Kenny shouted from the floor and the vision dissipated like a puff of smoke. I handed him the rope. I was reeling; I think I helped Kenny tie her hands and feet.

Finally, we were out of the house. It was a good thing, I thought, that the woman lived on acreage because we didn't have to worry about neighbors. Still, as we carried her to the truck, Kenny sweated profusely. Even though she was only a slight little thing, Kenny worried about leaving footprints. I pointed out that gravel didn't show them.

You'd know, wouldnya? Kenny rolled his eyes, saying that these days there were all sorts of technological thingamajigs and whatnots to find evidence. It might be better, Kenny thought, if we walked on the grass where nobody would be able to trace us. We sidestepped onto the lawn. Immediately I got bogged down where there was neither grass nor gravel but a flower bed, and when I told Kenny, he swore at me but, as he had his hands full, he couldn't cuff me. Still, purely on reflex, I dropped her feet. Kenny then really swore, and I had to move fast to grab her, and then we jumped back onto the driveway. We just managed to get to the truck when the woman moved.

She twitched her head, making a little gagging sound in her throat. Quick as lightning, Kenny threw her onto the back seat and we shot out of there. I drove. Kenny was halfway out of his seat, hanging over her, and he had the bat ready in case she had any funny ideas. However, she appeared unconscious. The poor thing bounced from side to side like a rag doll because I was forced to swerve constantly to avoid the potholes that pitted the back road we took. I would have slowed down but Kenny urged me to speed, thinking we might have been followed. We roared through the night like a fighter jet. Again, I had the strangest feeling. It was as if I weren't my own self, as if somebody else had jumped into my skin.

When we reached the highway, Kenny finally relaxed. Confident we were past danger, he began to enjoy the adventure, cackling and slapping his thighs and my shoulder. Then he decided to open a new bottle of rum. He drank and joked, and all the way up the mountain he never stopped smiling.

I pulled up at the porch. Hollering *you hoo*, Kenny jumped out of the truck and threw the now empty bottle into the bushes where it crashed with the other bottles that were already there. Then he did a crazy dance around the truck, shouting repeatedly that we were going to be rich.

Reveling in his high spirits, Kenny bucked like a randy buffalo. Seeing him so happy, I relaxed a little, knowing that we were safe in the woods. Although I shared his hopes, I didn't holler or throw bottles. I just stood there waiting to see what would happen next.

3

The next day, I woke up with a headache. It was hot and my eyelids felt as heavy as lead balls. I lay motionless on my bed, watching sunbeams make patterns on the walls, and I thought about last night. I imagined I might have dreamt the whole thing; however, a soft moan coming from the floor reminded me that the kidnap victim was lodged on a mattress next to my bed. I leaned over to have a look.

She lay in the exact position we had put her in, on her side, facing the door. She made sounds as if she were choking. Without thinking, I pulled the ski cap off her face. For a moment she lay still, stiff as a board, keeping her eyes closed. Then all of a sudden she lifted her head and tried to shake her hair away from her eyes; however, some of it was caught in the tape holding the rag in her mouth. Even from behind, I could see that she looked uncomfortable. The back of her shirt was drenched with sweat. Curled up like a fetus, she moaned, shuddering every so often, and I began to panic because I didn't want to be responsible for her dying. Not knowing what to do, I leaned closer to see if she was all right. She sensed me and lay still.

My head throbbed with pain. The sun cut through the holes in the blind like laser beams and the cobwebs looked like dream catchers. In this dreamlike state, I placed my hands over the tape and pulled it off. The woman spat the rag out. Taking deep breaths, she coughed, keeping her eyes tightly shut. She looked really scared. Or determined. It was hard to tell which. Her face was blotchy and she had bled from her nose. A thin trail of dried blood led from her left nostril down to her mouth, stopping just above her upper lip where the tape had been, then resuming on her chin and down her neck until the collar of her shirt absorbed it in its stitching. Further down, past the stain, there was more blood around her cleavage. Still, I didn't lose my head even though she looked awful; I could tell she had not been seriously hurt. I breathed a sigh of relief; having had no medical training, I wouldn't have known what to do, had she been injured. It was then the woman opened her eyes. Looking up at me, she stared, not saying a word. After a while I felt like it was up to me to say something, so I said, Don't worry, you are safe here, to which she responded with such a look that I said nothing further.

She continued looking at me, and I felt more and more uncomfortable. Just as I was starting to panic, she spoke, saying she wanted to use the bathroom. The manner in which she spoke took me by surprise; she sounded very sure of herself, not at all as if she were scared of me. For a moment I sat there mute while she struggled to get up; of course she couldn't manage it because her hands and feet were firmly tied. We couldn't afford to be sloppy, Kenny had said last night after we chucked her on the mattress unconscious, so we had secured her properly. Now, faced with her request, I felt torn; on the one hand,

I felt I should help her, on the other, I had received no such instruction from Kenny, and what with Kenny being such a stickler, I thought I'd better ask. So I went to tell Kenny. I knew that strict security measures would have to be adhered to from now on, so I locked my bedroom door behind me before I went to knock on Kenny's door. I knocked repeatedly but received no answer. After a brief hesitation, (entering without permission was strictly against the rules) I went in (this situation being so out of the ordinary, I reasoned, it would qualify as an exception).

Kenny was asleep in his bed. Naked from the waist down he snored, spread-eagle on top of the covers. The room was hot and Kenny was sweating. I tiptoed past him to open the window. I also pulled the blind down, and then I stood by and softly called his name. Aware how much he hated having his slumber disturbed, I stood a respectful distance away, but he didn't hear me and I had to come closer. Soon I abandoned the whispering and began to whistle, thinking it would help wake him up. It didn't. I whistled louder, in fact as loud as I could, but Kenny continued to snore and eventually I had to shake his shoulder, which I did very respectfully as I didn't want him to fly off the handle first thing.

Kenny … I shook him … K–Kenny … but he gave no sign of life. I realized I was in a pretty pickle. Confused about what to do I hovered, trying to come up with a solution. Finally I decided that the best thing would be to help her to the toilet myself. I tiptoed back to my room where I found her sitting up in a pool of wet. When I entered, she didn't acknowledge me. Hunched over her knees, she sat in the middle of the room, staring at the wall. Tears rolled down her cheeks, sparkling in the sunlight like dewdrops. Seeing her like this, I imagined what would happen if Kenny woke up now. Uh uh, Kenny would not be happy. He would probably slap her like he used to slap me whenever I wet myself. Not willing to risk Kenny's displeasure, I pondered whether she should change into new clothes—what new clothes?—and then she finally spoke.

I need to change, she said, nodding towards the wardrobe. As there weren't any doors, (they had been wrenched off a while ago when Kenny got mad after I forgot to stack up the stove) the woman was able to see that I had some tracksuit pants in there. I walked over and pulled out a pair, placing them on the floor in front of her, clear of the puddle of course, which in any case wasn't large, as most of the pee had been absorbed by her jeans. There was a long moment during which nothing happened. She didn't move, just stared at the pants, and I took this opportunity to examine her closely.

She looked to me about the same age as Kenny. Maybe a few years older. As Kenny had just turned twenty-four, that put her in her late twenties, tops. Who knows, she could be younger still. It was hard to tell because she wasn't looking her best that day. Her dark hair was disheveled but still, one could plainly see, luxurious and long. Cascading past her shoulders, her dark ringlets covered her breasts, which were small and perky. She was attractively thin and very nicely proportioned, and her legs were long, though she wasn't tall. She wore jeans, now wet, and a loose t-shirt with a picture on the front, but I couldn't make out what it was because of the bloodstains and the hair matted over it. Her face was shaped like a heart, with a wide forehead and high cheekbones tapering to a small chin. Her nose was slightly crooked, like a little hook. It was dainty, and her eyes were a most unusual shade of blue. Without a doubt, she was the most beautiful woman who'd ever set foot in our cottage.

She finally decided to end the silence when she said she'd like her hands untied. Jesus. I scratched my head. I knew that Kenny would not allow me to untie her, but I had to admit she needed her hands to change her clothes. I told her that I would untie her only if she promised not to try any tricks. I also pointed out to her that both the door and the window were locked. The woman assured me she understood her position, saying she only wanted to change. I then crouched beside her and attempted to loosen the rope; it wasn't happening, so in the end

I got our kitchen knife and sawed through the knots. She made a big show to let me know she had suffered.

Twisting her wrists ostentatiously, she grimaced, rubbing vigorously where the rope left a mark. I wasn't taken in; I noticed there was hardly any redness. When I cut her ankles free, she did the same thing. Again, it was just pretence, nothing to be concerned about. After she was done with her theatrics, the woman grabbed my pants and looked at me as if she expected me to turn away.

No way, I said, no way. Shaking my head, I gave her a knowing smile because I certainly wasn't going to give her the opportunity to whack me over the head with Kenny's bat, which really was mine, given to me by Kenny after Uncle Clem tried that funny business on me. Since then I always kept it in my room; indeed, it was in the corner, leaning on the wall by the door. Of course, now that she had her hands free, I would throw it in the kitchen.

We stood staring each other down. It was nerve-wracking but I didn't budge. Eventually, she saw my end of the argument because she very quickly unzipped her jeans and wriggled out of them. I saw her panties; I didn't mean to look but at the same time I couldn't help it, and I saw that she had very nice little panties on.

Of course, now it got really awkward; we stood looking at each other, her in her wet undies and me looking on like a fool. I might have blushed, I don't know, the whole thing was too bizarre to put to words. In the end I followed my instinct; I put my hands over my eyes and after I did that she took off her underwear and put on my pants. I stood stock still, with my eyes covered, thinking about her legs and her ankles; they were nice and slim and I reflected that it was probably a good thing that it was me standing here and not Kenny. It was definitely a good thing that my pants were much too big for her; with the waist pulled up under her armpits and the seat positively sagging, she looked like a clown, and I was glad because this way Kenny wouldn't be tempted to get romantically involved. I felt our position was complicated enough already.

After she adjusted the pants, she stood in front of me with the wet clothes in her hands. She seemed to be saying something but I was still thinking about her legs and missed it. I quickly tried to gather my wits. All things considered, we were in the middle of an awkward situation.

She asked me my name. Her voice, as soft and smooth as velvet, reminded me of those pretty ladies on television that Kenny always commented about. Sometimes Kenny went too far and I was obliged to bring him a towel, and then I had to wash the towel as well.

Anyway, her question took me by surprise. Without thinking, I blurted out Ricky. Why I said Ricky I don't know, but I told her this lie and there was no turning back. Besides, just then Ricky seemed to me as good a name as any. She might not have liked it though because when I said Ricky, she nodded as if her worst fears had been confirmed.

Ricky, she sighed, trying to smile. I wasn't taken in. Her nervous grinning reminded me of Fluffy, my scared little rabbit that Uncle Clem got me and which he let me keep; this happened before the funny business started but still, I eventually told Kenny about Uncle Clem's visits. Kenny flew into a rage and cut Uncle Clem on the ear with his trusty knife. He then threw him against the wall and beat him within an inch of his life. The same day, he threw out all the things Uncle Clem had ever given me, and the rabbit copped it too, but I didn't cry because I saw that it would have been pointless.

Ricky, my name is Kathryn, the woman sighed, looking 100 percent like poor old Fluffy. I can see you are a nice person and this is just a dreadful misunderstanding. She paused and once again attempted to smile, but I could see she was close to crying. She shot me a beseeching look. We can sort this out. No one needs to know, okay?

She looked up at me pleadingly, her ocean-colored eyes brimming with tears, and then she moved towards me. Remembering what Kenny told me about feminine wiles, I too moved. I stepped back to keep my distance, but she kept coming and I began to panic. Stop, stop lady, I wanted to scream, realizing she wasn't like Fluffy at all. I felt powerless, and now we were only a breath away from the door.

The door swung open. It hit me full force in the back and I pitched forward. Struggling to breathe, I fell on her, recalling, in that instant, her smile, which had pinned me against the door, and just as our bodies collided, I reflected that if circumstances hadn't brought us to this point, I would never have got to see it. I crashed into her and she fell backwards onto the mattress. As I lay against her belly, two soft mounds with the nipples clearly outlined appeared in front of my eyes. Straining against the thin cotton of her shirt, her breasts jiggled like jelly, making my eyes swim. I couldn't help myself. I inhaled, breathing in her scent, and a delicious shudder passed through me. Then Kenny's huge paw grabbed the back of my shirt, and, in the space of a single inhale, I flew through the air where the door had previously been closed.

4

The day I was kidnapped began as a regular Sunday. I woke up early and lay in bed, listening to Rupert snore. The sound he made was boring and predictable, a short snort followed by two seconds of silence. The snore never varied and I had long given up hope that it would; after all, Rupert was a predictable man.

I knew this from day one. From the moment we met, I was sure that this was a man I could handle. He was polite, clean and dependable, with habits as regular as clockwork. He had a certain dull wit, which I knew would displease my mother and that pleased me. I had, at the time, been going through a rebellious phase.

He's shifty, Mother declared after their first meeting, desperately hoping she could influence me. But I dismissed her diagnosis and fell head over heels in love. Mother learned to live with it. After all, we both knew this was not about Rupert; I could have chosen a leper to be my husband, for all the difference it would have made to Mother. She had simply hoped that I would always remain by her side where she thought she could protect me from Me. Me, of course, knew this and tried to stay out of her way, hiding deep within me when Mother was around. We had to be on guard almost all the time, as Mother had the habit of unexpectedly bursting into my room, hoping to catch Me in conversation with me. When she didn't succeed, she would try a different approach. At medication time, she sought to draw Me out, addressing Me as if she were a real person. But Me knew better than to get involved, managing to fool Mother some of the time by pretending that she had gone for good. The truth is that the summer I met Rupert, my dearest Me and I had been friends for over two decades.

Our friendship started with a big bang. Me appeared one day out of thin air, flying through the open window with the speed of a meteor and crash-landing on my bed where I lay reading. I must have jumped two feet in the air. Me took charge at once.

This won't do, she said, pointing to my book. She slammed it shut. You've had enough of that, haven't you, she asked sweetly then picked up my drawing pad and threw it into the waste paper basket. Then she grinned. No need to doodle now, she whispered. Me is here to stay.

And the rest is, as they say, history. Me turned out to be exactly what I needed, the sort of girl I had always wanted to be, a girl you wouldn't want to fuck with. She chewed gum. She wore army boots, fishnet stockings and a midriff top with dirty bra straps showing. She had spiky orange hair and way too much makeup. Chains, bangles and all sorts of crap hung from everywhere. To put it simply, Me was a dream come true.

Straightaway Me made me feel at home. Well of course we were at home, sitting on my bed, side by side, talking a hundred miles an hour. It was a day I'll never forget. It was just as I had wished it: I made me a friend. I was so happy I felt I was walking on air. It was a stupendous feeling; I had never had a friend before. Sure there was Mother, but she was old and always so busy building my career. At any rate, I couldn't have spared the time even if Mother had allowed other kids in the house; there was my work to think of.

My life had been mapped out for me from the very beginning. Being an only child of a rich widow given to cultural pursuits, my time was spent developing my many varied talents. And I was talented, everybody said so, not just my mother, who was expected to say such things, what with her being so proud of me and so devoted to the cause. It was money well spent, everybody told her when she told them how much she was forking out for the lessons—drama, dance, singing, gymnastics, story writing and painting classes. Yes, it was a sacrifice, and well worth the effort, maintained Mother, for I was destined to be a star.

Of course, the making of a star is painful, hard work, let's not pretend otherwise, Mother was always saying to anyone who'd listen, mainly the mothers of the other kids destined for stardom, who shared in the ambition and the grueling schedule. On this issue the mothers collectively agreed; putting aside their individual jealousies there was much sympathetic nodding backstage at all those pageants and talent shows. Yes, we were all in the same boat; hard-working, talented, artistic, or at least dedicated to the arts, as Mother used to say of the other kids on the way home when it was just me and her in the car. As a rule we talked a lot about my talent, Mother dissecting my performances as if she were a scientist and I an unfortunate frog. No pain no gain, Mother always said, adding that it would all be worth it one day.

Consequently, given my busy schedule, friends were a luxury I could not afford. I was too tired, at any rate. After the shows I would rest alone in my room, reading or drawing or just mucking about with the ballet barre mounted along the wall. Sometimes I would get lonely and then I'd wish for a friend. Sometimes I would imagine there was someone in the room with me. Of course, after Me came into my life, I stopped all that. There was no need to imagine anyone any more. She was there, coming and going as she pleased. And I'd never been happier.

My life changed completely in a matter of weeks. Me and I did such funny things together. Once we threw my ballet slippers out the car window just as we were passing over the river. Mother had a fit because we couldn't fish them out and we had to go buy a new pair, but it was no good because we had missed the performance. Another time Me cut up a brand-new frock I was to wear at a pageant minutes before I was due on stage. It was a hoot. Of course I couldn't go on just as I was in my underwear, and Mother nearly died of embarrassment. Then a few days later, at a recital where I was singing the lead, Me set my hair on fire after the interval. It was a scream, literally, with people leaping out of their seats left, right and center to get to the exit. Me and I were in stitches just looking at the mayhem, except I did have to go to the hospital to have my wounds dressed.

Predictably after that fiasco my career stalled; all my performances were cancelled due to perceived ill health. I was deemed a risk to myself and put on medication. Me and I didn't mind at all; being together in my room was much more fun. Mother, on the other hand, had a bit of trouble adjusting. She had a few run-ins with Me, frustrating, fruitless encounters that resulted in more medication being prescribed for me. Still, Me hung on and Mother sensed that she was in for a long battle. It was a real eye-opener for her, seeing all that hard work going down the drain.

Yes, for a long time Mother mourned the loss of her dream, but even she eventually accepted the death of My Brilliant Career and settled for me being alive. She came into my room and announced that she was happy as things were—all is well that ends well, to be precise— to which Me caustically replied, no pain no gain. Of course that sent Mother over the edge; she burst into tears and out of my room, leaving Me and me alone to do as we pleased. And we have been ever since. All this happened when I was barely into my teens. These days it's water under the bridge and hardly worth the mention.

All in all, having Me around has been terrific. One of the best things about Me is that she has always known when to show support. Take Rupert, for instance. Mother had been less than happy with the choice of my future husband. In complete contrast, Me had shown a great deal of enthusiasm.

He's perfect for you, Me had said, beaming at me slyly and thinking that Rupert would be no threat to her place in my affections. But Me was wrong. I did fall deeply in love and that love, for a few years, interfered with our relationship. Of course, we talked and I thought about Me a lot, but our contact was less frequent, our connection less intense, and I was learning to like it, thinking that Me felt the same. I was being naïve; all through my marriage, Me kept biding her time, lurking quietly within me and waiting for the opportunity to surface again.

On the morning of my kidnap, Me slumbered through my husband's relentless snoring with remarkable ease; however, I found the noise jarring. Rupert began to seriously irritate me, but to stop him I would have had to dig my elbow into his side, and even then he would have hardly missed a beat. It didn't seem worth the trouble, so I got up and went downstairs to make coffee. I had some breakfast and then went into the garden to do a little weeding. My doctor had recently recommended gardening to keep a healthy state of mind.

Rupert woke up elevenish and we had a leisurely lunch together by the pool. Looking at the sparkling water, I felt happy. On impulse, I reached over to my husband and put my hand on his.

What is it, Kathy? Rupert mumbled, looking up briefly from his newspaper. Behind his spectacles, he blinked wearily, appearing annoyed. Instantly, I felt my mood change. My happiness wavered under his stern gaze, shrinking away from me until it disappeared like a puffball in the wind.

Nothing, I replied and Rupert went back to reading.

I sat brooding, thinking we never seemed to find the time for a nice conversation anymore. After we married, our whole life had suddenly become a routine. On weekdays, Rupert went to work early and came home late, often traveling out of town and staying overnight, then returning straight to work without coming home until the following evening. On the weekends, he golfed. True, we were together at the golf club but always with other people, business cronies and their wives, whom Rupert felt duty-bound to amuse. On Saturday evenings, we'd go out for a meal with other couples. Then a late night movie in bed, followed by a Sunday morning sleep in, a leisurely lunch spent with the newspaper, afternoon drinks at the golf club, then dinner and the packing up of the overnight bag. A kiss on the forehead at the door and Rupert was off, because business is business and time is money.

To Rupert, the sacrifice was worth it. Take up a hobby, he advised when I complained that I never saw him. Join the gym, go out, enjoy yourself, he recommended when I pointed out that we were drifting apart. So I did. I joined water aerobics, the library, the Blooming Roses Association and the Crochet Society. I also bought a cat, a beautiful smoke-colored Egyptian Mau I named Kleopatra, who kept me company when Rupert was away. Thus my days unfolded, one after the other, without the least diversion, the weekly routine making me feel as if my life was slipping away from me. Until the day I was kidnapped.

The afternoon passed as per usual: we went to the golf club for drinks, then off to Waterlily's for an early dinner with our accountant and his pregnant wife. Conversation revolved, as per usual, around the stock market (that was the boys), golf and the recent housing slump (still the boys), and morning sickness (the pregnant wife). The woman spoke of her condition fervently, describing the minutest details with unrelenting passion and a great deal of repetition. Throughout her speech I nodded and smiled a lot, thinking about Me hiding quietly inside me, and knowing it would take much more than a boring conversation to rouse her. The evening ended as always, at half past eight with cognac and petits fours.

From the restaurant we went straight to the train station where

Rupert caught the 8:50 out of town; then I drove to the gym for my special women only yoga class. I got home just before ten, fed Kleopatra, and retired upstairs to read. Out of habit, I switched on the television. Although I never watched it, I liked having it on as the noise distracted me from my desire to talk to Me.

I lay on my bed, cuddling Kleo, when she decided she wanted to go out for a pee. She jumped out of bed and went downstairs. I heard her meowing at the door and realized I must have closed it when I came home.

The rest is a blur. I followed Kleo down the stairs into the kitchen and was hit over the head.

5

When I came to, I was lying on a smelly mattress with my hands and my feet tied, and my mouth stuffed with a filthy rag. I couldn't see a thing; my face was covered by a rough, hairy … something. The taste of petrol on my tongue was overwhelming and I felt scared and confused, and wished for Me to come.

Dear Me, I'm in trouble. I am in the middle of a panicky dream. Please help. I want to wake up NOW!

Of course, things are never that simple. I did not wake up. I continued in my nightmare: trussed up like a pig waiting for slaughter, I lay there petrified, and Me was nowhere to be found. I tried again.

Dear Me, I am tied up, LITERALLY tied up in this horrible dream. Please help me wake up. Please. I need to pee.

Nothing. Me continued to hide deep within me, leaving me all alone. All of a sudden, I felt a very strange sensation as if a cloud was lifting from my mind, and I began to grasp that this, perhaps, was not a dream.

It was certainly an intriguing idea worthy of exploration; however, at that point my head cover was unexpectedly pulled off my face, and the rag fell out of my mouth. I kept my eyes shut, afraid of what I would see if I opened them. To calm myself, I took deep breaths, all the while calling for Me. She didn't answer. Eventually, I had to face the situation on my own.

I opened my eyes. Bending over me was a boy, a thin, spotty teenager with hair like ropes sticking out everywhere, and he stared at me open-mouthed. He looked like a goblin. No. He looked more like a rabbit frozen in headlights. A large-eared, buck-toothed rabbit, with big, bulging eyes, scared stiff. The moment felt so utterly surreal that the thought struck me that I was being played. For a split second I imagined Rupert barging into the room; he would explain this as an insane joke, I would get angry but eventually I would see the funny side. However, when the kid stammered d–d–doanworry y–yousaifere, I knew.

This was no joke. Rupert wasn't going to come. This was real trouble and I was here alone to deal with it. A feeling of panic came over me, leaving me breathless; germinating from a tiny seed in the pit of my stomach, it quickly spread to my heels, my fingertips, and everything in between. A voice leaped out of my consciousness, whispering to me that I'd been kidnapped. The words splashed around me like children learning to swim. Some pulled me under. Why is this happening?

To find the answer, I tried to focus on what I knew, on what I remembered happening in my house. I was hit on the head. Then voices, two, maybe three, argued as I was carried out. They threw me down onto something soft. A car seat, perhaps. I smelled petrol. Then sweat. Sweaty leather. Car doors banged, and that's the last thing. When I regained consciousness, I was on the mattress, feeling sick and wanting to pee, hurting at the back of my head where they hit me.

The kid continued to stare, looking as if he were waiting for a cue. I told him I needed to use the bathroom. This clearly put him in a state of confusion. Avoiding my eyes, he shrugged. Then he jumped off the bed behind me and ran out of the room, locking me in.

When he left, I managed to sit up and take a look around. There wasn't much to see, only a bed, a window blind and a doorless wardrobe full of clothes; the furniture old, battered and hideous. And the mattress, torn and stinking of dogs.

I had never been inside such a place. Dust twirled in the filtered light where the sun came in through the holes in the blind, shooting rays the length of the room. Near the ceiling, cobwebs shimmered, their arms stretching thinly from corner to corner, with specks of peeling wall paint caught in the webbing. In several places the paint, what little was left of it, peeled in strips from the walls, exposing bare wood; large pieces of crumbled paint littered the floor along the skirting. The floor was linoleum and floorboards, more wood than lino and a lot of uneven edges. Where there was lino, the floor was the color of urine. I sat there with my eyes wide shut, thinking I was dreaming after all, and then the room began to spin.

Of course, I went to pieces, losing all control. I peed my pants and cried for a long time, hoping that Me would come rescue me until I realized that for Me to appear, I would have to stay calm.

I was still crying when the kid entered the room. He took in the situation and handled it quite well, going along with all my suggestions to help settle my nerves. Indeed, the kid seemed quite reasonable, as reasonable as one could expect any person in his position to be, and this boy was challenged, of that I had no doubt. I resolved to tread carefully.

I asked him his name. R–Rick–ky, he whispered, pronouncing the word reverently as if it were a new and precious thing.

I told him my name. Nodding once, he blushed. Feet slightly apart he stood in front of me, blinking nervously and swaying from side to side like a seal. He chewed a dreadlock.

I said something. It didn't register. He looked straight at me without seeing, his pupils, like huge luminous moons, reflecting Me. I heaved a sigh of relief. Me was here. She had finally appeared, releasing me from the stress of pretending that I wasn't scared.

Should you be?

Yes, Me. I should be. I've been kidnapped. Of course I am scared.

Me, looking doubtful, pulled a face.

Look at him. He is a child playing at being in charge, said Me, making a contemptuous gesture.

Indeed, seeing him through Me's eyes gave me a different perspective and the courage to try a new tactic. Taking a step towards him, I gave the boy a friendly smile.

There is no sense in this. No sense at all, I said, inching towards him and hoping he might see reason.

He didn't. He stood in front of me, looking sheepish.

I can't. P–pleeeez doan make me, he pleaded, wringing his hands, trying to stop me coming closer.

But I did come closer and he fell to his knees, visibly shrinking. Feeling hopeful, I took one more step. The boy dissolved at my feet like an ice cube. Then the door flew open and the boy tipped over, clutching at my knees. I fell backwards and he fell on top of me.

A man stepped into the room. For a moment, he stood framed in the doorway like a portrait. Broad-backed and muscular, he stood on the threshold with his legs spread wide and his thumbs hooked behind the brass buckle of his belt. The buckle, a Chinese dragon the size of a small plate, gleamed brightly, temporarily blinding me. But the moment passed, the glare disappeared and I realized who I was looking at—the Man In Charge.

Somewhere else, fear would be ice cream melting on your fancy clothes. I fear I've spoiled my dress. Here, looking at the Man In Charge, fear bore down on me like a tidal wave. The Man In Charge was a very short, very odd-looking person. Small but stocky, he was dressed like a cowboy; his tasseled leather waistcoat, oversized boots and his wide hat—the widest sombrero I'd ever seen—made him look ridiculous, but at the same time there was nothing ridiculous about him.

His physical appearance was truly bizarre. With his big head set squarely on top of his wide shoulders, he appeared to have no neck. Despite this, he looked well-proportioned, and somewhat geometrical. His torso was square. His legs made a perfect letter *o*. His face was a large flat oval and he had a wide triangular nose, big round nostrils, and precise rectangular teeth protruding from his slightly opened mouth. His lips were thin, pale lines, but his teeth were unpleasantly colorful. Some were black, some yellow, some reddish brown.

The man looked at me. Betraying not the slightest glimmer of thought in his cold, deep-set eyes, he stared me down and I began to tremble. Without blinking, the man slowly raised his arm and touched the wide brim of his sombrero, pulling the hat steadily lower until all that could be seen of his face was his massive pockmarked jaw, jutting out like a block of chipped granite. He was undeniably powerful. When he growled, he filled the room with a sense of menace as overwhelming as an avalanche. Without warning, the man pounced on Ricky and threw him out of the room. The door slammed and I found myself on the filthy mattress, feeling entirely alone.

6

After he found me consorting with Kathryn, Kenny, of course, set down rules. He made me write them out on a piece of leftover butcher paper I had to salvage from the rubbish. When I showed him what I'd written, he still wasn't happy, grumbling that if anyone found this, my handwriting would prove that we were involved. Then he ordered me to find the newspaper so I could cut and paste his instructions out of the printed words. I went to the crapper but there wasn't much left of the paper, only the television guide from which I was able to tear out all the right words, except for the word kidnap so Kenny let me write it in but only if I disguised my hand.

> Don't talk to the *kidnap* victim
>
> do not enter the room without permission
>
> do not leave the house without authorization

I read the rules to him while he rested on the sofa, drinking coffee. When I finished reading, Kenny grunted, which usually meant I was dismissed. Today, however, even though I knew he wanted to be left alone with the coffee and the TV as per usual on his day off, I hovered respectfully until he looked up.

What? He muttered during a commercial break.

I told him I was waiting for instructions regarding the woman.

Kenny furrowed his brow. I knew he was going to come out with a swear word so I mentally prepared to bleep it out as per Kenny's orders, which clearly stated I was to never engage in profanity.

Indeed, Kenny swore like a trooper as soon as he realized what I meant.

**** me Jerry! He cried out, slapping his forehead. The note!

This, in fact, was what I was driving at. The ransom note. The lack of, to be precise.

Where is the ******* note, you turd? Kenny yelled, looking as if he might cuff me.

Knowing my reply was to be negotiated delicately, I stepped away from the sofa and shrugged to indicate that I knew nothing.

Phoebus, you ******* turd! Kenny bellowed. Get on with it!

Much relieved that he didn't hit me, I quickly scurried over to the kitchen bench to get my pencil and the rest of the butcher paper. Then Kenny dictated the ransom demand, which went like this:

> *We have your wife. Do not tell the cops or she*
> *will die horribly. Leave one million dollars*
> *in a garbage bag at the dump at 8 tomorrow*
> *night and return home immediately where*
> *you will wait to be informed where to pick up*
> *your wife. If you do not do as requested, your*
> *wife is dead meat!!!*

Kenny made me write it all down, and then ordered me to cut and paste from the newspaper as before. Again, I could not find all the right words but Kenny didn't want to know. He gave me fifteen minutes to sort it out, and then he adjourned to the crapper, taking his coffee mug with him.

Feeling the pressure, I quickly substituted what I could not find, and on Kenny's return I had it all neatly pasted on the butcher paper. I ended up trimming the sheet because Kenny had noticed some stains that might have identified us, so after the trim, the note was kidney-shaped but the main thing, Kenny pointed out, was that the clown should know we meant business. Looking at the note, I thought the husband would grasp it straight away.

> We have your woman. Do not tell anybody or she will
> pass away in a bad fashion. Leave one million dollars
> in a luggage at the dump at 8 tomorrow night and go
> back to your residence at once where a telephone
> communication will announce where your female is.
> Remember do this or the lady is lifeless meat!!!

Kenny noticed I wrote million and dump by hand, and thought I did a good job disguising because normally my writing is not neat at all. However, he also thought the note wasn't scary enough. Apparently, we needed to put the fear of God into the clown. At Kenny's suggestion, I wrote the two words a bit more menacing, like this:

MILLION and **DUMP**.

Kenny approved.

The clown would never dare show this to anyone, he beamed. We'll have the money tomorrow and then bye-bye, Pristine Mountain!

Full of joy, Kenny slapped me between the shoulder blades, then folded the note in half and shoved it in the breast pocket of his denim overalls. Seeing him so happy, I was almost bamboozled into thinking we'd done the right thing. Deep down, however, I had my doubts.

Before he left, Kenny reminded me to follow the rules, which he made me put up on my bedroom door.

Without constant reminder, a blockhead like you might make a mistake, Kenny said, grinning into my face as I kneeled in front of him to lace his boots. I promised I'd behave. On his way out, Kenny playfully cuffed me and slammed the door behind him.

7

When Kenny left, I turned off the TV and went about doing my chores. I cleaned the kitchen and the lounge, and tidied up Kenny's room, throwing out all empty tomato juice bottles. Kenny was very fond of tomato juice and always kept a box handy under his bed. My job was to refill that box at the end of the week.

As I worked, I glanced towards my bedroom from time to time, wondering what Kathryn was up to. It was almost midday and she hadn't made a sound, and I was growing worried. I contemplated knocking on the door to see if she was all right, but the rules clearly stated that initiating contact was definitely strictly forbidden so, at first, I did nothing of the sort. I made myself a tuna sandwich and drank a full glass of water when it struck me that she hadn't had breakfast or lunch. This put me in a state because I remembered Kenny saying that we needed her alive. Faced with this dilemma, I chose between the lesser of the two evils, so to speak; deciding to break the rules, I made a tuna sandwich and a cup of tea for her.

I knocked and received no answer. I knocked louder, thinking that maybe she was hard of hearing but still, only silence emanated from the room. Eventually, I tried the handle. The door was locked. As Kenny always impressed upon me not to waste food, I decided to open it with my key. I couldn't find it; eventually, I remembered that Kenny took it because he couldn't trust me with the woman alone. Well, that's that. I stood there a while thinking about, I don't know, some other means of gaining entry, but the weight of the plate interfered with the ideas I was hoping would come, so I set the plate down on the table and went back to the door to listen for signs of life.

At first, everything was quiet. Then I heard the shhhhhh sound of bare feet sliding across the floor toward me. I realized she was right behind the door. She whispered through the keyhole. Begging, pleading, her words snaked through the narrow opening and hovered above me like a genie.

Let me out.

For a moment, I was unable to respond. Inside my chest, my heart fluttered like a hummingbird and my head was spinning, and it felt as if I were going back in time. Once again, I was a small boy locked up in that room, feeling lonely and scared and afraid that Uncle Clem would come back. I'd be very quiet but sometimes I would cry and then I would kneel by the door and talk to Fluffy, my rabbit, whose box was in the kitchen, through the gap between the door and the floor, and many a time I got a bump on my head when Uncle Clem, who didn't like me talking to Fluffy, suddenly opened the door.

Ricky? Are you there, Ricky? Her whisper broke my train of thought; I hastily replied that I was.

What is going to happen to me? she whispered, and her voice was so full of fear that I completely lost my head and went down on my knees and told her that I wasn't allowed to talk to her. Then she, all choked up, whispered, Pleeez, Ricky, I neeed to talk to you, and her heart-wrenching supplication made my head spin even more.

Before I knew it, I was telling her about the food and the drink, to which she responded positively. She said I was very kind. Of course, then I had to explain that Kenny took the key, and then she asked if Kenny was in charge. I realized I had made a dreadful mistake, a tactical error, because I let the cat out of the bag, so to speak, so I quickly said, Yeah, that's right, but Kenny is not his real name. Thankfully, she did not ask any more questions about him.

Could you open the door some other way? She whispered out of the gap, her words, like marbl—No, I hate those—like glass beads, rolled along the floor, leaving a trail in the dust until they stopped at my chin where they formed a most beautiful pattern. Vividly colored, the words pooled, making perfect sense, but still, I had to say no. I shook my head. Well, I had meant to shake it, but I found it impossible; what with my cheek pressed tightly to the lino and my nose wedged in the gap between the floor and the door, so I just said no, there was no other way, and we fell silent.

What about the window? she suddenly whispered in a much happier tone of voice. Considering this option, I told her I'd think about it, to which she replied that she would wait by the door so I could climb in through the window without worrying about her trying to escape, which she swore she wouldn't do after I had warned her not to try anything funny. I would be obliged to use force, I warned, not because I liked that sort of thing, but because of Kenny and what he might do, should the whole thing get out of hand.

I swear I will not move from the door, she pledged, promising cooperation and saying if I could just see her, I would know straightaway that she was sincere.

I tried to picture her face, how she would look all sincere, but as I only saw her once, it was hard to do. Anyway, to keep her happy, I told her I would try the window.

I went to the fridge and took what cheesecake was left and put it on the plate, next to the tuna sandwich. Then, armed with a knife, I went out the back door, carefully locking it behind me as an extra precaution. Outside, I set the plate down on an overturned bucket next to the crapper beside my window. Then I carefully inserted the knife into the crack where the two window panes meet. Pushing the knife upwards, I lifted the latch. Then I pushed the window open and grabbed the blind, pulling hard on it. It sprang up but only halfway, hanging all crooked on one side. Through the gap between the windowsill and the blind, I could see Kathryn's legs up to her crotch. She was standing by the door like she promised. I pulled myself up onto the windowsill and from there jumped onto my bed, and I said to her, no funny business, foolishly showing her the butter knife. Looking at the knife, she smiled and said she didn't want any trouble, adding that it was nice to see me again. Of course, I didn't believe her. Who would? Given the situation. Given the fact that she had met Kenny. On that score, I would not have been surprised if she had crapped herself, but still, I admit, it was nice of her to say what she said.

Well, she asked after she finally stopped smiling, did you bring me a drink?

I now realized that I would have to let her come up to the window to take the cup. A tricky, sticky situation. I wished I had the time to reflect on the proper course of action; however, she didn't let me think.

Well? She took a step towards me. I sprang from the bed and said: Okay, this is the deal. I'll tie up your legs and then you could stand by the window and take the plate.

She started to shake her head. Pleeez don't tie me up, I swear I won't do anything, she pleaded but I was stone-faced, and she could see how entirely serious I was, so in the end she consented. I bid her to sit on the floor. Seizing the rope I had so carelessly left behind, I thanked my lucky stars; I mean, she could have done herself harm while she was alone. Obviously, she wasn't that bright because if she had, let's say, hung herself, we would have been in a pretty pickle because kidnap is one thing but suicide quite another, and I felt that neither I nor Kenny was equipped to deal with nutcases, so it was a good thing she hadn't thought of it herself, which testified that she wasn't crazy.

We did as I proposed. I tied up her ankles; as an extra precaution, I decided to tie her right hand to her back. Seeing she was like a china doll, so little and delicate, I took care not to bend her arm painfully or uncomfortably, only just so she would stay still. When that was done, I climbed out of the window to pick up the plate, which I handed up to her. The plate wobbled on her palm and she almost spilled the tea; in fact, thinking the tea would scald my face, I let go of the windowsill and ended up in a heap by the crapper in a totally undignified pose. She heard the racket but she knew better than to look; as she promised, she did not come any closer to the window. By the time I got back to the room, she was sitting on my bed, sipping the lukewarm tea and eating the sandwich. I sat on the floor with my back against the door. As I watched her eat, huddling over the plate like a small, defenseless child, it dawned on me that I had nothing to worry about. To think that I had fretted that an iddy-biddy thing like her could overpower a grown man like me—really!

When she finished all the food, she thanked me, saying that tuna and cheesecake were her favorite. She must have been telling the truth because she didn't leave a scrap, only a crumb on her chin. Sensing she might appreciate the gesture, I pointed this crumb out to her. Indeed, she was grateful. Smiling at me, she wiped her mouth with the tip of her little finger. Then she asked to be untied.

When I loosened the rope, she kicked it off and stretched her legs in front of her. My too-long pants were bundled about her ankles, almost covering her feet. Her toes poked out and I noticed that her toenails were painted pink, a very pale pink that sort of sparkled. I was surprised to find that she had no corns or dry skin; in fact, her feet were very pretty if one can say that about feet. I'd only ever seen such feet on TV, and I had assumed it was tricky photography. I dare say, she noticed my stare because all of a sudden she wriggled her toes.

Morning Frost, she said, smiling brightly and then, thinking I wasn't getting it, she specified. The color is called Morning Frost.

I didn't blush or anything, I only coolly remarked that it was pretty, and then, out of the blue, she said that she and her husband had no money, not the kind she would imagine people might want, and the best thing would be to just think about this calmly.

She completely caught me by surprise. Consequently, I uttered something, which, on account of the impact it had on her, I immediately regretted uttering. I said, What makes you think we want money? Right away, her face crumpled and fear—no, more than that—sheer terror, flooded her eyes. Panicking, I quickly said, okay, it is money we want, and she was able to calm down.

Acutely aware that by now I had broken all the rules, I peered into her tense face. Really, I reasoned to myself, what's the harm in discussing the terms?

I asked her how much money she thought her husband might be able to come up with for her safe return.

Well, Kathryn cautiously replied, we have some savings.

Aha, I uttered just as cautiously. Like her, I wasn't prepared to show my hand. That was all I said. I left the ball in her court.

Well, she said when she realized that aha was indeed all I was prepared to say, how much are you asking for?

In reply, I flipped my palm back and forth in a gesture I find speaks for itself.

Indeed, it had the desired effect because she blurted out they only had about twenty thousand and that was only in equity but maybe the bank could pay up against the house. At that moment, I was glad I was sitting down. Had I been standing, I would have keeled over. Our note clearly demanded one million dollars; I could see how this new development was going to cause trouble. I certainly did not fancy imparting the news to Kenny.

Are you sure? I mumbled, which just testified I wasn't thinking. Obviously, I didn't want her to get any insight into what was going on, but she sensed something because she abandoned the smiling. An anxious frown marred her otherwise smooth brow when she whispered, what's wrong? To which I could only reply with a shrug.

8

I excused myself soon after an uncomfortable hush descended upon us. Not because I was unable to handle it, of course I was; after all, I had plenty of experience. Whenever I tried to join in at school, the very same hush accompanied me, or even preceded me. No, immersed in the hush, I suddenly realized that we had been chatting a while. Expecting Kenny to return at any moment, I told Kathryn it was time for me to go.

It's for the best, I told her as I retied her legs and her arm. She didn't struggle, not even when I tied one end of the rope to the wardrobe. I had explained to her it was Kenny's explicit wish.

Kenny's a stickler, I told her truthfully. If he finds out about my visit here, there'll be hell to pay.

She grasped it. Saying that our meeting was our secret, she put a finger on her lips and then, just as I straddled the window ledge, she told me again that her name was Kathryn.

I know, I replied. Looking at her smiling at me, in that friendly, welcoming manner, I too gave a little smile. Clearly, she wanted to forge a connection between us. Like it was going to make any difference to Kenny what her name was.

But to make her happy, I said, If it makes you happy, I will call you Kathryn.

Her face lit up like a firecracker. Beaming, she said she would like us to be friends.

Finally we parted. Her smiling at me made me want to wish her a nice day, but I realized she might take it the wrong way. Let's face it; pleasantries aside, she was our captive, so I only waved at her before I plunged out of the window. I pulled the blind as far as it would go, and then locked the window from the outside. Really, I had been careless because the window had not, until now, been secured. Ah well, no harm done.

I went back to my chores. From time to time, I listened at her door; she remained as quiet as a mouse. As the hours went by, I began to feel anxious. It was getting dark, and still there was no sign of Kenny. When eventually Kathryn knocked on the door, asking to use the crapper, the bathroom actually, my nerves were worn to a frazzle.

I solved the problem by throwing her a bucket through the window. When she was done, she wanted to pass it to me, but I thought that risky, so I said she might as well keep it in there. I calculated the bucket would hold a couple of more goes, especially since she'd only had that one cup of tea. Then I locked the window. At a quarter to eight, I brought her canned spaghetti and a big bottle of water, but I refused to stay because I was expecting Kenny to come home. Kenny, however, did not show and I passed a restless night. I had the TV on so she wouldn't hear me walking around. I smoked heaps to keep me calm. I thought that maybe Kenny had been caught.

9

The first night was very hard on me. I couldn't sleep, and neither could Ricky. I heard him moving next door; he might have been talking to himself or even crying at times, it was hard to tell over the hum of the television. I tried to keep things in perspective.

Dear Me. What is going to happen to me?

I don't know.

You saw Ricky, didn't you? When I told him how much money we had, he was petrified. I don't understand why.

Don't you? Me answered, looking me straight in the eye. I'm going to sleep.

Me evaporated on me, leaving me confused. I felt exhausted and lay down on Ricky's bed to rest. I kept thinking of Rupert. He would have to know by now that something was wrong. After all, I would have never left home without telling him where I was going and when to expect me back. It stands to reason that he would be worried by now and that's a good thing. So I should just concentrate on keeping a cool head. Just think clearly and logically. Put my faith in Rupert, who would soon be looking for me. Perhaps, he was already looking for me. Perhaps, he had called the police. Clinging to hope, I imagined everyone in town was looking for me at that very moment. I will soon be rescued, I told myself, resolving to think positively from then on.

Well, of course, I soon lapsed into despair. Any which way you looked at it, my situation was grim. I had no idea where I was. I was possibly in danger of my life, and there was nothing I could do to help myself. How could I expect to be rescued?

Feeling agitated, I found myself unable to rest, so I got up and paced up and down the room, taking stock of my position. Was anyone likely to have noticed my absence? No one last night. Today? I couldn't think of one person who would miss me. I was a housewife; I had no employer waiting for me to show up first thing in the morning. Mondays were my lazy days; I usually rested in bed with Kleo and a good book, seeing no one. Therefore, there was no one but Rupert to discover me missing. And relying on Rupert could be tricky, I now realized, feeling a sense of irony I wouldn't have thought possible. After all, I had married a very predictable man. And ironically, it was this very predictability that now threatened to be my undoing.

I could bet my life that Rupert wouldn't have called me today because he never did. So Monday was gone. That left only one option—tonight—for him to realize that I'd been taken. But. There was a fifty-fifty chance that he had not come home. It was possible he might have decided to stay out another night as he invariably did if there was business to attend to. If that were the case, I knew I was doomed because Rupert would have simply left me a message on the answering machine.

All night, I swung between hope and despair. It was exhausting. I walked around a bit; from time to time I lay down, attempting to sleep. Failing miserably, I tried to rouse Me, who remained obstinately uninvolved.

Towards the morning, things got worse. I thought I was losing my mind. Maybe I dreamt it, maybe I didn't. I don't know. But there was someone there. A man came out of the shadows. It was Kenny, as one-dimensional and flat as cardboard. He laughed at me, his teeth as white in the dark as sugar cubes. He looked like a rabbit. Or a dead man.

10

Phoebus! Phoebus, you turd, get up!

Kenny's voice penetrated my consciousness like a spear. I lay listening to him berating me and I felt relieved; I felt as if I were sinking into a warm bath and the world around me was full of lovely things: candles, clean towels and musical notes bursting with joy. I was so happy, I could have shouted out loud: Dear God, I thank you for keeping him safe!

When I opened my eyes, Kenny was sitting at the foot of the sofa, taking off his boots. He complained that the TV had been left on and that the sink was full of weed. He said I was a slacker and that slackers were not to be tolerated in his household. Then he slapped me on the back and ordered me to cook him breakfast.

I kept him company while he ate, making sure he had plenty of everything. Seeing he was interested, I reported on everything I did the day before, leaving out boring details. With regard to Kathryn, I only told him that everything seemed to be okay. I knew this, I pointed out, not because I tried to communicate but because I heard her moving. Kenny, however, was not the least bit concerned about Kathryn's welfare. Dismissing her as a non-issue, he gestured for me to sit down across the table from him.

Everything is set to go, Kenny said, reaching for his toast. I watched him take the note out of the mailbox and I can tell you right now, he got the message.

Smiling, Kenny munched the toast. As I poured his tea, he went into particulars how the husband stood by the gate: motionless, uncomprehending, clearly shaken, he had stared at the note. Then he shoved it into his trouser pocket and went inside. The lights went on and off all over the place; in the lounge, the lamp stayed on all night.

He's flipped, Kenny chuckled, revealing how in the morning the husband got into his car and drove off like the house was on fire.

To show how pleased he was, Kenny clasped his hands and rubbed them together.

We're in the money! He shouted, beaming like a lighthouse. Looking at me as if he expected a show of appreciation, he began to pick his teeth with a toothpick. I tried to feel happy, but I could not entirely share his mood because something was niggling at me. Eventually, I ventured to voice that niggle.

Kenny, I murmured as I topped up his tea. What about her?

Whadabouda? Kenny roared, and I only just managed to move the hot jug out of the way before he jumped up. Cuffing the air in front of me, he spat sideways and shouted that I should mind my own business.

A few moments passed. We stared at each other in silence. Then Kenny resumed picking his teeth and after a while whatever he found there he flicked at me, so I knew his good mood had been restored. Indeed, it wasn't long before Kenny thawed out completely and we spent a pleasant hour in conversation. Well, Kenny talked and I listened to him outline the second phase of his plan, which involved collecting the money and speeding off into the sunset with it.

After breakfast, Kenny went to bed. As usual, I helped him off with his clothes while he issued directives for the day. Scrub the kitchen floor. Kenny sat down on the bed and stretched his feet towards me. Pack some food. I knelt in front of him and took hold of his right foot, and began to rub. There was to be absolute silence, Kenny stressed to the swish swish of my rubbing, so one (he meant himself) could reenergize for the long drive ahead. Wash the truck. Yawning, Kenny shifted so I could massage around the ankles where they tended to swell. Don't forget my tapes. After the ankles, came the shoulders and then Kenny's temples. Finally, I was dismissed, but not before Kenny ordered a hot bath to be waiting at six PM when he planned to take a light supper. I enquired about the menu. Surprise me, Kenny replied, winking good-naturedly. Then he dived under the blanket. Close the door.

As I went about my day, I was tempted to visit Kathryn; however, I knew that after a night out, Kenny was prone to restlessness so I did not risk it. I only passed her sandwiches and bottled water, not the real thing, just tap water in my old school water bottle, but she was grateful nonetheless. She beckoned to me but I did not engage in conversation. I only indicated with a mimed slash under my chin that there would be repercussions. She seemed to grasp it; she thanked me for the food then quietly tiptoed from the window.

When Kenny woke up, I had everything ready. I had a warm bath waiting and while he bathed, I made him an omelet. After dinner, I shaved him and trimmed his toenails. Then Kenny decided to take one last crap in this crappy dump, he quipped, slapping me on my back on his way out to the crapper. He charged me to clean up the kitchen and then wait for him in the truck. When he had gone, I tiptoed to my bedroom door and knocked, very very softly. Kathryn was behind the door in a flash, wanting to know what was going on. I whispered to her that everything was all right, and that she would be going home soon. I had planned to tell her that she'd be free in the morning, but at the last moment I thought better of it. I didn't want her to know that we were leaving the house. Kathryn seemed reassured and said she was okay with everything. So I left her alone and went to clean up the kitchen, and afterwards I went to wait for Kenny in the truck.

I thought about my plan; I had made up my mind to send a note to Rupert, telling him where to find Kathryn as soon as we crossed the border in the morning. Of course, I wouldn't tell Kenny about it, I'd just do it. Perhaps I was being foolish; after all, it would give the game away, the cops would be after us, and who knows, maybe even hunt us down, but I felt that it was the right thing to do. Besides, Kenny had always wanted to go out in a blaze of glory.

All the way down the mountain, Kenny never stopped talking. He was very excited. He drank rum, bubbling with optimism like a pot of horse stew. He had it all planned out. The life we were going to lead. The house we were going to have. I could even go back to school, Kenny said. If I wanted to. I could enroll in some fancy college. I gave him a slightly doubtful look. Kenny laughed. I was to have everything. Braces. Speech therapy. New clothes. Books. Girls. Whatever I wanted. We were driving into the sunset, and it was as if Kenny had lost his mind. In a good way.

By the time we arrived at the dump, night had fallen and it was difficult to see; to distinguish a shape on the dump heap, which rose before us like a mountain, was nigh impossible. Nevertheless, we turned off the lights and we sat in the truck until Kenny was sure it was safe to venture out. At eight-oh-five by Kenny's watch, Kenny bid me to go search for the money while he kept an eye on things from the truck.

It was pitch black. Even though Kenny gave me his lighter, I could not see a thing, but I did not think it wise to go back to the truck empty-handed, so I poked around in the heap just where I stood, and eventually I did pull out something. It was a bag, a lady's handbag, which had bugger all in it, so I chucked it right back. Meanwhile, Kenny grew impatient and got out of the truck. Swearing under his breath, he wanted to know what the **** was taking me so long. He fumed and attempted to cuff me, but he couldn't see me, which only exasperated him more. In the end, he gave up on the idea and fumbled about in the rubbish, and then we both got a fright when a set of lights appeared close to where we parked our truck.

****! Kenny swore and I realized he was very near because his spit landed on my left cheek. I gauged he was about a foot above me. I was able to tell that quite accurately because Kenny was a head shorter than me, and, since I am only five foot six, this made him, well, a head shorter. We never spoke of the difference and really, Kenny always acted very tall, so it was hardly noticeable. So now, blinded by the headlights, we immediately ducked down.

The vehicle pulled up almost parallel to our truck. A person emerged. In the glare of the unknown vehicle's lights, we could see the person's silhouette. It was a man. He walked over to the boot, opened it and pulled out a bag, a big sack, which he threw on the heap but not anywhere near where we were. Then he drove off. Kenny moved with the speed of lightning. I was right behind him, but he got to the sack first. Catching hold of it, he howled like a madman and then, out of sheer joy, he punched me in the chest. For a moment, I could not draw breath. I collapsed at his feet and so it happened that Kenny was the first to discover the remains of a dead pig in the sack.

****! Kenny uttered in an I-don't-believe-this-is-happening kind of voice but it certainly was because the blood dripped from his hands, which he had plunged into the sack. Holding the lighter close to the opening, Kenny peered inside. What a sick joke. Pulling a face, Kenny declared the money was at the bottom. Consequently, it was my turn to plunge my hands into the sack; still, the dead pig was the only thing there. After we realized, Kenny kicked into the carcass for a long time, swearing he would kill that clown. He meant the husband. That clown was going to pay one way or the other, Kenny swore, uttering threats, which due to their fantastic nature I was not alarmed about, but when he said, that bitch back home is going to get it, I was jolted out of my complacency, and it was then I suggested we go buy a torch. A big strong-beamed one, I said, and then surely we'd be able to find the money, which had obviously been deposited earlier somewhere else on the heap. Kenny brightened up considerably. All the way to the truck, he playfully cuffed me.

I drove while Kenny smoked and took swigs. From time to time, he cackled; spitting phlegm, he watched it streak the window and I knew he was feeling better. The journey passed quickly. Within a couple of hours, we were back with not one but two torches we got at a petrol station a long way off where the shopkeeper didn't know us.

Kenny attacked the heap with renewed energy. Whistling happily, he rummaged through the rubbish, expecting to find the money at any moment. I, on the other hand, suspected we were in for a nasty surprise, which indeed we were at sunrise the next day when we concluded our search. Exhausted beyond measure, Kenny was a pitiful sight, like a deflated balloon. When I suggested we go home, he only sighed. Might as well.

In the truck, I put on country music and before I knew it, Kenny fell asleep.

11

I spent the day having a conversation with Me. We argued a bit about what to do. Me thought we should just wait and see, but I thought just the opposite. We had to do something, I urged Me, begging her to help me think of a plan. I wanted to escape. However, we couldn't agree on anything and Me grew tired, eventually withdrawing from the battlefield. With Me quiet, I prayed to God, to be kind enough to make an exception. To save me. In between, I used the bucket.

It was a day like no other. The boy came once to pass me food and water, whispering platitudes and promising freedom. But his face looked as bleak as my future. He left and I listened at the door.

When the sun went down, I finally crumbled, sprawling on the lino in a steeeeewpor. I never even knew the meaning of the word. This then is how stupor feels. My eyelids like soggy clumps of earth. My head steaming like fresh manure. Thoughts moving about awkwardly like so many dung beetles. Eventually, one burrowed through to the surface. You are alone in this house.

My very own brainwave. I felt as if I was coming out of a bad dream.

Ricky! I called into the gap under the door.

Ricky! Ricky! Rickeee! I screamed, my voice sneaking out to fill the empty space on the other side.

I began to move about the room as far as the rope would let me. I wanted to see if there was something I had missed that I could use to free myself. There was nothing, only a plastic bottle and a plate, and books under the bed. Seeing those, I suddenly had an idea. It was so simple, I wondered why I hadn't thought of it before. I would write a note to throw out the window. The room throbbed, glowing like a horny woman, applauding me. I was seizing the moment.

In no time, the moment dissipated like so many scattered clouds. I cried with frustration. I didn't have a pencil or a pen. I sat there with a book on my lap, crying. Eventually, I read something. The words ran into each other like blind dogs into lampposts. I gave up, and the room shrank to a single living cell.

Kathy? Kathy, where are you? Kathy? Rupert's despair bounced off the walls in a crescendo of a thousand voices; all around me, thumbs pointed down. You are about to die. I felt myself lifted, crawling along the wall like a worm. There is nothing you can do.

12

I parked the truck under our big tree so that Kenny would have shade to safeguard his slumber. I stretched his legs the whole length of the back seat and I got him a blanket. I also rolled down the window a bit to ensure flow of air. This, I hoped, would help him get a much-needed rest, and so the chances of him blowing his stack when he woke up would be diminished.

Back at the house, everything was just as before. Not a sound was heard from Kathryn's room, for which I was grateful because I was exhausted. I crawled onto the couch and when I woke up, it was four in the afternoon and I still had my boots on. I went and washed my face and then went to listen at Kathryn's door. Silence. I contemplated knocking but then I heard Kenny clearing his throat outside, so I quickly put the kettle on, as well as the big pot which I used to heat up water for Kenny to wash in. Kenny took his time. Swearing, he coughed and spat, and in between he hollered at me to open the door. When I opened the door, he fell into my arms, groaning. He clutched at his temples as I helped him to the couch where he collapsed with a massive headache. Of course, I did everything to ease his torment, but somewhere between the headache tablets and the warm foot-soak, he remembered we didn't get the money and his temperature began to rise.

I'm gonna killa, Kenny whispered from underneath the wet tea towel, which I had folded over his face to soothe him.

Of course, you will, I murmured, gently stroking his brow. Kenny made a gesture as if to get up but he couldn't manage it. Sinking back onto the cushions, he moaned in a weak, tired voice and I sensed that he was receptive.

Kenny, I whispered, swallowing hard because I was nervous, there might be another option.

Kenny, however, wasn't prepared to listen. Saying what would you know, you turd, he waved his hand to dismiss me. Nevertheless, I judged it appropriate to reveal the information I had regarding Kathryn's financial position.

13

What? You knew they didn't have the money?!

His voice roared through the wall like a charging bull. All day, I had been drifting in and out of consciousness; disturbing dreams floated around and wild ideas came to me in regular intervals, but it was only when I heard Kenny that I came to. I couldn't help but stare at the door where I expected him to be in the next instant, and I prayed he wouldn't take long to kill me. Then I heard a big thumping noise, a thud and a slap, and then Ricky cried out. Stop! Stop! Slow down! he cried, but Kenny wasn't listening. The blows kept coming, thick and fast, as if poor Ricky was nothing but a punching bag. I placed my hands over my ears and prayed it would be over soon.

14

Of course, as usual, Kenny overreacted. I was prepared; when he sprang up yelling like a mad man, I dropped down behind the sofa and pulled out his trusty punching bag from under it. At the sight of the gleaming leather, Kenny rolled off the cushions and punched the bag with all his might. Fearing he'd aggravate his back trouble, I pleaded with him not to exert himself too much. Gradually, the exercise wore off some of his rage, and I was able to continue with my explanation. I told him how Kathryn called out they only had twenty thousand in the bank.

She called from behind the closed door because, of course, I did not talk to her, I reassured Kenny, who was back on the sofa, moaning. To ease his anguish, I sponged his feverish brow with the tea towel.

Twenty thou, he moaned, twenty thou. Clenching his fists, he thrashed his head from side to side. I'll killa, I will ******* killa, he mumbled, going off into morbid fantasies, but eventually recovering his composure to the point where we were able to have a rational discussion.

Kenny, I said, kneeling by his side, what if we lower the ransom?

Yellow saliva, foamish in appearance, surfaced from his mouth.

I gently wiped it off, telling him that if he was willing to wait, maybe the clown could sell a few things; the boat, the car, and maybe some pool equipment too, or white goods and other such appliances, and then maybe he could cough up, like, a hundred thou.

After I finished speaking, Kenny looked at me without saying a word. Then he turned away and stared out of the window, contemplating his tree. It was a truly beautiful tree, a centuries-old stately oak, mossy, with magnificent knotted branches and shiny leaves that rustled against the window ledge, producing a lovely, soothing sound. As a rule, Kenny wasn't sentimental, but the tree was his soft spot; right now, he stared at the very place where he'd once nailed our fathers' death notices. Gazing at his tree, Kenny waved me away. I took this as a good sign. Filled with hope, I tiptoed from the lounge and closed the door behind me.

15

Mercifully, the fight ended quickly and the house lapsed into silence again. I sat on the mattress with my back against the bed. I felt lonely and alone. The first scream had sent Me into hiding; she now lay useless, shriveled inside me like a piece of old skin. I cried a little, thinking about one thing. Why did this happen to me? Why pick us? We have no money to speak of. You only need to look at the house to know that we're not wealthy. Rupert runs a pool supply business. A new venture, it barely pays the bills right now. I don't have a job. I used to work. I was once an actress; I had a small part in a soapie, but they killed me off, and I haven't been able to get an acting job since. I've tried, God knows how hard I've tried because acting is all I want to do. When

I act, I feel alive. Acting is in my blood. But I just haven't been lucky. Anyway, my lack of success plunged me into a depression and I was advised to give my acting a rest. It was hard, at first, giving up on the idea, but, in the long run, things worked out for the best. I did need to take a break. Apparently, I am emotionally fragile, so when the doctor suggested a change of lifestyle, a little yoga, embroidery, not too much reading, Rupert had said yes to everything.

We moved out of town. It's quiet where we live. Rupert, of course, doesn't spend much time there. He'd like to but there's his business to think of. Rupert is very ambitious; we're going concrete instead of fiberglass. Soon, he means to say someday, we'll expand. We'll have another store in a better location. When we have the money to open up new premises. When is definitely not right now. Right now is barely getting by. So why us? Why?

I couldn't answer that question. I had no idea about anything. Nothing that's happened in the last two days made sense, and I knew I was thinking too hard and going nowhere. What I really needed was a plan. Or Divine Intervention. If there is such a thing. In my present position, I am inclined to Believe. I decided to try a little prayer.

Dear Lord, if you're up there—

Are you not aware of the irony here? A voice piped up out of nowhere. It was Me, rudely interrupting my moment.

Ignoring her, I continued.

Please help me—

That ought to do it. Me laughed, letting out a condescending snort. The sound irritated me so much that I lost my train of thought.

Have you a better idea? I barked at Me, feeling like a fool.

I might.

Let's have it, then. I can't think of a thing I haven't tried to save myself. And you.

Me sighed.

I seem to recall you once walked through a nightclub with your skirt tucked into your underwear.

I did do that. Yes, I walked through this crowded place with my skirt tucked into my g-string. Revealing, amongst other things, my bottom. Until recently, My Worst Nightmare.

Dear Me, why are we talking about this now?

Because, dear Kathryn, paying attention to detail is important. It's a lesson you've learned the hard way.

I had to agree with Me. I did learn that lesson the hard way. Some time ago in the space of a few months, I twice ran into this woman I knew. No one important, just someone I used to nod to. The first time it was she who stopped me for a conversation, just as I was about to nod in passing. She asked me about my life. I uttered some platitudes. I made a gesture. She didn't take the hint. She stood in front of me with this silly grin on her face. Clearly, she expected something more. Oh dear, we are forging a friendship, I thought to myself, regretting the waste of my time.

So what's new with you? I sighed wearily, but she didn't reply. Just stood there, grinning from ear to ear. Look at me, her smile seemed to say. She wore a shapeless sack and orthopedic shoes. Fat as ever.

You've cut your hair, I murmured, thinking that really, between Me, Rupert and Kleopatra, my world was full.

The woman stopped smiling.

I am pregnant, she said and promptly departed, leaving me behind stammering congratulations to her diminishing back, leaving me behind to figure out what lessons might be learned from this.

Of course, I felt embarrassed about not noticing. Guilty, even, about doing the stunned mullet to her face. I duly considered. Eventually, I came to realize that a) a fat woman might just be pregnant and b) some time in the future, the fat woman would have given birth some months ago.

I ran into her again after she had given birth. Only I didn't notice. Okay, she didn't have the baby with her. Okay, she was still fat. Okay, I should have done the math. I get it: it's a case of shoulda, woulda but didn't—because I wasn't paying attention. But she wasn't letting me go, she asked about my life and of course, I had to return the favor. So I foolishly asked when she was due. It didn't go down well. There was a scene the result of which is a lesson learned: paying attention to detail is vital.

All right, then. I will pay attention to detail; I will be vigilant, alert, discerning, clever and devious. And hopefully, all of that will bring about my salvation.

I sat on the hard floor, hugging my knees, feeling full of hope until voices drifted in through the gap underneath the door. Kenny was making noises, humming along somewhere in the house. I knew it was him, his voice cut through me like razor blades through paper. I curled up on the mattress and closed my eyes, praying for him to leave me alone. I wished that he would go away, disappear and never come back. I wished.

16

Kenny was due for a night shift at eight. When he woke up in the late afternoon, he told me to organize a new note.

We'll go with the hundred thou, he grunted, and I was so happy I could have kissed him; needless to say, I did no such thing.

At dinner Kenny was in a pensive mood, grumbling over his chops about the choice of the victim.

I could have picked someone richer, he sighed, dejectedly plunging his spoon into the mash. Pouring the gravy, I nodded in sympathy and told him that it was a rotten piece of luck he chose them; in hindsight, we should have checked out the prospective victim more thoroughly. This observation earned me a cuff, but Kenny admitted he had been misled by the blurb in the social pages, which portrayed our victim as the wife of a well-to-do businessman. Indeed, in the photo Kathryn looked prosperous as she cheerfully smiled into the camera, one hand on her hat, the other wrapped around a champagne flute full of bubbly. She later told me they snapped her at the races where she had been happy to oblige the local paper, but she had never told them she was well-to-do.

Kenny philosophized throughout the entire meal.

Perhaps the clown told the cops, Kenny remarked, slowly sucking on his chop, in which case it was only a matter of time. On the other hand, cops are such a stupid lot they'd never figure it out. Burping loudly, Kenny threw the bone onto my plate and gave a good-natured laugh. Naah, we're safe, my friend.

We'll deliver the note tomorrow. Pausing, Kenny frowned, his face a picture of concentration. He was thinking about how much time the clown would realistically need to get the money together, eventually deciding to give him forty-eight hours. Problem solved, he set to mopping up the leftover gravy with his usual gusto.

I set to my task as soon as he left for work. I cleaned up the dishes, wiped the table and then brought out the glue stick which was almost dry but as I only intended a short message, I was confident it would do. The note would read something like this:

Last chance!!! You have 48 hours to deliver one hundred thousand dollars to the place you know! We are deadly serious!! If you value your wife's life, get the money!!!

Recalling Kenny's instructions from when we wrote the first note, I anticipated a lot of emphasis in all the right places, provided I could find enough exclamation points. I needed at least seven and I couldn't vouch that, not in what I had left of the newspaper. What I thought I had left of the newspaper. When the moment came to substitute my handwriting for the printed words, I went to the kitchen draw where I usually kept the paper but there was nothing, and I realized Kenny had taken the last sheet to the crapper, so I went out there to check. Sure enough, a lot of it went down the hole. The scraps that were left did not contain enough printed words to compose my message. A tricky, sticky situation.

Eventually, I went and got my cookbook and looked for a blank page. There was one between the page where it said Essential Cookbook and the page where they listed the recipes. I tore it out. I also sharpened my pencil and then I left everything on the table while I made Kathryn dinner: spam and cheese sandwiches, tinned baby mushrooms, and a cup of tea. I put the lot on a tray and I was just on my way out the back door when I noticed that Kenny had left behind his jeans. Hoping he might have forgotten the key to my bedroom in one of his pockets, I rifled through them and found it; thus, I was able to open the door and deliver the dinner straightaway.

17

My prayers were answered. Kenny left the house. I felt a real sense of relief, especially when, a little while later, Ricky brought me food. It wasn't anything I would normally eat but I knew I had to keep up my strength so I took everything he gave me.

While I ate, Ricky sat on the floor opposite me. He was quite obviously watching me, even though every time I looked up, he'd look away. I thought he was nervous. He was all flushed, his ears as red as stop signs and he fidgeted, nervously picking bits of cotton from his jeans.

Dear Me. I think he fancies me.

He does fancy you. Use it, Me piped up all of a sudden, smiling in a very open, friendly way. There was a grin on her face as big as a watermelon wedge. I was taken by surprise; Me had not been all that supportive up to now.

I thanked Ricky for the meal. He was so pleased he didn't know where to look. Casting glances like a virgin bride, he smiled at me, saying nothing. As the minutes went by, he looked more and more confused, more and more like someone who was in over his head.

We sat opposite each other, feeling ill at ease. Where do we go from here? I thought, reminding myself to be strong. I had had a long time to think about what I would say to him but now, looking at this boy, my courage failed me. How could I explain to this innocent what I was feeling? I miss every single molecule that is my life. He has his life right here. I love Rupert with every fiber of my being. What has he to love? I didn't know. I didn't want to think about that. Dear Lord, give me strength.

Rupert is looking for you now. Survive. Sur.Vive. Me whispered to me gently, seeing my resolve was fading.

I pulled myself together. Yes, Me is right. Rupert is looking for me. By now, he knows I've been kidnapped and he is doing everything he can to find me.

I stared past the boy, imagining my rescue. It would be a fairy tale. A beautiful princess sits locked in the tower, waiting for her prince to magically appear. The hero comes, slays the ogre and carries the beauty away on the back of his white horse. Off to the sunset they go, intending to live happily ever after.

Of course, nothing in real life ever happens the way you dream it should. Real life has a way of intruding, appearing when you least expect it, ready to wreak havoc like a freak snow storm in the middle of summer. Right now, it was the boy who spoiled the moment. He called to me from across the room.

K–Kathryn, he stammered, snapping me back to reality. He looked anxious, there was about him a sense of desperation, or doom, as if he were about to plunge out of the window or change the world. It was obvious to me that he had something of importance to tell me, but he sat quietly for a little while longer, regarding me with suspicion, and it was only when I smiled that he began to talk, stuttering awkwardly in his weird fashion, his syllables cautiously se–pa–ra–ted from each other as if he were sorry to part with them. It grated on me, but I was conscious that this boy was my only hope, so I listened carefully to his every word.

18

She sat on the bed with the plate on her knees. I sat in my spot on the floor with my back against the door. I knew I was nervous because I fiddled with my trousers and pulled on the rope that was tied to her ankle, but, in light of what I had to ask her to do, I found my anxiety a reasonable state of mind nonetheless.

Kathryn.

Slowly, deliberately, I repeated her name. She appeared not to have heard me the first time; she only looked like she was going to cry, and I started to panic because I am no good comforting people, but then suddenly she was all attention, and I was able to proceed. I told her we didn't get the money. I also mentioned that Kenny was upset about that and now it was up to us, her and me, to put this right. Not wanting to unduly alarm her, I refrained from mentioning unnecessary details; despite that, she went to pieces the moment she grasped the situation.

Throughout my speech, she gaped at me with eyes round like saucers, she gaped as if I was not of this world, and then, blinking, she said, no wonder the money was not there, I told you we didn't have a million dollars. Oh, Lord! Clasping her hands tightly to her chest, she put her face in her palms and cried out, Rupert must be going out of his mind! Then she rocked back and forth over the plate, moaning repeatedly, dear me, what's going to happen? Dear me, what's going to happen? But I kept my wits about me and said, this is what we'll do.

I presented her with the blank page from the cookbook and the pencil. She wrote out the note like I dictated, and then I allowed her to write I love you, Rupert, and to sign her name. She wrote her name as Kathy in a very shaky hand, but she assured me Rupert would recognize her handwriting. She also told me she thought forty-eight hours was a very short time to get that much money.

He'll have to apply to the bank, she said, pointing out that Rupert could not tell the bank people it was to pay ransom. The bank takes longer than forty-eight hours, she whispered, all choked up with tears. She made a few weird swallowing sounds, and then she just went plain hysterical. Shrieking, she fell on the bed face down, emitting all sorts of wild noises; her whole body shook as she flailed about. The next instant, she reared up like a wild horse and her eyes went back in her head, and then snot came out of both of her nostrils so I was obliged to clear out.

19

Dear Me, I feel all my insides are bleeding.
I know. It'll pass. Wipe your nose.
What's going to happen?
Rupert will save you.
You promise?
I promise. Go to sleep.

20

I delivered the note early the next morning. We went as soon as Kenny returned from work, which was around five. He was tired so I didn't bother him with details of how the note got written. I only said I had everything ready, and then I drove in silence while Kenny stretched in the back where he listened to Moody Blues. As a precaution, I parked a little further away from the house than the first time. After I switched off the motor, we sat quietly for a few moments, and then Kenny told me to go put the note in the mailbox.

There were lots of trees and shrubs close to the house, providing a good cover. Or so I hoped, because my heart palpitated as I imagined Rupert spying me from his kitchen window. Consequently, I sidled up as quietly as I could with those dry twigs underfoot. Finally, I drew near the gate. Watching the house, I saw that all the windows were closed and all the lights off. Holding my breath, I gently, noiselessly slid the note into the box and then just as silently returned to the truck where Kenny lay sleeping. Taking care not to drive over potholes which might have jolted Kenny out of his slumber, I headed back towards the mountain, but as we neared the town, he woke up on his own and ordered me to drop him off at Janelle's, who used to be a waitress at the truck stop where we worked, but now worked as a stripper in town. About three times a week, Kenny drove to see her at the club.

I drove straight to the back entrance and pulled up by the staircase leading up to Janelle's room. Everything was quiet; the club was closed, the customers gone and the girls were sleeping. I turned off the ignition and we went up the stairs to the third floor where Janelle shared a room with her friend Lien. I began to feel nervous. I also hoped it would be Janelle who opened the door because Lien would stand there with hardly anything on, just this mocking smile on her face. I would go red all over and she would laugh.

Kenny rapped on the door.

Nothing stirred. Not a sound was heard from within.

Kenny knocked again and called out to Janelle to open the door. He pleaded with her. I cringed. Seeing him down on his knees like that tore my heart.

Then we heard them giggle. In no hurry to let us in, the girls laughed at us. Outwardly, Kenny remained calm but I suspected he planned to sort them out, once he and Janelle were married.

Eventually, Janelle spoke to him. Hello, Bid! She called out happily and I breathed a sigh of relief. She appeared to be in a good mood. She had used his special nickname, Bid, which means beloved in Chinese.

Lien opened the door. She lit up the doorway like a flame, her silky black hair shimmering and her almond-shaped eyes shooting stars. She tapped me on the hand; the touch of her finger was as soft as silk. I don't know what she said. As usual, I couldn't recall a thing until the door slammed behind me and I found myself squinting into the bright morning sun. Then I remembered Kenny's instructions. He had told me to pick him up in forty-eight hours.

Back in the truck, I reflected that things had turned out better than I expected. I had worried about Kathryn and Kenny being in the house alone together after I went to work. Knowing that Kenny would spend the day here put my mind at rest.

I went straight to work and stayed there until two PM. When I returned home, Kathryn was asleep. No, more than that, she was dead to the world because I was able to kneel next to her face and she never moved. Asleep, she looked peaceful; arms by her side, she breathed so lightly that, when I lowered my head close to her chest, I could only just detect her nipples under her t-shirt, a mere shadow disappearing with each breath. With her pouty lips slightly open and her hair strewn about my pillow, she looked like a mermaid. Her eyelashes, long and silky, fringed her eyelids like a half-opened fan. Looking at her, I was only thankful that it was me here and not Kenny. Really, it was a good thing he never even saw her at all after he put the ski cap on her.

I could have stayed there all afternoon, but I didn't fancy having to explain myself in case she woke up, so I placed some food and water next to the mattress and I left. On my way out, I took the full bucket to rinse outside. That done, I put it back in her room. Then I quietly locked the door behind me and went to sleep on the couch.

When I woke up, it was dark outside and Kathryn was at the door, calling me through the gap.

Ricky? Ricky, are you there? She called out softly.

I switched on the light in the kitchen and told her to step away from the door. Then I switched on the light in her room. The switch, mounted on the wall in the hallway, I had always regarded as a nuisance, but now it came in useful as it prevented Kathryn from manipulating the light. I mean, she could have signaled to the outside world or something. Well, nobody ever came out here but still, I was glad the switch was out of her reach.

When I came in, she was back on the bed where she sat curled up into a ball, hugging her legs. There was a smell of fresh pee in the air. I glanced at the bucket. Indeed, it was half full already. Kathryn saw me glancing and blushed.

I need to use the toilet, she said, pursing her lips like she found it distasteful to have to mention these things, which I suspected she did.

Aha, I said and, as delicately as I could, indicated that there was plenty of space in the bucket. I told her that she didn't need to worry about toilet paper because I would supply her with all that she needed.

She went crimson all over.

I would like to use a real toilet, she whispered.

For a moment, we stood there regarding each other. I tried to think of some other alternative. What would Kenny do? Would he bring the paper? Would he let her? Pretty soon, however, I abandoned that line of thinking because it had occurred to me that Kenny would have never allowed himself to be bothered by crappy details like this.

Meanwhile, Kathryn looked like she was going to cry. I had to make a decision quickly.

Okay, I said to her, I'll take you to the toilet. But I'll have to leave you like this, I pointed to her ropes and she nodded.

Okay, leave the ropes.

I untied the rope from the leg of the wardrobe and held onto the end of the rope, very tightly, while I instructed Kathryn to pull the ski cap over her head, right down to her neck, and then to walk slowly three steps in front of me. At first, she was worried about bumping into things but I navigated her carefully through the kitchen and out the back door, and to the crapper where there was another exchange about the practicalities of the situation, which we solved satisfactorily by leaving the door ajar. While she was in there, I whistled a tune so that she wouldn't think I was listening to her business, and when she was done she thanked me, and she also commented that I whistled very well. Slowly, we made our way back under the porch. Then Kathryn did something unexpected. She asked if we could stay outside.

Her request took me by surprise. I stood there thinking what to say to her when she started complaining that she missed the fresh air.

It stinks in the room, she explained, begging to stay outside. Please, Ricky, can we stay here? Pleeez …

She certainly had a point. It did stink in the room, what with the bucket there and those dirty jeans and the windows closed all the time. I decided to let her have five minutes.

Okay, I replied, five minutes.

I could tell she was smiling underneath the hat. We walked around the yard but she kept tripping over things, so I rolled the hat up a little so she could see where she was going. Her nostrils were free to sniff all the air she liked, and she was really grateful, and she looked very cute with only the tip of her nose showing and that big smile on her face. I walked her up and down the porch while she breathed deeply. We talked about nothing in particular. She said the air was very fresh, not like in the city, to which I replied, What makes you think we're not in the city? She just shrugged and said she didn't know where we were, she was just saying. She stopped smiling and after the five minutes was up we went back inside.

I locked her in while I prepared a meal for her: fried sausages and a big slab of lasagna that I got from work. She liked it, even said I made really good tea. After dinner, she sat on the bed and I on the floor by the door facing her, and we made idle conversation. It was hard going because there wasn't much I could tell her about me or Kenny, and I knew she'd get upset if we talked about her life, so mostly I told her about the weather and the TV guide. Out of the blue, she asked to have a wash, which I did not think an outrageous request at all, seeing she hadn't washed for the last three days. Honestly, I could smell her from where I was sitting, so I told her that I would think about it, and then left to think about it in the kitchen.

21

When Kenny showed up on my doorstep at six AM, I wasn't thrilled. I had been asleep, happily dreaming of my own wonderful death, imagining a quick, merciful end to my earthly life when Kenny woke me up with his knocking.

Janelle, please, he called, rapping sharply on the door. Let me in. Please …

Moments ticked by while I lay quietly in my bed, wishing he would go away.

He didn't. Knock, knock, he persisted, scraping at the door like a turtle backed into a corner.

I pictured him standing outside, just under the doorknob, clutching his sombrero to his chest, sweating and trembling, begging to be let in. In spite of myself, I was filled with pity. Poor Kenny. Scaly-eyed, flat-nosed, with skin like a vegetable grater, he is a scarred little soul, inside and out, having just one wish: to be loved. But men like him do not inspire love. Indeed, I found it impossible to imagine anyone who would love him voluntarily. Excepting little Phoebus, I couldn't think of a soul. I certainly was never meant to be Kenny's girl. To me, Kenny would always be nothing but a stupid old Bid, an ugly, dull, unlovable turtle, perpetually banging his head against the wall. Beside me Lien stirred, her skin gleaming in the sunlight like the petals of a lotus flower. I watched her sleep, marveling at her beauty. In my mind, we are the only people in the world. We live on a white sandy beach the shape of an enormous heart. I love Lien. When she speaks, her words sound like wind chimes. When she touches me, her fingers flutter like butterfly wings over my body. In her presence, I am a snowflake melting.

I am a girl in love. My desires are simple; I want only to be happy. In a perfect world, I would be. In a perfect world, I would not dance to sleazy tunes in a sleazy bar in front of sleazy desperate men waiting to be pleasured. In a perfect world, Janelle the dancer wouldn't exist. In a less-than-perfect world, things are what they are; in the here and now being Janelle takes up most of my time.

My name is Mai Lin. Six weeks ago I murdered a man. He was a good man, generous to a fault, an honest fisherman with a heart of gold, always happy to lend a hand without looking to profit. His name was Jim. He looked like a vulture and laughed like a hyena. We called him Old Buzza. So happy to be alive. The poor bugger died needlessly, with his eyes fixed on me till the very last breath. He pleaded for help but I didn't listen. I let a good man die. And now I'm paying the price.

Knock. Knock.

Bid keeps on knocking, trying to knock his way into my heart. He lives in a fairy tale; we all do. Mine is the Lotus Flower and The Turtle, a twisted adaptation of the classic; it goes without saying that in my story the turtle is bound to remain a beast. Ah. But circumstances are beyond my control.

Knock. Knock.

The boy, now. I hear him. P–please, open the d–door.

I could. I could get up and open the door, but now is not the time. Lien is fluttering her eyelashes, coiling her body around me like a snake. She is a snake, a beautiful, mysterious serpent. I look at her and see her through other people's eyes. I see me through other people's eyes. We are whores. We speak English funeee. We are poor things spinning endlessly in our own orbit, two foreign girls with no future. What will happen to us when we're old? I don't know. I can only pull a sad face. Nobody notices. How could they? You can't read a Chinese face. All them Orientals look the same, the old men say. They do not mind as long as we do what we're paid for.

Knock, knock, knock. Pleeez Janelle, let me in.

Bid again. Using his Janelle voice. At the sound of it, I bury my head in the pillow. Good Brethren, we will have to let him in. Eventually.

Time passes through my mind like a river through a tunnel. Listening to Bid, I feel sad for all of us. We deserve better.

Six weeks ago we were friends. We worked together at the truck stop, and we made quite a team: I cooked, Lien served drinks in the cocktail bar and Kenny pumped petrol outside. The pay was pitiful but Lien made heaps extra on tips and as we never paid for food, we managed. Kenny, on the other hand, was always short of money. Having to support Phoebus, he could barely make ends meet. So one day he devised a scheme to supplement his income; for a fee, he would send tourists on a wild goose chase to find waterfalls in the mountain. His spiel was very convincing and he got a great many people interested, so after a while Lien and I began helping him, priming people in the lounge, directing traffic to him for a cut. We worked for coins but it was fun.

Eventually, everyone in the shop got involved. Our kitchen hands, the German twins, Deep Fryer Fred and Onion Hans, spread the word in town in the German club. A client of mine, a baker, put up a poster in his bakery and Old Buzza sent day trippers to us from as far as the bay. When little Phoebus came into it, we had him distribute flyers on his paper route. Of course, from time to time, there were complaints, but Kenny dealt with those in his own special way, without jeopardizing the scam.

Inevitably, we all began to spend time together, going out for a picnic or a ride in the truck, and it was all very pleasant until Kenny fell in love with me. At first I didn't worry, I thought it would pass, especially as Kenny knew that I plied business on the side. Kenny, however, was determined to "rescue" me from the life I was leading. His dream was to make enough money to take good care of me. What a dreamer. How could he ever make that much money? Relieving unsuspecting tourists of loose change wasn't going to do it, and Kenny never seemed to come up with anything else. He tried. Every week he had a different plan, one crazy notion after another, but they never amounted to anything. It was plain to see that Kenny was fated to remain a colossal failure, a loser incapable of rising to the occasion, doomed to living hand-to-mouth in the woods forever and ever. And now, this loser is standing at my door.

I wish he would go. I wish I never had to see him again. But circumstances dictate otherwise.

Eventually, we go open the door. Lined up on the threshold, the boys look awkward. Phoebus, ears flared like flaps of veal, stares down at his weird lace-up boots. Having caught a glimpse of Lien in her nighty, he is all confused; he stands there chewing a dreadlock, rocking on his heels like a seal. Behind him, Bid with that stupid hat. He looks defeated and as ugly as ever. Dismissing Phoebus with a tug on his shirt, Bid waits till the door shut behind him before advancing towards me. He comes at me with open arms.

Wheh du munee? I ask him point blank, cutting him off with a gesture as if he were nothing but a customer. I can tell, I know from the way he shrinks to the floor that he hasn't delivered on his promise.

Bid shrugs.

Of course he doesn't have the money. He is a fool and so am I for believing him. Out of desperation, I believed. All I wanted was to be able to leave. Now. Today. Yesterday, if possible. And he promised. I am going to get you out of here, he swore to me after I killed Old Buzza. But he lied. From day one, this flesh-eating bug told me nothing but lies.

Bid's apologizing.

Everything's on track, he splutters, wringing his hands like an anxious child. Next time you see me, I'll have it. I promise.

I. Promise. Retreating into his shell, he pleads. Scrape, scrape, his heavy boots drag him closer to me. But my heart is as hard as a rock. I do not love you, Bid. I look at my girl and my heart softens. I am worried about what Lien will say.

Lien is not angry. She takes a step towards him. Bid. Smiling, she reaches down and takes off his sombrero. She puts it on her head, pushing it down over her eyes. Ah plomise, she pouts, mocking Bid. He has no choice but to laugh.

Eventually, we make coconut balls. Loh Mai Chi, Lien says. I just love the way the words leave her mouth. We drink cha out of mustard jars. We have no muneee. Not yet.

22

The fresh air lifted my mood. I felt confident that things would work out. A hundred thousand dollars was manageable.

Me was of the same opinion. He'll borrow. He'll steal. He'll even ask your mother for a loan, Me whispered to me soothingly. Do not worry. You will be home soon.

The thought of my mother cheered me up. She had always been a tremendous help to me. Indeed, until I met Rupert, my mother was my best friend. My best *real* friend. Then I fell in love and Mother distanced herself while she digested the shift. Mother's a trooper. By the time the wedding came along, everything was fine.

I talked to Ricky about having a shower. Surely five minutes alone in the bathroom can be arranged, I reasoned, and I could tell from the expression on his face that he thought it was a good idea. I told him I needed to change my clothes, and again he agreed, saying I could pick anything I liked out of his wardrobe.

Dear Me, anything you like. Of course, it wouldn't do to laugh. I thanked him and after he had gone, I went through his clothes. I picked out clean underwear, a pair of faded blue trackies and a yellow t-shirt, which, in the end, I decided not to wear because it had Pristine Mountain written across the chest. As Pristine Mountain is about a half-hour drive from my place, it had occurred to me that maybe this was where we were. I felt that under the circumstances it would have been foolish, even dangerous, to wear the shirt, so I hid it under some other clothes, choosing a black singlet from the bottom draw instead.

I sat on the mattress with the clothes in my lap. Waiting for Ricky, I thought of Rupert, imagining his anxiety, the feeling of utter devastation at my disappearance, and I felt like crying. I closed my eyes; one by one, memories of our happy life passed me by like frames in a slide show.

There's the first moment when our eyes locked across the crowded room; I knew instantly that we were meant for each other. There's our first movie date, our first dinner, our first kiss. The first weekend away and the first time we went to see Mother, the first time we argued, the first time we made up; all those firsts undulate towards me one after the other like models down a runway. Here comes a big one. It's Rupert, down on his knee, in the middle of a busy street, asking me to marry him. I was so happy I could hardly believe it was happening. Tears streamed down my cheeks when I said yes. Rupert picked me up and we twirled and swirled, dancing in the street the way they do in romantic comedies.

The wedding took place on a lovely summer day. I take you, Kathryn. For better or for worse. The church was full, the reception perfect, the wedding night a dream. A honeymoon in Spain followed. We stayed at a charming place and we did all the things honeymooners do. On the last day, we drove to the beach in a convertible, the roof folded and my hair tangled in his fingers. He kissed me. He loved me. And I loved him.

That's the way it should have gone on. It is what I deserve. But do I get it? No. I sit in this filthy hole, clutching some half-wit's rags, as helpless as a child.

Dear Me, this hideous bug hole is slowly sapping me.

23

It took me a while to work it out. When I had it all planned, I went back in Kathryn's room and explained that we didn't have water or electricity in the bathroom.

However—seeing her frown, I had to smile—there is a bathtub.

This cheered her up. She stopped frowning and gave me a most beautiful smile. When I told her that I was willing to fill the bathtub with warm water for her, she literally jumped for joy.

That's fantastic, she grinned, making a move as if to touch me, but I quickly stepped back. I put up my hand to stop her and said: Hold your horses.

We went over the rules. I absolutely insisted the door stays ajar like before, I said, and I think she knew what I was referring to because she didn't argue. I then explained that I would untie her hands but leave the rope tied to her leg. I would then sit outside the door with my back to it and hold the other end of the rope. After her bath, I would retie her hands before we left the bathroom. That was my plan, take it or leave it. Of course, Kathryn agreed to everything because she knew she didn't have a choice.

I began preparations for her bath. I stoked the fire and filled two big pots with water, and while I waited for the water to heat, I washed the bathtub. I only had a bit of detergent left, but I did what I could. I scrubbed the worst spots with Kenny's back-brush so when the bathtub was full, it looked reasonably clean. Then I lit a candle and placed it on a small plate on the window ledge in the bathroom so that I would be able to see from my position by the door what Kathryn was up to. Looking at the window, it occurred to me that although the opening was small and narrow, it was probably still wide enough for her to get out, so I went outside and dragged Kenny's steel locker off the porch to block the window. Having taken these precautions, I was convinced I left no opportunity for escape.

Back in Kathryn's room, Kathryn sat waiting on my bed. She was ready. I gave her my towel and then we went to the bathroom. I didn't bother putting the hat on her; I saw no harm in letting her see the house. Still, I didn't think it wise to let her see the outside, so I made sure all the blinds were down. As a last thing, I got rid of the note on my door, the rules concerning the handling of the kidnap victim. I took the paper down and hid it in the kitchen draw because I felt it showed us in poor light, now that we were on different footing. I mean, we were talking and interacting like normal people. I felt confident that she wouldn't do anything stupid; after all, I was doing her a good turn by letting her wash, and she would have been foolish to spoil things.

In the bathroom, I showed her the soap and the shampoo. I also showed her that I had a big pot of water ready by the door, which I was going to throw at the candle if she had any funny ideas about burning the place down, but she shook her head.

Oh no, she said, I would never do such a stupid thing.

Nodding to show that I believed her, I said I would be ready all the same. I warned her I would be just outside the door. Seeing I was leaving the door open, she looked unhappy, giving a suspicious glance, so I assured her that she had nothing to worry about because I wasn't any kind of pervert. Smiling nervously, she assured me that she had no worries on that score because she knew I was a gentleman. This, I could tell, wasn't strictly true because her lips were twitching and there were beads of sweat on her nose so clearly, cleeear-ly she was anxious. Finally, I untied her hands and left the bathroom.

Holding onto the rope, I sat down by the door in the hallway. The gap accommodating the thickness of the rope was not very wide; still, it afforded me a clear view of the bathtub. When I heard splashing, I counted five seconds, and then I briefly glanced inside. Indeed, Kathryn was in the tub up to her chin; the only thing I could see was the back of her head resting on the edge. She lay very still. I shifted to get a better look.

She lay with her head tilted, showing her profile with its smooth, high forehead, the sculpted nose, and the full lips with their upturned corners. Her ringlets hung over the edge, almost to the floor. Seeing her like this, I crossed my legs and made myself comfortable, unzipping my fly; I only wished I had put on music so I could really enjoy the sight in peace. A few minutes ticked by. In the soft light of the candle Kathryn looked like a painting, a divinely beautiful portrait, and I felt happy. Then suddenly, she looked over to the door and I was forced to retreat because I didn't want her to think I was spying on her. I sat behind the door feeling unbearably tense; I thought she had seen me and I felt I was going to pass out, when I heard her splashing. I forced myself to look; she sat with her back towards the door and she was washing herself. With her arms lifted, she repeatedly slid the soap over her body, up to her neck and back down over her little boobies, which I could only imagine were there. It was then that I completely lost control and my jam flew out of me. It splattered over my jeans and some landed on the floor beside me but I was paralyzed and could do nothing about it.

24

I lay in the bathtub, submerged to my chin. I felt deliciously warm; the water gently rippled, and beneath the surface my body glowed, shimmering like a pale horizon. Choosing to ignore the last seventy-two hours of my life, I was having a moment. The moment stayed true to its nature. Suddenly, I felt his eyes upon me. He sat as still as a cat, and he was watching me. I washed as quickly and privately as I could.

I called to him when I was ready to step out of the tub. I knew he was there, listening. But I didn't want him looking.

Ricky, I am ready to dry myself, I said, hoping he'd take the hint. I'm getting out of the bath.

He told me to go right ahead. But I wouldn't move just yet. Something was not right. He sounded upset. I wanted to know if he was okay. He replied that he was. I jumped out of the bath and grabbed the towel.

Ricky shifted about outside the door, calling out to me that he had accidentally spilt some water on his jeans. He was obliged to take them off but I should not panic because as soon as we got back to the room he was going to find new trousers to wear. Apparently, I had nothing to worry about.

During the course of this speech, I dried myself and put on the clean clothes. The tracksuit pants were too long and the t-shirt came down to my knees but I didn't care. It felt good to be clean again. I asked Ricky whether he'd mind if I washed my underwear. He said to go ahead and even offered to take the washing outside to dry.

I wrapped my hair in the towel. I was rinsing my underpants when Ricky knocked on the door. He waited until I invited him in and then he only just stepped over the threshold. He stood in the doorway with his jeans tied around his waist like an apron. In spite of everything, I felt like laughing at the sight of his skinny legs.

Uh–uh had an a–accident, he whispered, avoiding my eyes. Looked down at his feet. Looked sheepish. No. Looked like a sheep. A little lamb shivering with fright. He seemed altogether frightened.

Of course, he is frightened, Me whispered, nudging me to move closer to him. There's a big bad wolf about.

What? Me? A big bad wolf?

Yes. You. Think about it.

But the boy gave me no time to think. He turned away from me and pulled the rope, gesturing at me to hurry. I tagged along, looking for a way out. Or a weapon to use. We marched through the kitchen like ants. I looked at everything and saw nothing. We reached the bedroom. We entered. When the door slammed behind me, my insides turned into cosmic winds. I felt as if I had wasted a chance.

W–what's wrong? Ricky asked, sensing something.

I pulled myself together, telling him that I needed to dry my hair. He took the towel off for me.

25

Her hair spilled over her shoulders and her breasts were barely discernible under the loose fabric; her thick tresses in which tiny droplets sparkled like diamonds, covered them entirely; nevertheless,

I was aware of her chest rising with each breath she took. Standing close to me, her forehead was just under my chin and her skin radiated warmth; she was confusing me. I felt I had to get into a pair of pants immediately. Retreating into the wardrobe, I grabbed my black trackies and pulled them on.

That's better, I said and she took it as intended, as a sign that we were on safe ground once again. She went to sit down on my bed, and I sat by the door. A heavy, uncomfortable pause hung between us like a wet curtain until she decided to end it. Looking at the cobwebs above the door, Kathryn said she had always enjoyed baths better than showers.

I asked her why.

Kathryn shrugged; she didn't know why, it just felt better. She looked up at me expectantly so I told her that it's been a while since I had a shower.

You prefer baths then? She asked me, trying to sound interested.

I nodded. Yes, I preferred baths.

With nothing more to add, we lapsed into silence.

I wasn't thinking about anything in particular. I tried not to stare at her but it was difficult. She really looked very pretty with her hair gleaming and her cheeks glowing. All of a sudden, she asked me whether I had a comb. Taken by surprise, I stammered out that indeed I had one and if she wanted to use it, I would bring it for her. She replied that she would appreciate it.

I went to get it from the bathroom. The comb was filthy so I cleaned it at the kitchen sink. I was aware that I was under no obligation to clean a perfectly serviceable comb, but I wanted Kathryn to remember me as a nice person when I was gone.

I gave her the comb and loosened the rope so she would be able to use her right hand. She began combing her hair, patiently separating strand from strand in an even motion, her head slightly tilted to one side. Occasionally when she came to a knot, she grimaced and when she saw me wincing as well, she smiled, saying that she didn't mind my watching her. I could whistle something, she suggested, so I whistled Kenny's favorite song, a country tune, but she didn't like it much, I could tell she wasn't the type for country music, even though she complimented me, so I just asked her if she had any requests. She stopped brushing.

I caught my breath. She sat still, looking at me, her gaze as pure as an angel's. Indeed, the thought struck me that perhaps she was a messenger from Heaven, only I was too stupid to know what the message was.

Feeling confused, I began to panic. I knew she only had to walk out of here and I would do nothing to stop her. But she didn't move, and slowly my panic ebbed away and I was able to calm down. Clearly, her beauty was messing with my head. Her tresses, coiling around her face, reminded me of the Virgin Mary; she, too, had looked questioningly upon me whenever I kneeled in front of her during my churchgoing days. Indeed, right then Kathryn looked so sad I would have done anything to make her happy. So I told her I would whistle anything she liked. She asked for a hymn.

The haunting melody made Kathryn cry. At first, only tears rolled down her cheeks but soon her distress intensified and she began to sob, and I was forced to whistle louder and louder, until eventually I stopped. Watching her suffering, I was overwhelmed by my own feeling of utter helplessness. I don't know what I was thinking but I got up and went over to her and patted her on the shoulder, telling her that everything was going to be all right, only one more day and she'd be home.

Then everything went crazy. As soon as I touched her, she sprang up like a coil. Don't touch me! She screamed at the top of her voice. At the same time she chucked the comb and lunged at me. I didn't lose my cool. I grabbed her and struggled with her, and eventually was able to tie her hands behind her back. She fought me like a tigress though. I never would have thought a little thing like her had so much strength. She clawed at my cheeks. She sank her nails into my neck. She scratched my forehead and drew blood but I never once let go. She shrieked and twisted, and when I finally overpowered her, she spat at me. The spit landed on the pillow.

Get off me, you ******* freak! She screeched. Get off me!

I got up and left her. I locked her in and went to sit down at the kitchen table. I knew I would have to clean myself up, disinfect the wounds but I was too shaken to do anything straightaway. I kept thinking about what happened and I was truly worried about Kathryn, about her state of mind. For a moment there, she had seemed truly insane and her eyes looked like they did not see me at all. Trying to stay calm, I now had a sinking feeling that we had made a terrible mistake, and I wondered how this whole situation was going to end.

26

My dream is about to unfold. As always, it begins with the sound, the irregular, hollow clang of the dinghy bumping against the pier. My heartbeat quickens. To keep balance, I hold out my arms as I walk down the plank to join Old Buzza and Lien, who are waiting for me in the boat. Lien looks a picture in a flowery summer dress, Old Buzza well-worn in his tattered shirt and rolled-up trousers; under his wide straw hat he is smiling. Stepping into the boat, I take the seat opposite Lien. In between us, a chicken and champagne picnic spread on a checkered cloth. The pleasant aroma of the freshly cooked chicken sits delicately above the damp, salty smell of seaweed, creating a whole new scent.

Old Buzza plays the gallant.

Champagne? The man grins stupidly, showing his rotten teeth.

We graciously accept.

He takes us out of the bay. We chat. Old Buzza is full of life. He has a secret to tell. And we are the only people he wants to confide in. The nature of our relationship dictates that we should listen. We make admiring noises. What a clever man you are, Jim.

I look out towards the horizon. The sun is sitting right on it, sparkling like a giant mirror ball. Old Buzza drones on but I am not listening. The dream is taking a new direction. The boat starts to spin and Lien screams like a child. She cries, pleading. I imagine she is pleading but truly I don't know, it's a dream and I only see her on and off like a flickering light.

Mai Lin, wake up …

In our room, Lien shakes me awake.

Old Buzza long gone, she whispers urgently. It never happened.

Her words are soothing. Perhaps we could go on pretending that we were never there.

I feel like kissing her but she doesn't let me. She points to Bid who is snoring on the other bed, and giggles. He is a funny sight. Wrapped in Lien's green blanket, Bid looks like a caterpillar. A short, fat one. Lien reaches across the narrow gap between our beds and pulls the blanket over his head. It is a matter of beauty.

We go back to sleep for the rest of the afternoon. When we wake, it is almost time to go to work. Bid sits on the edge of my bed, looking unhappy. Yawns. Tries to say something but I haven't the patience to listen. Lien and I are due on stage downstairs.

Mooov, I frown at him; I am pulling on my fishnets and he is in the way. He just stares. He is beginning to irritate me. Fancy coming here out of hours and without the money.

Wheh du munee? I say. You plomise. Ploh. Miss.

Bid stares. Looks dense.

I realize I need to be firmer. It is time to raise the stakes.

Noh munee, Ah noh luv you.

Bid nods frantically. I will fix it. I will, he insists, pleading to be allowed to kiss me.

But kissing is out of the question. I slam the door and go downstairs where I twist around the pole. Physical exertion allows me to think clearly.

Lien comes running. There's a rumor, she pants, her eyes as big as moons. People say Old Buzza used to come here. They say he had a thing for young girls. And the widow is curious. Lien looks worried; she might be on the verge of a meltdown. I need to reassure her that everything will turn out all right.

Good Brethren, I sigh, rolling my eyes dismissively toward heaven. There's always a rumor concerning old men and young whores.

Still, to use an old phrase, time becomes of the essence.

From her cage, Lien smiles at me. A delightful smile she has. Crooked to one side where a stitch had healed badly. It doesn't detract from her beauty. Well, it just shows you, there is such a thing as true love.

We go on dancing till dinnertime. The club is slowly filling up, a sign that we will have customers tonight. Lien goes on her break and Bid comes down for his feed. Sits hunched at the bar in all his chelonian glory. Before long, Phoebus turns up to take him away.

27

I cried and cried until I had no tears left. Then I cursed. I cursed my bad luck, my bad temper, Kenny, the boy, the whole world. Dear Me. What a mess. I don't know what possessed me. Possibly, the tune. Hearing my wedding song made me mad. Desperate. Frantic. Something. I don't know.

Whatever the reason, I must have hurt the boy. He had staggered away with his face covered in blood. A lot of blood. It dripped onto the floor, leaving a trail. There would have been pain but he didn't say. He went away without a word, locking the door from the other side, leaving me sobbing on the floor.

All night, I sat up waiting for him to return. He never came. Even though I called to him, he never made a sound. What was he doing? I imagined he might have gone to Kenny and told on me, but somehow the idea of coming face to face with that man again didn't scare me half as much as the thought of being left abandoned. But it was so quiet I had to consider that Ricky might have gone. For good. What would happen to me if he had? I knew I couldn't get out.

Deeply worried, I sat on the floor with my back to the door and my legs tucked under me, hoping that Ricky would come. Then, out of the blue, Me popped in to give me a lecture.

You know, don't you. Me frowned, nodding repeatedly like a small furry animal, a squirrel perhaps, or a beaver. A something with eyes like bottomless wells and a mouth full of sharp little teeth.

Yes, I do. I fucked up.

You've done this before.

Yes, I've thrown a fit before. Many times in front of Rupert.

How does Rupert handle it?

He doesn't. He goes away.

And?

He sulks.

And?

And what?

What do you do to make things better?

I pretend it never happened.

Do you think that's going to work here?

Good question. Looking at Me's raised eyebrows, I quickly realized a change of strategy was called for. After all, this was a matter of life and death.

Okay, I will apologize, I reply, looking straight at Me. She doesn't look convinced.

I've apologized to Rupert, you know. Many times, I say in my defense. It's true. Sometimes it is easier to back down. It gets me what I want quicker.

You promised you would never behave like this again, Me says quietly.

Yes, I did promise I would never behave badly again, I repeat, thinking Me has a point to prove.

But you do behave badly all the time, don't you?

I nod. I do behave badly. Sometimes I just can't help myself.

There is nothing more to be said. Me goes in one corner, I in the other. We sit in our separate worlds without saying another word. For a long time, I sit watching the black fade into grey, thinking and dreaming and feeling very fragile.

When I woke up, I found a bottle of water, a plate of cheese sandwiches, and two apples on the floor beside my bed. It was my breakfast. While I ate I thought about last night, with every detail of that stupid scene garishly colored in my mind, every painful moment of my bad behavior parading in front of me like clowns taking a bow. Eventually, I shook off the stupor. I had to put things right. My life depended on it. I called out to Ricky.

28

I drove to Janelle's straight after work. I had our things packed in the truck like Kenny told me and I was there right on seven, knocking on the door. No answer. I persisted. I knocked on the door until Lien opened it. At first she cursed in Chinese mainly, which I didn't mind; it was charming the way she gestured for me to go but I stood my ground.

Where's Kenny? I asked her firmly, placing my foot in the

doorway.

At that, she broke into English.

He downstair, she murmured, kicking off my foot. Then she slammed the door in my face.

Of course, I forgot Kenny always had dinner at the Club. I should have gone there in the first place, I reflected as I sat on the doorstep, massaging my smarting ankle. Indeed, when I got there, Kenny was eating a pie at the bar. He sat in his usual position, on a stool with his feet tucked under him. Hunched over his plate, he ate quickly while he watched TV. Absorbed in a trashy talk show where a wet t-shirt competition was in full swing, he paid no attention to anything else, and I had to tap him twice before he acknowledged me with a slight nod. Even after I told him it was time to go get the money, he never looked away from the screen; he was waiting for the winner to be announced, and he was oblivious even to Janelle, who was doing splits right next to his pie. We left only after the credits ran.

I drove. Kenny chewed on a toothpick and whistled under his breath, and he looked really happy. I wanted to savor this moment so I didn't say a word. We got to the dump right on eight. I switched the ignition off and we sat in the truck, same spot as previously, and quietly listened to country music. Kenny adored country music, so for his birthday I made a compilation of his favorite tunes and recorded him a whole tape, which I now played as we waited for our money. After the last chorus, at eight-oh-five, Kenny told me to go. I switched on my big torch and set off towards the designated area where I attempted to locate the money same as before. However, despite being methodical, I still could not find it. At precisely eight-fifteen, Kenny became interested. He rolled down the window and yelled, Phoebus, you turd, ezatefefteen. What the ****'s going on?

I responded with a shrug because I truly didn't know. Kenny, it turned out, was after a more specific answer. He got his torch and joined in the search.

We toiled like miners all night with no result, eventually giving up at sunrise. The journey back to town passed in a somber mood; Kenny, beside himself with rage, carried on like a madman until I was forced to turn off the radio because there clearly was no point in turning up the volume.

On the way to Janelle's, (even though I never told Kenny, who thought we were going home, I knew Janelle's was the only place he could possibly go in the state he was in) I stopped at a liquor store and bought a bottle of rum out of my pay. I cruised the town for a while and when we finally docked at Janelle's, Kenny was legless.

29

Lien comes off the stage at three AM. I get rid of my customer just in time to have a shower and change the sheets. He wasn't a slob; nevertheless, I stick to my routine, soaping up and scrubbing vigorously until not a trace of him remains. Most importantly, I wash my hair; the stink of sex tends to linger there. Finally, I'm ready for my sweetheart to come home. I put on a fresh nightgown and set about brewing a pot of jasmine tea.

I think about Old Buzza, about the way he died and how the whole thing has turned into such a mess. If only we could leave here without arousing suspicion. But we can't, I know that much. The reality is grim and no amount of wishful thinking is going to change that. I know that. I so know that and yet, I'm still hoping for a miracle. I'm still waiting for something to happen. And it's all this misspent energy, all this going around in circles, that's making me weak. And weak is dangerous. To get through this, I need to be strong, so I'm going to have to focus on the positives. Right now. Let's see. So far no one suspects a thing. No one has connected us. Touch wood, we will continue under the radar. Eventually, everyone will forget what happened to Old Buzza. So, fingers crossed, time is on our side.

Out of the blue, the power of positive thinking conjures up a most delectable vision of Lien. In my mind's eye, Lien sits perched up on a cloud, painting her toenails. She winks at me, tells me she's never been happier in all her life. She looks so cute I feel my heart melting at the sight of her, and it feels good. As always, she knows just the right thing to say when I'm feeling down. We are going to leave, Mai Lin, she calls to me from her cloud, trying to cheer me up. She talks about our future. Just the two of us, far, far away.

The sweet smell of jasmine fills the room, interrupting my thoughts. Ah, our tea is almost ready. It is now past three o'clock and Lien will be home soon. Indeed, here's the sound of her key turning in the lock. My love steps into the room, a weary smile on her beautiful face. Waving her delicate hand, she heads straight for the bathroom. Well, it's a tap fixed at head height. There is a curtain now. I put it up when Bid came to us. I don't want him looking.

A little while later, Lien and I snuggle in my bed with our cups of steaming tea. Lien speaks, whispering sweet, lovely nonsense to me and her soft words sound like wind chimes, look like paper lanterns strung from a fishing line. There's an orange. For those who are hungry. There's a necklace of exquisite beauty. For those who need to be adorned. There are other worldly goods. For those things matter to Them, Lien whispers, her eyes full of her fear. I nod. Then I help her light an incense stick.

Thus we dream. Inhaling, Lien smiles blissfully, suffusing my mind with the bittersweet scent of eventually. The past, the present and the future pass me by like painted horses on a carousel. The past comes, waving to me like a long forgotten friend. Hello! Remember me? I was there. I do remember my past. I spent it waiting. To be noticed, loved, fed. But orphan tales are such an old hat. Better move on. The here and now is less conventional. A dead man, an unwanted lover and two whores, all in it together looking for a way out. Looking for a happy ending. And here it comes. The future, mine and Lien's, lies unbearably tantalizing at the end of the ride.

Our time together is suddenly interrupted by a knock, and Lien goes to open the door. The boy stutters in the doorway, looking at his feet.

Aah. You 'gain, Lien frowns at his flaps of veal. Pulls her petticoat tightly around her. What a silly boy you are.

Nevertheless, we go downstairs to fetch Bid who, at this hour, is as drunk as a lord. Good Brethren, I sigh. I'll bet he doesn't have the money.

30

Lien cursed as soon as she saw me at the door. Janelle, too, looked like she didn't want to know me, but when I promised them twenty dollars, the girls came downstairs with me, and all three of us got Kenny up to bed. Kenny, on the verge of losing consciousness, belched mightily, saturating the air with a foul smell of rum and barely digested meat, then turned over and fell asleep. Holding their breaths, the girls retreated to the other bed and grumbled, glowering at me as if I were to blame. I judged it a good time to leave. I turned to go just as Lien jumped in front of me and put out her hand, barking at me to pay up. Even though she scowled, I still thought she looked breathtaking in her silk camisole underneath which her lovely breasts jiggled with every little movement she made. I gave her the money and she let me out.

It wasn't until I got half way up the mountain that I started to get emotional. I pulled over and cried like a baby, feeling wretched, confused and very scared. I remembered my mum, and how I cried when she told me she was leaving. It felt like I was falling into a black hole and there was no way out.

Now I felt the same confusion except it was worse because then I had Kenny, who took charge and made all the decisions for me.

If only there was someone to advise me. If only I had stuck to religion. A memory demurring at the edge of my universe took a step forward. It showed Uncle Clem standing at the door, his hand on the handle and his voice pouring through the gap under my door, making a puddle at my feet. Coloring pencils under his arm, Uncle Clem pulled the handle down. But I locked the door.

That was then. Maybe if I prayed hard enough now, my wishes would come true. In the movies, the good people always pray. Well, I'm a good guy. Perhaps it's worth a try.

Clasping my hands in front of me, I prayed.

Dear God, I am in a fix. I told Him the whole story. Once again, He didn't come to my rescue. And I didn't feel any better. Only worse, I felt stupid.

Oh Jesus. I sat in the truck and cried.

31

Sure enough, not a penny. Lien and I go through Bid's pockets: trousers, jacket, shirt. Lien picks up the sombrero, running her finger along the hem. Nothing. It is clear that Bid has failed us once again.

There is nothing we could say that hasn't been said before. We are resigned to another day of waiting. To keep busy, we cook. Lien decides to make an omelet. I help to chop the ham and then I go to sit on Lien's bed. I like watching her work. She looks beautiful and her beauty gives me strength.

Bending over the stove, her hair covers her face like a soft curtain, with only the tip of her nose showing. A vision of loveliness, she reminds me of a precious stone, a diamond cut to perfection, but the feel of her skin is pure velvet. When she blows into the pan, her lips are as red as cherries. I feel very much in love with her. I slip into a dream. In it, Old Buzza doesn't exist. He never lived. He never died. And we were never there. Never.

A shadow streaks the window. It is a bird flying. I imagine the tips of its wings are touching on the upward rise. I imagine where it goes. Somewhere warm. Sunny. I imagine I am that bird.

32

Centuries flew by punctuated by nothing more than my heartbeat. When I finally realized that I was alone in the house, my bones turned to water. The thought struck me that I might be able to escape. It filled me with hope and a sense of adventure. I wanted to tell Me but I couldn't find her. She had disappeared. I decided not to worry. It would do me good to think for myself.

I came up with a simple plan. I would cut through the rope, wrap myself in the quilt and crash through the window, hide in the woods until darkness fell, and then find my way home. A vision of Rupert sobbing in my arms spurred me on. I quickly searched the room for something to use to cut the rope, but there was nothing I hadn't already considered. I felt frustrated but tried not to panic. Determined to succeed, I forced myself to slow down. There might be something I'd missed, there had to be, otherwise I was doomed. Finally I spotted it. The bucket handle.

33

I sat in the truck crying for a long time. Eventually I ran out of steam. The feeling of self-pity subsided and I felt better. I felt I was ready to fight whatever came my way. But first things first. I blew my nose. Then I looked in the rearview mirror to check for signs of my recent distress. I decided to wash my face in the creek. The cold water further revived my sagging spirit; as I trudged up the hill back to the truck, I put all my energy into thinking and for once it worked. I came up with an idea to save the situation.

As I drove back to town, I reflected on the simplicity of it; the scheme was so straightforward, it was bound to succeed. I would send Rupert a new message, asking only for the twenty thousand I knew he had. I reasoned that he wouldn't need much time to get the money together and that I could have it this afternoon. Then, when I collected the cash, I'd go to Janelle's and give it to Kenny, and hope for the best. Yes, it was that simple. With that much cash in our pocket, we'd be free to leave, I reasoned, feeling more and more confident about my idea. Of course, I felt a little apprehensive about Kenny, about keeping him out of the loop, but I also knew I had to act quickly and be done with it. So, by the time I reached town, I convinced myself that my plan would work, and decided to go right ahead. I had an hour to spare before work, which was just enough time to execute my plan.

I stopped at the nearest stationer where I bought a horticultural magazine, a sheet of paper, a pair of scissors and a little tube of glue, and then I sat in the parking lot, composing my new message.

Leave 20 thousand in a brown paper bag by the dead pig at the dump by 4 pm or your wife dies.

I folded the note and then drove like mad to Kathryn's house. I mean, it was a mad thing to do because it was daylight and I could have been seen, but I didn't have the time to be careful. I just drove the truck right up to the gate and chucked the note in the mailbox. I noticed there were open windows in one of the rooms downstairs but I didn't wait to see if Rupert came out. I just bolted.

I made it to work on time. I spent the morning in a dream, worrying about everything. The plan, Rupert finding the note, Kathryn alone in the house, all of it. And I hoped that Kenny would sleep the whole day through. I planned to pick him up at Janelle's around 4:30 PM with the bag of money in the boot. I hoped he would understand. Sure, he might feel cheated at first, but I hoped that the sight of that much cash would ease his disappointment, and we would drive away happy. Once we were safe somewhere far away, I planned to make an anonymous phone call to Rupert about Kathryn. I imagined their reunion and the thought put me in a better mood. I whistled through the rest of my shift until three-oh-five when the world came crashing down.

34

The bucket handle was a joke. It was plastic and as such did me no good whatsoever. God knows I tried. First I hoped to pick the lock, but the handle was too wide to fit through the hole. Then I slid it under the door and swished it back and forth with the expectation of catching hold of something I could use to free myself. As a last resort, I began to saw through the rope with it. Later, drained of all hope, I slumped on the floor with my hands sore.

I thought about everything, mulling it over endlessly in my mind.

It was getting me nowhere. The thought of Rupert sitting alone in our kitchen, sad, destroyed, unable to eat, drove me mad. I imagined him gazing vacantly out of the window, an anxious frown across his forehead, sweating, nervously perspiring.

Dear Me. He is out of his mind with worry. Waiting by the phone, he is praying for me. Well, maybe not praying, Rupert's not a believer, but you know what I mean.

Me didn't answer. Staring at me wordlessly, she uttered a sigh, insinuating that I had it all wrong. But I was determined to be right. I continued my fantasy, pointedly ignoring Me.

Back in my kitchen, the newspaper lies on the table unopened, the financial pages neatly folded, unread. Rupert, unable to hold back his grief, sits there wringing his hands in despair.

Yes, dear Me, you may think what you want, but I know that Rupert loves me.

Me continued looking doubtful, gazing at me reproachfully. I know that look; Me was trying to tell me I saw my life through rose-colored glasses. And perhaps I did. But I prefer to see my glass half full, so I went right on thinking about Rupert, about the little things we did together that mattered only to us. I thought about our Sundays and the fun we had doing what we liked.

The day would begin with a leisurely breakfast in bed, followed by a brunch by the pool. Rupert read the paper and I served coffee. When he finished the sports section, we talked. I talked about everything that happened to me during the week, and Rupert listened, deeply interested in everything that I had to say.

After brunch, we set off to have lunch at the golf club with other couples. In the afternoon, we did our own thing: Rupert played golf with the other husbands, and I played at being one of the girls with the wives at the clubhouse bar.

Thinking back at it took me close to my breaking point. The feeling of nostalgia I now felt was a true revelation; after all, I had always hated playing that role. Being *one* of anything had never been my destiny, but now I longed to be one of the gals again. How I wished I was there, immersed in the boredom of it: sipping martinis in the club lounge, discussing renovations, holidays, marital sex. The conversation did little to break up the monotony of watching our husbands' endless play. Still, we drew comfort from each other, huddling together like penguins waiting the winter out.

The afternoon ended around five. As a rule, Rupert and I dined at Waterlily's. Where people know your name, Rupert often joked, and I laughed with a contented sigh, at ease with the expectation of the expected. The shop talk. The dessert. The wine. Then back home for a quickie before the late night news.

Of course, I realized we were slipping into being a married couple. There were no surprises. Things had been said once, twice; they were being repeated as regularly as clockwork. Over his chops, Rupert warbled on about his pool shop. I sipped my wine, nodding dutifully, nudging the conversation in the right direction, yes, darling, expansion is the answer. Meanwhile, I thought of planting ferns under the verandah. I mentioned it to Rupert. Yes, dear, whatever you want. The house is your domain, he replied, loosening his trouser belt. We shared the dessert. It felt comfortable to be so comfortable.

Remembering my life, I fell to weeping. I wanted to be home with my trusty, predictable husband. I wanted to be where people knew my name. I wanted to be a sounding board.

Shhh, shhh.

I can't help it, Me. I miss him so much.

I know you do. It is a good thing. Perfectly normal. You love your husband and you want to be home.

Me, I am so scared. What if Rupert can't find the money? What then?

He will find the money. You will be home soon.

You really think so?

I know so. Now relax.

Me had the right idea. I could use a little rest. I stretched out on the bed and closed my eyes. I wasn't quite asleep; nevertheless, I had a most beautiful dream. I was walking down the aisle in my white dress. In the gallery above me, the organ played the wedding song and I measured my steps to suit the beat. The pews were packed—at least in the photographs the church was full—but in the dream I saw only Rupert, waiting at the altar in his white suit.

We stood side by side like a pair of turtle-doves. This was the happiest day of our lives. Then a door banged and the noise startled me. My daydream vanished, melted into oblivion like a snowflake.

I sat up with the speed of a bolt of lightning. I heard footsteps and realized that somebody was running through the house towards me. I jumped up and fixed the handle onto the bucket. I was shaking.

Sit on the bed and look the part. You'll be fine. It was Me, making sure I knew what to do.

I went back to the bed, telling myself to remain calm. I could do this; after all, I had been an actress, a successful actress paid to make people believe. Acting is in my blood. I have my apology ready. I am going to be contrite, truly remorseful, really sorry for my bad behavior.

The door flew open.

I'm so sorry, Ricky, I started my speech but got no further. The moment Ricky set foot in the room, I knew he brought bad news. His face said it all.

Dear Me. We have arrived at the heart of the matter. Finally, I will know where I stand. Feeling excited, I gave Me a little smile. This then is my moment of truth.

My moment of truth began with a show of despair. Ricky burst into tears. Standing in the doorway, he shook like a leaf.

What's wrong, Ricky? I asked him softly, trying to control my nerves, which were getting the better of me. I could hardly contain myself; I was like a flooded dam about to burst.

In one leap, Ricky crossed the room and went down on his knees in front of me. Looking ready to pass out, he shoved a piece of paper, a glossy magazine page, into my lap.

R–read th–th–this.

I recognized the publication, a real estate magazine advertising local house sales. I knew it well; we browsed through it every week because Rupert likes to keep an eye on the market. I looked at the page; in the middle of it was a photograph of my house.

It was a good picture. The house, taken from the front, shone like a flower in bloom. It looked lovely, well cared for with the raked driveway and weeded rose beds, dew sparkling on the blossoms closest to the camera. It was a house where surely only happy people lived.

I took in the caption. Not to be missed, it said. Well, I couldn't have put it better myself.

Dear Me, I am finally playing the role I deserve. This is as close as I will ever get to seeing my name in lights again.

I read the blurb underneath the photo, the words undulating in front of my eyes like silly old whores doing a tango. Mr Rupert Calliper is making an announcement to the world. About Me. About Mrs Kathryn Calliper. She has gone on a study tour to Egypt and won't be back in a hurry.

Dear Me, what a lucky girl that Kathryn is. For after all, it is she who is visiting ancient monuments overseas while I rot here alive. It is she who is collating her experiences while I wallow in my own filth. And it is she who hopes to publish those on her return. Well, well, dear Me. It is good to see her spreading her wings.

And what about that enterprising Mr Calliper? He is a tower of strength, isn't he? Prepared to sacrifice, offers unflinching support. The research, so crucial to the success of … is expected to take some time … Here, I imagine, Rupert makes an expansive gesture at his captive audience, a gesture which they can appreciate. Yes, yes, everybody nods sympathetically, we know all about research. It takes time. Who can say when she'll return?

I've never seen him change color. As a rule, Rupert doesn't blush. Now, however, a pinkish glow appears as the enormity of his altruistic, selfless, charitable act dawns on him.

I am selling the house to pay for her lifelong dream, Rupert tells his golf club buddies, who are quite overcome by his goodness. It sits attached to his side like a colostomy bag. And it's getting fuller with Rupert's every word.

Of course, I will be joining her on her travels very soon, Rupert clarifies, gulping air theatrically. His emotions are getting the better of him. She is the love of my life, my Queen of Hearts. The audience cheers and somebody hands him a glass of water. Rupert takes a grateful sip. Consequently, the business is also winding down. I'm selling everything, lock, stock and barrel, just to please her. The audience applauds his decision and Rupert's flush spreads from his head to his toes. Bag and all, his goodness is a force to be reckoned with. I imagine a great ball of fire sitting in his ass, just waiting to explode.

The tango approaches the finale. Executing the last, most difficult turn, the whores are barely able to stand up.

Offers are currently sought for the Calliper residence (pictured). Interested parties are to contact R. Calliper on blahblahblahblah after hours.

35

Bid wakes up.

What time is it? He asks me, grimacing painfully. It seems he has a headache.

Late, I reply.

It's half past twelve in the afternoon. Lien has gone down to the Club already.

Bid takes a shower. I sense he wants to talk, but I have nothing to say. I feel he has let me down. He promised me money, enough to take us a long way from here. A long way from the dead man, and from my conscience. He promised and he's come with nothing.

Bid wants a cup of tea. I point to the kettle. There it is.

Finally, the silence is too much. He talks and soon his words begin to make sense to me. I look at him, disbelieving. Bid's words pierce me like daggers. He's kidnapped a woman. The ransom was not paid. And now, Bid is at a loss. What should he do?

The look on his face is priceless. I don't know what he should do, but I'm getting an idea what *I* should do. I should get Lien and leave town before the cops come after him. They'll be asking questions about other things too. Old Buzza had been seen with us, people are whispering and I feel it is only a matter of time before pieces fall into place for everybody. I should have known Bid would do something stupid.

Understandably, I want Bid to go. It's for the best that we part ways now, before any more damage is done, I tell him, wanting him to understand that our association has come to an end. There is no point in keeping it up. It's every man for himself now, I say to him, but he stands firm. He will not give up on our love.

Making the decision is easy. I have so much to lose. Let Bid come and I will deal with him later. I pull his trunk from under the bed and pack quickly.

36

Kathryn stared. I half expected her to lose it like I almost did when, at three-oh-five, I sat down to my lasagna, and Fred, who works the deep fryer, announced that he was rich. Me und Hunz, the old man said, jerking his head to the side where his twin stood holding a shoe box, inherited zis muny from Jim. Hans put the box down in front of me and lifted the lid with his trembling hands. We looked inside. A pile of money filled the shoebox to the top; I felt like pinching myself to see that I was not dreaming.

Vun hundret souzand, Fred grinned, leaning across the table. Ve vill be u houz buyink.

Jim would have wanted that, I stammered, thinking the world had gone insane. Jim had no money. Fished all day on the bay without catching a thing. Played cards for peanuts. In between, he grumbled about his rich wife who never gave him a penny. Where would he have got a hundred thousand to bequeath? The very idea was laughable.

The twins appeared blissfully unaware of my doubt.

Pulling a copy of *Pristine Mountain Realty* out of the front pocket of his greasy overalls, Hans leaned closer to me. Silently he pointed at the front page, to the photograph of Kathryn's house.

It was a beautiful picture, expertly taken, the vivid colors virtually leaping off the page, the text large and bold. I read the whole thing from Not To Be Missed!! down to the phone number in one breath.

Niize, eh? Fred grinned toothlessly while I gaped like a stunned mullet. It was only when Fred asked, Vot's vronk, Feebuz? that I was able to pull myself together.

Yes, very nice, I replied and shook his hand. For the rest of the shift, I took refuge in the kitchen, taking care not to speak to anybody. If I had, I would have just howled, and then everybody would have thought I was mad.

For a long time, I didn't know what to do. Clearly we were not going to get any money; Rupert was selling up and leaving town. All he had to do was pay the twenty thousand. But he wasn't going to. He put the house up for sale just this morning. After he knew we only wanted the money he had available in the bank. Where does that leave Kathryn? I didn't want to think about that.

If only it was up to me, I would let her go. I never cared for the money; in fact, this wasn't my idea, none of it, and if it had been up to me, we wouldn't be in this mess in the first place.

Christ, we're fucked, I swore out of desperation but only inwardly so it hardly counted as breaking rules. Maybe we'll just let her go and disappear, I daydreamed while cleaning the grills, and I almost fooled myself into thinking it was a viable plan. Deep down, I knew Kenny would never go for it. I grappled to find a solution, to find a way out of this predicament so that nobody would get hurt. It was just as well I had a lot of dishes to wash because being a slow thinker—a dimwit, Kenny always said—I needed a long time. Eventually I came up with something.

Quite simply I decided not to tell Kenny anything. After work, I would go to Janelle's to pick him up. I would pretend we were going to collect the money at the dump, but instead I would take the highway and head for the border. At some point Kenny would cotton on, and then I'd own up that we were saving our lives this way. Oh, I knew I'd cop it, Kenny would go crazy, but I was prepared to take the risk because I was determined to save Kathryn. We were in enough trouble already. Above anything else, I could not bear the thought of parting with Kenny. They would definitely split us up in jail and I knew that I wouldn't be able to survive without him, so clearly I thought my plan would have to work. Of course, I planned to call someone about Kathryn, not Rupert and not the cops, but maybe that nice man at the petrol station where we bought our torches, who joked and laughed with me but not at me.

I said goodbye to Fred because Fred had always been good to me. As a precautionary measure, I didn't make a fuss, so Fred never stopped chopping garlic; as usual, he just grunted, See you tomorrow, Feebuz, over his shoulder. I drove off, taking a copy of *Pristine Mountain Realty* from the front counter. In the truck, I tore off the front page, folded it into a neat square, and put it in the back pocket of my jeans. I knew I would have to produce it for Kenny in the early stages of executing my plan, maybe right after Kenny cottoned on that we were not going to the dump, which might be right after I missed the turn-off or, with a bit of luck, a long way from here if Kenny decided to have a little lie-down on the backseat, in which case he would not notice that we missed the turn-off. At any rate, I felt very nervous about the whole thing. As the strip club came to view at the end of the street, I began to sweat. By the time I parked the truck, a thin trickle had formed in the hairline near my temples, and I was obliged to wipe my face.

The club was eerily quiet; the rickety wooden stairs didn't make a sound under my footsteps. Feeling like a condemned man, I took one step at a time. Eventually, I arrived at Janelle's door. For some inexplicable reason, the image of Kathryn flew by in slow motion and I found myself whistling a hymn. Kathryn was on her knees, begging me to let her go. She never knew how close I was that time she brushed her hair. But that was then. And now I felt a whole lot worse. Realizing that I had no strength to face Kenny, I began to cry.

It was Janelle who opened the door.

Feebuh, she grimaced, shaking her head to indicate she did not wish me to come in. Not now, she frowned, flapping her hand impatiently towards me. Go away.

Her mouth made an angry red circle. She was wearing the same peignoir Lien had on yesterday, which showed her legs as well as her breasts to advantage; however, under the present circumstances I was not able to appreciate this view fully.

Go, Janelle repeated, but of course, I did not move.

I need to see Kenny, I said in my shaky voice. By the time I got it all out, she stopped flapping and looked at me intently.

You cly? Janelle whispered, stepping over the threshold towards me. Why?

I'm okay, I lied stupidly. You could see the tears on my cheeks.

Sum thin happen? Janelle asked, reaching up to touch my chin.

I shook my head. I'm not crying.

Taking my hand, Janelle drew me inside. She sat me down on her cot, and then she went over to the sink where she poured me rum. She brought the glass over to the bed.

Dat bedda, Janelle murmured when I downed the drink in one go. She gently patted me on the shoulder, standing so close that her hip bone was almost touching me. I closed my eyes, inhaling her. She smelled of rum and perfume. Her scent, a curious mixture of flowers and alcohol, reminded me of Lien. A fleeting memory of times gone by flickered from me to Janelle, and for a moment, our minds joined. Lien, you are a snake shedding your skin. I will slowly peel it off you and bury myself in it to preserve the perfection that is You.

Feebuh, Janelle barked suddenly, jolting me out of her consciousness. Her face looked blurred and puffed, and somehow not connected to the rest of her. She took a step back, and then another one, and then she bumped into Lien's cot where she sat down facing me, with her peignoir firmly folded over her knees.

Whachuwann?

I need to see Kenny, I replied, looking at those knees. I noticed a cut just below her right knee; it was fresh and it was bleeding, making a dark stain on the hem of her nighty.

I pointed at it. You're bleeding.

She kept quiet and when I finally looked at her face, I saw that she was watching me with a most peculiar expression.

He gone, she said.

I stared.

He gone, she repeated. You noh?

I didn't know.

Look. Bending down, Janelle pointed under her cot where Kenny had kept his trunk.

I looked.

See? Janelle nodded firmly, even though I didn't see anything. But I kept looking, peering under the bed as if compelled by an invisible force, and, to my horror, Janelle's words soon made sense to me.

A large shiny rectangle in the dusty floor left no doubt that a trunk had previously lodged there, and I slowly pieced things together. Clothes. Cassettes. Shaving cream. All gone. I knew there had to be an explanation, but was I brave enough to hear it? I didn't think so. My scared little heart raced like there was no tomorrow. My thoughts, hundreds of them, were all questions, and they screamed at me, and I felt I was about to drown.

Where is the trunk?

Janelle shrugged.

Kenny leev. Took tlunk. He fuck off. She stood up. You go now.

37

I stared at the picture of my house. There seemed to be little else I could do. Obviously, I was having a nightmare, one of those slow-motion dreams where you can't lift your knees to take a step because your bones are too heavy, and when you breathe, you don't get enough air. And you have to wake up soon.

Rupert will not pay, Me piped up out of the blue. She stood in front of me, and her eyes were as big and hollow as cart wheels.

Of course, he will, I retorted, trying to sound believable.

Me gave a sad little smile. No, he won't.

He's selling the house to pay the ransom. As soon as the property sells, he'll have the one hundred thousand.

He can't sell the house. It doesn't belong to him. You know that. His only option is to ask your mother for the money. She could easily pay up. But he hasn't done that. Ask yourself why. Me shook her silly little head in a gesture of resignation. But I wasn't going to give up that easily.

I know what you're thinking, dear Me. But you are wrong. He loves me.

He's telling people lies.

Having said everything there was to say, Me evaporated into thin air like a thought. In the room, only Ricky remained huddled on his knees, his huge doe eyes filled with tears.

I aaaskt foh t—twennythousand, he announced, spitting the words out like poison. He made a gesture to express his despair; the way he shrugged said it all.

You haven't got the money? I whispered to him foolishly as if I needed to be told. Inside me, my hope unraveled like a badly stitched sweater; the yarn snaked along the floor, looking for an exit. Soon, there would be nothing left.

In front of me Ricky sobbed like a child, looking through me as if I no longer occupied space. Only his lips silently moved. Finally, his words came out, loud and clear.

Kenny's left me.

With that, the last of my hope disappeared under the door. I looked Ricky in the eye.

Rupert has left me, I heard myself say.

38

Kenny's left me, Ricky pronounced clearly and then he shifted closer, quietly asking me to turn around. I don't know what I felt. Relief. Confusion. Disbelief. Anger. Maybe all and every single emotion I ever felt brewed inside me like a bellyful of bean farts, while outwardly the good Kathryn remained calm.

Ricky untied my hands and my ankle. Y–you can g–go.

I stretched my legs. I rubbed my wrists. I told Ricky I wasn't going to tell.

It d–doesn't m–matter, he shrugged in a hopeless gesture of acceptance. His eyes were filled to the brim like buckets left out in the rain. He turned away from me.

I walked out of that bedroom and out the back door. A half moon looked down at me. Smirked. No it didn't. It would have, if it could. A half of a whole can't do anything. A wing on its own. A seedling without soil. A marriage of one.

Ahhh, but you are wrong, says the half moon, making a loop in the sky. It's being witty. Half a pair of shoes worked for Cinderella.

I gave him the finger.

I stood on the porch not knowing what to do. I had no idea where I was.

Wrong. I did know where I was. In the shithouse. With my head in the bowl.

Ricky came out.

I'll d–drive you. He wiped his face with his sleeve.

I wanted to know where we were.

P–Pristine Mountain, he replied, saying the cottage was close to the summit and that he'd better drive me to the main road because I would get lost in the woods. He stood in front of me, dangling the key to the truck on his finger, waiting for my decision. The thought struck me that he might drive me somewhere remote and kill me; it was a silly idea, seeing we had been together in this remote place for almost a week. If he had wanted to kill me, he would have done so already.

I climbed into the truck, leaving behind clanking, brittle, dense memories I knew I would have no need for. Tins on a string tied to a limousine. Chocolate flakes on a wedding cake. Sand in my hair and seaweed between my toes. My heart. My soul. My mind. Cast aside like useless junk.

We drove in silence until a roadhouse appeared on the left. Then Ricky indicated to me that he would stop there if I wanted to.

I w—work here, he said, slowing down to turn, but I told him to drive on.

I can't be seen looking like this, I explained, and Ricky nodded, tearfully agreeing to take me all the way home. The rest of the journey passed somberly; spiraling down the mountain, we pondered our own thoughts and our misery grew with every turn.

Ricky switched on the radio. "Turning Japanese" filled the cab with sound and me with additional sadness.

Rupert had sung this to me at a karaoke bar on our first wedding anniversary. I had laughed then at the sight of him gyrating at our fellow diners, and I had felt proud my husband had such a sense of adventure, but now I recalled the occasion with embarrassment.

And then there was Rupert's office party, where he insisted on repeating the performance. There I felt distinctly uncomfortable because I had caught a glance between the receptionist and the courier, and I saw that they only clapped because Rupert was the boss. Thinking about it now, I couldn't help cringing. Perhaps I had been foolish to adore him unconditionally; perhaps I should have held him accountable. If I had, we'd both have been better off.

My house came into view. In the glare of the brake lights, a huge FOR SALE sign rose before me like a warning: Do Not Enter.

Ricky pulled up close to the gate; behind it, my house slumbered in complete darkness. Ricky turned off the ignition. For a moment, we sat motionless, saying nothing. I knew he was expecting me to go. But my legs had turned to jelly.

What day is it? I asked him, looking into the distance at my house.

Ricky replied that it was Sunday.

Sunday. The thought of it filled me with great sadness. Sundays were our days. On Sundays, Rupert played golf in the morning, and in the afternoon we usually went out. Sunday evenings, if Rupert was home, we spent together in bed, watching television.

I looked towards my bedroom window. There should have been a blue light illuminating the life we once had. Well, there was nothing for it. I had to go. I opened the cab door. The sound alerted Ricky and he gave a start, turning towards me.

S–sorry, he murmured, looking as if he were about to cry again. S–sorry 'boud ev'rything.

Nothing is that simple.

Goodbye, Ricky, I slammed the door behind me, determined to resist the temptation to forgive this silly little boy. My only wish was to never see him again. But he had one last thing to say.

Ricky stuck his head out of the window.

K–Kathryn, he called out, m–my name's F–Feebus.

39

I went straight to the back door. I tried it, thinking that maybe Rupert went out to get takeaway as he sometimes did when I didn't feel like cooking. As always when he stepped out, he would leave the back door open. It was locked. I carefully felt my way around the pool fence to the shed to fetch the spare key we kept under a loose brick by the flower pots. Then I let myself into my home where everything seemed as if nothing ever happened.

The kitchen was tidy; scrupulously tidy I found when I ran my finger along the window ledge, which I hardly ever dusted. In the living room, I smelled the newly cleaned carpet. Upstairs, more surprises. The spare bedroom was refurbished from top to bottom. Previously a storage room, it now shone with a new identity. New curtains, new furniture, bed linen, rug, wallpaper. Everything matching. Vibrant. Immaculate. Pulsing with expectation of good things to come. Amazed at the transformation, I couldn't look away. Like a drawer full of knives, the room held my attention. I wondered what other surprises were in store for me.

Eventually, I moved on. Gliding along the corridor, I decided to play a little game of I spy. I entered my bedroom.

I spy with my little eye … my vanity table. De-cluttered. Devoid of spots. Taken care of. Unlike me. So not like me. Quite the opposite of Me, who like me was feeling deluded, deranged, devalued.

I spy with my little eye … the alcove. My side of the bed vaguely reminiscent. Just vaguely because here, too, changes had taken place. My dressing gown, usually found on top of the linen box, was gone, as was my teddy bear. The frayed tips of my beloved slippers did not poke out from under the valance. There was not a thing of mine in sight; my space had been cleared of my presence. And the surprises did not stop there.

On my bedside table, silk flowers, beautifully arranged in a crystal vase neither Me nor I could recall buying, lent a certain ambience to the room. The drapes were different. Last week pink polyester hung from the bed frame, now luxurious blue velvet provided a discreet shade. Well then, what a difference a few days can make. On Rupert's side, things remained pretty much as they always were; his side remained distinctly his. His jeans casually draped over the armchair. His work tie hanging down the backrest. Spare watch on the table as always. Yes, Rupert's space remained protected.

Facing the facts was an intensely painful experience. I realized I was being left behind, and the hurt was excruciating, full of sharp little teeth lined up in a row, like hungry little orphans begging for food. Those lost souls, those filthy little urchins. What will become of them? Those desperate, forgotten things, always hoping. To be used, noticed or just to be in the minds of their loved ones.

Feeling sorry for myself, I began to cry.

Dear Me. If only I could …

What? See him? Hold him? Speak to him?

Yes, dear Me. There is an explanation. There has to be.

To my surprise, Me laughed.

You're priceless, you are … she smirked sarcastically. Of course there is an explanation. You know it and I know it. Are you telling me that you didn't realize where this was going? Me looked at me with a most peculiar expression on her face.

I shrugged. I didn't know what to say. I had not expected things would turn out this way.

Me stood there with her arms crossed, shaking her head at me. I could tell she was really angry. I could tell she thought I didn't have the sense to deal with this. But I do. I have sense enough to deal with this situation as I see fit.

All I ever wanted was for Rupert to love me. And now he's done this to me, I blabbered to Me, wanting her to understand but she wouldn't listen, abruptly withdrawing from the conversation to leave me on my own. I knew I was feeling fragile. I should have just taken a sedative and gone to bed but I was too restless. I resolved to wait for Rupert.

I sat on the edge of the bed, brooding. All sorts of ideas ran through my mind and got me nowhere. I was irrational. All of a sudden, a change came over me and I felt better, full of hope. We'll sort this out, I said to myself out loud, deciding to think positively. Go downstairs and make a pot of coffee. Everything will be fine.

Passing the hallway mirror, I caught a glimpse of myself. I paused in shock, staring at this mess that apparently was me. I looked like a scarecrow. Ricky's tracksuit hung off me in folds. My face looked drained, greasy, the pores clogged. My forehead shiny with oil. My hair was literally a bird's nest. This will not do. I must have a shower.

I returned to the bedroom to get fresh clothes. When the wardrobe slid open, I was dealt yet another blow. My half of the wardrobe was bare, not a single article of my clothing to be found there. Rupert's side was full to bursting.

New clothes. Beautiful, expensive clothes. Shirts, suits, underwear, shoes. Everything tailored, imported. He'd been shopping while I feared for my life. In disbelief, I fingered the suede of Rupert's new sports jacket and thought I was dreaming.

There was nothing else to do but to check the bathroom. As expected, all of my toiletries were gone. From the en suite, I went straight to the study. Same story. My notebook, pictures, painting supplies were all gone. There was not a trace of me left anywhere.

40

On my way home, I drove to our local and bought a bottle of rum. There was a new man behind the counter; looked like a nice friendly sort, and he wanted to chat, but I frowned and he stopped smiling and just stared at me. Then he asked me whether I was okay. I lied, telling him that everything was super because I didn't want him to get involved. It was none of his business how I felt. After all, if Kenny didn't give a stuff, why should a complete stranger care?

As I slowly spiraled up the mountain, I recalled that glorious afternoon when Kenny took me to the movies. We'd just started living together again after mum left and Kenny chased off Uncle Clem. In the movies he bought me popcorn and ice cream, and we had the best seats because there was hardly anyone there, and we talked the whole time about the movie and other things, and it was the best afternoon. I loved the film, it had sword fights and heroic knights in pantaloons who spoke of honor and friendship and loyalty to their king, and they all stuck together through thick and thin, and I liked that very much, and when I told Kenny, he said we were like that, all for one and one for all, and he made a gesture to show how tight we were by crossing, well, almost crossing his fingers. Of course, he didn't quite manage it all the way because his fingers were simply too short to be manipulated like that, but still, I foolishly believed him. I believed it was us against the world.

I never even cried when our fathers died. We didn't know them very well. In any case, Kenny always said they were filthy animals, and I only cried a little when mum left, but really only because I felt most people would have cried if their mother had left them. And I always wanted to be like other people when I was young. Then, as mum began to fade from my mind, things changed and I began not to care what people thought. Eventually I stopped caring altogether. I did not even mind people calling me Uturd. It was an honest mistake on their part because Kenny was always saying Phoebus youturd, very quickly like it was one word, so it was only natural that people would assume my name was Phoebus Uturd, and when they found out it wasn't, they were very surprised. Like that man in the video shop where Kenny once sent me to get a video. The owner knew me by sight because he said, I know you. You're young Uturd. When I told him that Uturd wasn't my name, he was staggered and he apologized, but he didn't lend me the video because I was under age, and he said I should not even have been interested in that sort of thing, which, of course, I wasn't, but I didn't tell him that. I just left to face Kenny's wrath, which indeed, he showered upon me.

All for one and one for all preyed on my mind all the way home; I cried like a baby because in all my years with Kenny, I never expected this.

41

The boy leaves. I collapse on Lien's bed. I am exhausted. It hurts when I breathe. I am injured. In every possible way. I wish. I wish. I wish but I am still here. The pain of being alive congeals around me like the blood on my knee, suffocating my every pore with its thick, crusted surface. I lie on her bed, curled up around her space, spooning. The space is small. Comfortable. The way it used to be. Outside, the world keeps on living. Somewhere nearby, a clock chimes five times. The afternoon is determined to go on. Eventually, I dream.

Fried chicken and champagne, a perfect day. Lien, stripped down to her bikini, sings, and poor Old Buzza can't take his eyes off her. The song ends. Old Buzza stops rowing and fills up her glass. Tiny froth bubbles spill over the glass and flood her fingers like myriads of fragile spiders. Smiling, Lien sips her champagne. Old Buzza begins to talk, confiding more of his secrets. Talks about his shoe box. It is full of money he's hidden from his wife. We nod, smile. We are happy for him. That is why we are here. Old Buzza is pleased. Life a party iz.

42

After I checked the study, I returned to my bedroom and sat on the edge of my bed, waiting for Rupert. I couldn't think. Without Me, my mind was the shape of water. I seemed to have lost all feeling; my body was a jellyfish and somebody was poking. Out of the holes came nothing.

43

I got home before sundown. Numb from all the crying, I had no feeling left so I simply went about my chores. I cleaned the bathroom, the lounge and the kitchen. Then I chopped up some vegetables and put a roast on like it was a special occasion, but this time I sprinkled plenty of caraway seeds over the meat. I laid them on thickly, the way I always wanted to but was never allowed, because to Kenny the seeds looked like worms. I had tried to reason with him many times but once Kenny made up his mind, he never budged.

After I tidied up the kitchen, I went and cleaned my bedroom. I aired it out properly and stripped the bed, and got rid of the mattress, the rope and the pee bucket. I swept the floor and sorted out the wardrobe; in less then half an hour, no trace of Kathryn remained. After that, only Kenny's room was left. I hovered by the door, struggling with my desires, wanting to carry on as if nothing had happened, and knowing that everything had changed. In the end, I chose not to open the door, realizing that I was not at his beck and call anymore. Besides, I felt he didn't deserve a nice clean room to welcome him when he came back.

When everything was done, I sat at the kitchen table, drinking rum straight out of the bottle. Looking at Kenny's favorite tree, I wasn't thinking about anything in particular, I just sat there, hoping to, as quickly as possible, obliterate the past, the present and the future, which I could feel bearing down upon me like a tonne of bricks. I took deep swigs and imagined I was still in my old life, imagined what Kenny's reaction might have been if he ever found me passed out. Kenny, who had never allowed me to drink alcohol, would have had a proper fit; who knows, in his effort to save me from myself, he might even have broken a chair over my back. Buoyed by the thought of his triumphant return, I kept drinking, spinning fantasies and releasing them into thin air where they wafted about, tantalizing me like delicious smells.

44

I sat in my bedroom for quite a while. I simply didn't know what else to do. When the moon came up against the window, the room came alive under its silvery glow. It gave me energy; I got off the bed and went downstairs into the living room. I switched all the lights on. All around me was a house made ready for sale and nothing more. There was not a shred of evidence to suggest that Rupert's life was off course. As a matter of fact, things looked very routine. Rupert's favorite programs were duly circled in last week's television guide, the magazine, as usual, neatly tucked in the coffee table drawer. When I checked the calendar in the kitchen, I found a golf session penciled in for this afternoon, and underneath it, a new entry, a surprise dinner date:

Peter Colliert, Waterlily's, 7.00 pm

I stared, disbelieving, at the narrow handwriting. It seemed to mock me. This is the way the cookie crumbles, the letters smirked. I felt sick to the pit of my soul. Despite my disappearance, Rupert was enjoying himself as per usual. I could just see him at the restaurant, stuffing his face with pâté, amusing our accountant with his silly sayings, his idiotic one-liners and innuendoes while waiting for the main course, and the scene conjured up a most delicious memory of lamb shanks and glazed vegetables. My stomach growled, reminding me that I had not eaten since lunchtime.

In the fridge, I found an empty carton of orange juice, a bottle of milk and a jar of olives. Not usual. It was clear that my husband had been dining out a lot. I went into the pantry and managed to put together a peanut butter sandwich, which I ate standing up over the kitchen sink. The clock above the stove chimed eight times. Outside, my garden slumbered peacefully in the moonlight.

45

Forty-four dreams in as many days. Life a party iz. Round and round it goes, a slight variation on the theme is all one can hope for. I wake up to find myself still alive. A red moon is rising just outside my window, hanging on a tree branch like a big fat cherry. There's a breeze, I can smell the sea in the air. Nothing has changed.

I go through the motions. I get ready for work and drag myself downstairs. The club is very busy. For the first time in my life, I feel I need to be here, in this cage, writhing like a worm cut in half. There might or might not be new bodies twisting around the poles. I don't know; I only see the tops of their heads below me. Lien is here too. I feel her near me. Singing, whispering, she's making me listen. Heaven is above. Her words stick to me like clouds of fairy floss. It seems to me I could touch her with my eyelashes but I choose not to raise my eyes. Down here, pushing and grinding makes things go bump in the night.

46

A quarter to ten. No sign of Rupert. I'd eaten two sandwiches and drunk two cups of coffee, and sat patiently waiting at my kitchen window. The minutes ticked slowly by. Even the moon, who'd been keeping me company, eventually yawned and disappeared behind the bushes.

I am left alone in the dark with my thoughts.

I imagine a pitiful, sad, vile creature worshipping a painting. He is an unlovable, disgusting thing bent on destroying. He has a dungeon in which he will skin you alive. I am He. And you, Rupert, are the blind woman.

I am angry. Desire burns in me like the three fires from which it springs. Anger, greed and foolishness are to blame. Therefore, I desire you to suffer, to be trampled on, to be destroyed. You. You. And you. Yes. All good things come in threes.

Shhhh. This is getting us nowhere.

Dear Me ...

Shhhh. Listen ...

No. No. You listen. Everything has gone wrong. Rupert doesn't want me. I can't find my cat. My house is up for sale.

Me took a while to reply. When she finally spoke, she made no sense, advising me to let go, to lay the whole thing to rest and get on with my life as best I could.

It was all I could do not to laugh out loud. Silly little Me, I replied, feeling like a dead girl come out of a well, I know what I'm doing. I am looking for an even distribution. Rupert is to blame. Kenny is to blame. And Ricky, sweet stupid little Ricky, will have to pay too. They will all pay for what they've done to me.

I grabbed the phone and dialed.

47

At half past nine, the roast was ready. I had forgotten to bake the potatoes but I had onions and green beans and they would have to do. I set the table for one and was just about to carve the meat when I heard a noise outside. I turned off the light and crouched by the window. The noise, a low hum, intensified. It seemed that a car was approaching. I lifted the blind and peeked outside. Sure enough, in the next heartbeat its headlights appeared in the window. I dropped to the floor. As I lay there with my eyes wide open, beams of brilliant white light traveled across the ceiling and along the walls, and when they finally merged, a cavernous wormhole opened up at the foot of the wardrobe ready to swallow everything in its path. In that instant everything became crystal clear. This was the moment I had spent my whole life waiting for. I always knew it would come, but I had hoped I could somehow dodge it, or pass it over to someone else. In the end, I had fooled myself into thinking this moment would never arrive.

The headlights died. Outside, car doors banged. Leaves rustled underfoot. Voices whispered. I heard them under the window; they were messengers, soul suckers, bad, bad seeds. Eventually, they stepped up to the porch; the floorboards creaking under their weight made it plain, and with each footstep I understood a little more how futile it was to go on resisting Destiny. I clearly saw the inevitable beckoning to me with a smile and a friendly nod, but when I tried to stand up, I felt such weakness in my knees, I knew I was powerless to move.

There were two of them. The short fat one I recognized the moment he set foot in the kitchen. He was the cop who had vouched for Kenny at the roadhouse so Kenny would get the job. A kind man, though rough around the edges, of whom ordinarily I would not have been afraid. The other cop, a tall thin fellow with a squeaky voice, I didn't know. They had called my name several times before they entered the house through the back door.

We're coming in now, Phoebus, the cop I knew said, and the other called out, We are entering the dwelling. And then I heard the fat cop, who was in charge, telling him off. For God's sake, Wally, he grunted, he's just a kid. I imagined he would have been shaking his head but then they entered the dwelling and found me crouched under the window.

48

I had many questions I fully intended to ask Rupert when I grabbed the phone, but a flashing light on the answering machine caught my attention. Without thinking, I pressed the button. It took precisely fifteen seconds to answer many of the questions I had. A woman's—a mature woman's—voice rang out. Hi, it's me, darling, the woman said, giggling like a schoolgirl as she reminded Rupert about tomorrow night. She wanted him to come to her place. Then her voice dropped to a husky whisper. I miss you so much, partner in crime, all of you, you naughty boy. The message ended with a noise, an intimate sort of noise that left me in no doubt as to the exact nature of their relationship.

Me and I looked into each other's eyes. I see my jealousy reflected in hers, as green as algae and spreading with each breath I take. I calmly walk over to the television set and turn it on.

You don't need to do this, Me says, looking as if she is about to cry. She's pleading; she knows what is going to happen.

Oh, but I do, I reply.

I make my move, lunging towards her with the speed of a shot glass sliding across the bar. We make contact and I start to choke her. She fights back; rolling on the floor, gasping for air. She clutches at me, begging me to stop. But I don't. I shake her off and I stand there laughing, filled with rage and growing bigger, bigger and bigger, like an inflatable balloon. I scream. I shout. I am having a good old rave. The rage spreads, filling the room like a fart, penetrating all my senses. I throw a punch at the sofa. At the pillow. At the footstool. And so it goes, I punch and punch until a newsflash bring me to a standstill.

The intersection between the 66th and the 67th kilometer of the Pristine Mountain highway is closed to traffic at this time until further notice, the newsreader announced, describing an auto crash between a sedan and a semi-trailer. Stern-faced, the steely-haired man warned against the following images, they were graphic and bound to distress some viewers. He was right. As soon as I saw the cowboy boots and the belt buckle, I was affected.

The deceased, whose names have not been released, were apparently traveling at a high speed when the female driver lost control of the vehicle and collided with oncoming traffic. The driver of the semi-trailer has been taken to the District Hospital where he is being treated for shock. As the newsreader voiced over the bloody debris strewn along the road, my mind raced ahead. Poor Ricky.

49

Throughout the fat cop's speech, I remained immobile. Standing over me, the tall cop's body blocked the glare coming from the naked light bulb above the kitchen table. Illuminated, their grave faces descended upon me like a visitation from above.

Is there anyone we can call for you? the fat cop asked me after he finished.

I shook my head. No one.

What about your mother? He squatted down to my level and I caught a whiff of him; he clearly was sweating in the nether regions, for there was a dark stain in the crease of his crotch where his sturdy thighs spread outwardly towards me. The cop rested his forearms on them, and he entwined his fingers as if he were getting ready for a finger play. This is the church and this is the steeple. Uncle Clem's favorite from a long time ago. He had liked to play it with me, but I always had to sit on his knees, and after a while I didn't like sitting there, so I never played it any more, and naturally I thought I'd forgotten it, but now it seeped into my mind and I could have told the cops the whole rhyme.

I'm fine, I said, asking them to leave, which reluctantly they did.

If you need anything. The fat cop tucked his card into my shirt pocket.

I nodded. Okay, I will. Through the kitchen window, I watched them get into their cop car.

50

I finally lose it in the break. In our dressing room, Lien's fan lies carefully folded in my draw. My lotus flower left it there. Even now, her words chime in my ear. I love you.

We share everything, I cry. We shared everything.

The police are here to tell me. They stand awkwardly behind my makeup chair; I see their faces in the mirror. They spout the formula. They are sorry for my loss. I can tell they are trying to mean it. But there is going to be paperwork. They will come back at a better time. The cops are as efficient as machines. They don't notice a thing.

Once upon a time, the past, the present and the future passed us by like painted horses on a carousel. Now, there's only death according to Lien. She hovers, unrelenting, whispering, and her soft words fall to earth in rose petal showers. The Good Brethren will come, she whispers. I cry, knowing she is right. I see Them in my dreams. They come swirling, howling, swooping on my door.

A policeman hands me a tissue. He follows his job description. He means to be sympathetic but I know better. I fake orgasms. I blow my nose. The police leave. It's for the best. I want to be alone in my misery.

51

I woke up at half past three in the morning, on the sofa with Me curled up next to me, taking up space like an imaginary friend. The television was still on, and maybe, if I had had my credit cards, I would have bought the foot massager. It looked like something I could use.

However, as all my credit cards were gone, there was no point in wallowing. I switched the television off.

Rupert, if you could see me now. The irony of it. I am lying on the sofa fully clothed. Writhing. Despairing. Torturing myself with jealousy I didn't know I was capable of feeling. How could you do this to me? To us?

I pictured her. The Other Woman. The growler. Just the type I thought Rupert would never find attractive. Ne-ver. I should have listened to my mother. She had always known.

Never say never, my mother warned me when I told her Rupert never even looked at another girl since we met. She had wagged her finger meaningfully, but of course I rejected her counsel because Mother had never liked him. Ingratiating, she said. Smooth. A person of limited appeal. She gave me to understand I was being foolish.

But, trembling, I rose from the chair, leaping to my beloved's defense. I swore, declared, revealed.

Mother listened quietly to my argument, my pretty words coiling around her like tinsel until she disappeared in the glitter.

End of story. I married then moved away. Nowadays we saw each other rarely, but spoke on the phone frequently, especially after an argument with Rupert, when I called her to make me feel better.

Thinking about Mother, I realized I had not spoken to her for over two weeks and decided to call her straightaway. I knew she wouldn't mind being woken up this early.

I will not say anything about my troubles just yet, I thought to myself as I walked up the stairs to the study where I kept my interstate numbers. I will only let her know that I am home, in case she called last week.

Upstairs, I went straight to my desk, expecting to find my phone book in its usual place. I had forgotten that Rupert had cleaned me out.

It wasn't there.

Dear Me. Where is it? Irritated, I gazed into the empty drawer. This really is going too far. A hot wave of anger gripped me and I ripped the drawer out of its rails. I never realized drawers had wings. Aah. They don't. The drawer hit the wall and bounced, eventually landing on the sofa.

The drawer. A funny, pragmatic little object, insignificant until a hole in its space reveals your place in the Universe. Then it becomes the very centre of your world. In my world, the false bottom of the drawer revealed a file marked House Title Deed. I pulled it out. Looking at it, I began to understand the rules of engagement.

Dear Me, this is where we're at. Rupert is really trying to sell our house. Has he gone mad? Our house belongs to my mother. Of course, she's letting us have it, but the title is in her name. He knows that and yet he is prepared to risk everything. Why? What have I done to him?

Me shrugged and I, looking at my mother's signature authorizing Rupert to execute the sale of the house on her behalf, suddenly felt like laughing. My mother would never sign such a thing. My wits gathered round me like witches. Clearly, her signature is forged. It is. I can see it in the way the letters are formed. Smooth. Confident. Perfect. Like Rupert. I would never have thought it would come down to this. But here we are. Rupert did it. He did it to get rid of me.

I sat at my desk, staring at the paper. The forgery had really brought it home to me. I was being abandoned, trampled on like an old mattress waiting to be discarded. I sat staring at the paper for a long time, feeling defeated, feeling used, crooked and damp, like a wrung out dishcloth. Eventually, I would dry into a funny shape.

In the end, I had to wake up. I picked up the drawer and put it back in its place. Then, for no reason at all, I pulled out the bottom drawer. What I saw there took my breath away once more. Secured by a rubber band, a pile of money clung to one side of the false bottom of the second drawer. A big pile, thousands of dollars perhaps. I took the notes and spread them on the desk to count them. All in all, there was twenty thousand.

Aah. All my life, I'd been a dreamer, a wannabe full of hope that things would turn out the way I'd dreamed. Well, they didn't. All I ever seemed to do was to let other people run my affairs while I sat idly by, a mere spectator in my own life. I watched it slip away, moment by moment, and then those moments turned into days and those into a haze, a grey-blue-white haze of nothingness. Up to my nostrils in it, I finally panicked. I geared up one last time and tried to change, to become someone that mattered, someone other than me.

Oh, dear Me. It hasn't worked. A dreamer trying to be a schemer looks to be another colossal failure in a long line of many. No wonder Rupert wants out. No wonder he is sick of me. I am sick of me. I really don't like me.

Clarity is a terrible thing. I put my head down and sobbed. I sobbed until my eyes came away in my hands.

52

Strangely, I didn't feel anything after the cops had left. I mean, I felt no sadder than before; it was as if nothing, not even Kenny's death, could top his leaving me. I would have understood if he had said to me, I'm taking Janelle and I am leaving, or if he said he was out of patience and therefore it was up to me. If he had walked out then, I would have understood. That I could have dealt with. Only, he did none of those things. It simply didn't matter to him what happened to me. It didn't matter to him whether I lived or died, and that was very hard to take. His death was just an unexpected twist; it really made no difference that I had not said goodbye because Kenny had already made that choice for me.

Feeling no sadder, I remained still with my head pressed against the lino for some time. I thought about mum. I knew I ought to tell her about Kenny but I had no idea where she was. So I pictured her in my mind, I pictured how I would break it to her, how she would cry and then, of course, she'd get drunk and I would have to deal with it. Poor mum. She wasn't always bad though. When she was sober, she could be nice. Once, a long time ago when I was little, she took me to a zoo and we had a lovely time and I told her I wanted a pet and she promised to get me a puppy. Of course, it never came to anything because on the way home she met a man on the train and the puppy thing got forgotten, but still, it's the thought that counts. Later, when she left us and Uncle Clem was in charge, I got my wish when he bought me my bunny but there was the other business, too, the memory of which even now made me feel like crap.

For a long time I lay on the lino, feeling powerless. And scared. Of the future, of all the things to come. It was as if I had gone back in time. Once again, I was nine years old, lying on the floor in my room, talking to my rabbit through the gap under the door, and I remembered how good it felt knowing that he was there, and I wished he was here now to comfort me. But Fluffy was long gone. It was Kenny who let him go because Fluffy reminded him of Uncle Clem. I begged him to let me keep him because I loved my Fluffy, but Kenny wouldn't hear of it and I was left with nothing. And now, six years on, I'm still left with nothing.

Remembering my bunny made me feel angry to the point of shaking. The anger felt good. It gave me energy. I got up and went outside to look for my axe. I found it by the shed and used it to stop my shakes.

Kenny's tree fell just before dawn. I threw the axe behind the shed and went to lie down in my room where I fell asleep the moment my head hit the pillow. I had the strangest, most beautiful dream. Kathryn and I were in the truck, going down the highway. Kathryn had her hand out the window and was catching the wind, and her eyes laughed because I whistled her favorite tune. On her lap, my bunny lay contented, and a cat in the back seat softly purred. In the distance, a picturesque town came into view. It was a lovely place, I imagined, filled with nice families living in clean, neat houses with tidy gardens behind picket fences. There were children in those gardens, playing ball games and swinging from swings their fathers hung from cherry trees, and everybody was happy, even Kathryn, who looked radiant, sitting next to me in my truck.

There! She exclaimed excitedly, pointing towards the town. There it is.

I veered off onto a dirt track and stopped the truck. We sat a while, looking at the lovely vista before us and then Kathryn put her hand on my shoulder.

Ricky? She whispered, peering anxiously into my face. Ricky, wake up.

PART II

I see her in real time. She is as strong as an ox and full of confidence. She gives me a wink. Not long now until They come for you. I should be pleased. Instead, I cry. I cry because I am a weak, defenseless being, both guilty and innocent. The Good Brethren know it. I feel Them coming and there is nothing I can do to stop Them.

1

Peter cancelled on me at the last moment. I briefly contemplated returning home but, as the restaurant came into view, a vision of Rosetta's lamb shanks beckoned and I swerved into the car park.

The restaurant was pleasantly quiet. A young couple in the recessed alcove, and a table of four on the terrace was all the traffic. I strode past them straight to my spot at the round bar.

Evening, Mr Calliper. Rosetta beamed from behind the open grill; she placed a menu in front of me the moment I sat down. We bantered easily about nothing in particular. I watched her work; reaching for her utensils hanging overhead, Rosetta smiled, her shapely bosom filling her cleavage in a most attractive way. Not for the first time, I envied her husband.

What a lucky guy, I thought. A sensuous wife, bosomy and a good cook. I ruminated over the excellent starter of smoked chicken salad peppered with walnuts and tossed in orange dressing. A transient thought of my own wife, God rest her soul, temporarily clouded my sunny mood; remembering her culinary skill, I privately shuddered. My wife. A chapter closed, I hoped, with the sale of her—ah, my house—in the near future. A sudden nervous flutter in the pit of my stomach made me start. Refusing to give in, I rapped my fingers on the table. Touch wood, I'll be a rich man very soon. Thus reassured, I finished the entrée and turned my attention to the hostess.

Superb, I complimented the charming Rosetta, who, bustling busily about, looked delectable. Attractively flushed, her skin appeared as soft as butter, her lips as luscious as ripe strawberries, and her curves … I fell to wondering what it would take to possess such a complete woman. Beautiful, confident, full of promise, Rosetta stirring a sauce seemed to me the pinnacle of womanly perfection. I tried to find fault with her, tried to picture her raving and ranting and crying incessantly over the littlest thing the way my late wife did, but it was hard. I could not picture Rosetta crying over burnt eggs; indeed, I could not imagine Rosetta burning eggs in the first place as my wife did every time she braved the stove.

My wife, I recalled with a pang, had not been bosomy, had not been sensual and had not been a good cook. I had fully expected to find those qualities in her, for a man goes into marriage expecting something in return for the loss of his freedom; alas, I was not to be compensated. Of course, to start with, Kathy had beguiled me with her big eyes and innocent demeanor. I had been fooled into thinking that I was fortunate to have married a virgin, and of course, the house and the money her mother had put up for my business eased the pain initially, but in the end it counted for nothing. They trapped me, plain as plain can be, Kathy with her artlessness, and her mother with her generosity. Inside three months, I began to suspect that the old bag played me for a fool, for Kathy turned out to be difficult, demanding and prone to temper tantrums.

Is it any wonder, I asked myself over Rosetta's succulent lamb shanks, it's ended this way? I shrugged. Not really. Savoring the exquisite taste, I thoughtfully chewed. No wonder at all.

Having recently arrived at this answer, I took comfort in it more than I cared to admit, for my initial response a week ago when I pulled the ransom note out of the mailbox had been vastly different.

> We have your woman. Do not tell anybody or she will pass away in a bad fashion. Leave one MILLION dollars in a luggage at the DUMP at 8 pm tomorrow night and go back to your residence at once where a telephone communication will announce where your female is. Remember do this or the lady is lifeless meat!!!

Walking up the driveway, I stared at it, thinking it not so much a bad joke as nothing at all; it certainly made no sense to me until I set foot in the hallway and, through the open kitchen door, perceived the cat sitting on the bench.

Kathy! Peeking into the kitchen, I called to summon my wife. She, however, did not appear. Instead, Kleopatra—spelt with a K, Kathy had informed me the day she brought the wretched thing home—jumped off the kitchen bench where she had been licking her paws. Meowing, she advanced towards me. One look at the cat's bowl told me that the creature had not been fed.

Kathy! Feeling my bile rise, I persevered. I was in no mood for Kathy's theatrics. That woman has far too much time on her hands, I thought irritably as I stepped over Kleopatra who had not ceased meowing. She rubbed against my calves and continued making an unbearable row.

Kathy! I tore through the house, positively seething. The kitchen held no signs of dinner simmering quietly on the stove and I felt most horribly inconvenienced. Would you show yourself! I raised my voice impatiently, stomping into the bedroom. With one swoop of my muscular arm, I slid open the wardrobe. I had expected to find her standing there in her stupid monkey pyjamas; she would be giggling foolishly and she would express a most innocent surprise as to why I was "grumpy." I would have told her that she would have been better employed in cooking a decent meal for once instead of scribbling silly notes, but she wasn't there. As I stared at my suits, I realized that something was not quite right.

2

I dawdled over the dessert. It deserved to be dawdled over for Rosetta's cheesecake was something out of this world. Delicious, simply scrumptious, a mouth-watering treat. As I sat sipping my port, I thought what a pity it was that I was leaving town. Alas, leaving town was an essential part of my plan; a component not to be altered under any circumstance because leaving town meant a new beginning and peace of mind.

The first ransom demand threw me. I felt conflicted, confused, and I had sat up all night, thinking things through. From time to time, I read the note. I fingered the greasy paper. I even smelled it to make sure I wasn't dreaming.

What if it's for real? This thought occurred to me when I stared into my wardrobe, looking for Kathy. I promptly fished the note out of my trouser pocket where I had previously placed it and looked at it again. One could be forgiven for thinking it was a prank, it looked so silly, this cut-and-paste newspaper job, just the sort of thing Kathy would come up with to be funny. But now, as I studied the message, it came across as quite serious. It might just be the real thing. The phrasing was ridiculous but I knew what the note meant to say. Pay up or Kathy will die.

What if it's a joke? This thought occurred to me again much later in the night, when I determined I had all the answers, and long after I had decided to let the thing run its course. The thought had jolted me out of my complacency, for if this was Kathy's idea of being funny, I would be in very hot water indeed.

Why didn't you pay? she would ask me after she'd come home. She could even be waiting at the dump where I had no intention of going, to see whether I had the courage to face her "kidnappers."

Why didn't you pay? she would ask.

What would I tell her?

Visualizing the scene, I shuddered. Perhaps it was a joke. It would just suit Kathy's insecurities. She never stopped harassing me, constantly demanding I prove my love for her while she plagued me with over-the-top protestations of hers.

In the end, I flipped a coin. Heads it's a joke, tails it isn't.

I am a lucky tail man so when the coin stopped spinning, I was not the least bit surprised. However, it moved the stakes up a notch and I realized I would have to think things through very carefully indeed. I lit a cigar and eased myself into the sofa to be comfortable.

By dawn, I had a plan. A perfect plan. Shape-wise I knew I had a circle. A simple, uncomplicated curve along which I would travel easily from A to B, C and D, naturally progressing from one thing to another without the least difficulty until I reached my desired destination. Feeling happy, I decided to cook a hearty breakfast. I put on my bacon. I put on my eggs, and, while waiting for the coffee to brew, I watched the sun rise over the pool. Shimmering brightly, the water reflected prettily, and I brimmed with optimism.

3

The hardest thing, I decided, would be to negotiate Kathy's mother. The old hag had never signed the house over; she had deemed it unnecessary, she declared at the wedding, for we were all one family and therefore it made no difference whose name the house was in. Of course, we had nodded and clinked glasses, no difference at all, and I thanked her profusely. I made a speech and acknowledged the kinship, the family ties that now bound me to her, but the witch had only replied with a knowing smile.

However, I was not fooled. I had noted the glint in her eyes and I knew she did not trust me. Yes, definitely the hardest thing.

But first things first. To those few who cared, I let it be known that Kathy had taken off overseas. Funnily enough, everyone had remembered Kathy mentioning her desire to travel. Oh yes, the monuments, one woman said. She had stood next to Kathy at yoga a few times and she distinctly recalled Kathy's intention. She liked them Egyptians, the woman disclosed when I ran into her at the gym's reception where I cancelled Kathy's enrolment. The receptionist, too, nodded. Yeah, the pyramids. After the gym, I had only one other errand. At the library, I spread the same lie. The clerks charged me with best wishes, and these I faithfully promised to deliver. And then it was time for Mother.

Mother, a tough nut to crack, to be sure. However, I stuck to my plan and came up trumps. After hours of agonizing over how to approach this delicate matter, I finally decided on the boldest, simplest move of all. I would not tell her. Of course, I smacked myself in the forehead, the very simplicity of it guaranteed success. The more I thought of it, the more sense it made, for, however hard I tried, I could not come up with a believable story. Kathy's mother would never go for the "overseas trip" crap. She knew Kathy too well. She would smell the proverbial as soon as the words reached her hearing. Oh no, telling her would never do. Well satisfied with my decision, I turned my mind to the next item on the agenda. Mother's signature.

I knew I would have to practice because Mother wrote in fanciful characters. A real witch's brew that woman conjured up within the nine letters she had to play with, and it took me a good part of the day to master it, but in the end, it became second nature. The deed was done. Oh, I knew the thing wasn't legal but what's life if not a gamble?

It appeared to be paying off. I had an offer on the house this very afternoon. A local man, an elderly invalid of limited intelligence, willing to pay cash for a good deal which I hastened to offer him in exchange for a speedy conclusion, a condition to which he readily agreed. Just a few hours ago, we had shaken on it, a gentleman's handshake but binding nonetheless, and now I was celebrating my last night in my boring life.

I was one of the last customers to leave Rosetta's pleasant establishment. See you next Sunday, she called after me, and I turned and waved goodbye. She stood behind the cash register with her elbows on the counter; leaning forward, her heart-shaped face cast a shadow over her matching cleavage. I sighed. I could have … I might have … a lot of maybes in another lifetime. Feeling somewhat fragile, I decided to finish off the evening at Janelle's.

4

I had been seeing Janelle for the better part of my marriage. She was a tiny girl with a lot of attitude, who knew what I liked, and twice a month, without fail, she delivered it. I had discovered her at the club I'd been frequenting since I started the pool business. Proprietor Wong had purchased a spa bath and we got to talking. Then one thing led to another and a month later I found myself a member. Initially, I had not been particularly keen on Janelle; being small in stature she reminded me of my wife, but Wong hinted at untold delights. Don't judge a book by its cover, were his precise words, and indeed this was the case. All resemblance to my wife vanished the moment Janelle opened up her fan. One flutter of her eyelashes could make a man weep. Thinking of her magic fingers, I now shuddered in anticipation of the evening ahead, and not for the first time thanked my lucky stars, for such expertise is hard to find.

Not long ago, I asked Janelle to devote herself exclusively to me. She wasn't the least bit surprised. Promising to duly consider my offer, she went upstairs to do her sums, but when she reappeared she told me I didn't have that kind of money. I recalled feeling stunned, for I had thought I was in when I watched her come down those stairs. Delicately placing one high-heeled sandal in front of the other, Janelle, lithe as a tigress on the prowl, undulated along the spiral, keeping eye contact with me, and for one fleeting moment, I thought I had her.

Yes, I'm yours, I read in her face, and of course it was only when she said: You noh munee foh mee that I realized a Chinese face is not to be read in the ordinary way. But that's all the skill I had, and I knew I had to find the cash somehow.

Enter Zelda.

Thinking of Janelle, I drove down the highway like a madman. I felt a wonderful sense of freedom. Only a few more minutes and I'd have her all to myself. I glanced at the wad of money lying on the passenger seat, mentally counting the folded notes … one hundred, two hundred … yes, thanks to Zelda, I'd have my skillful Janelle all night.

I took a sharp right off the highway. A rabbit, making his way across the road, froze in my headlights. Ah well, I never liked animals. As I steadied the car, my eyes again strayed towards the notes. Fresh they were, crispy, brand new, full of possibilities. I took one out and smelled it. Thank God for Zelda.

Stop that! I shouted out loud. I was almost there; the neon sign of the club well in sight, and the last thing I wanted to do was to think of Zelda. Zelda Old Money Bags, Zelda the Mistress, Zelda My Biggest Fan, An Altogether Capital Girl. I don't know where I'll be without you. Certainly not off to buy pleasure, for my pleasure doesn't come cheap. You noh munee foh mee. I had to find the cash and I did. I found Zelda.

5

Who is Zelda?

An ageing widow with money to burn. A foolish romantic hungry for *lurve*.

Zelda sailed into the pool shop one day, a broken pool hose in hand. Smiling shyly, she flashed that gold tooth at me and extended her friendship in a most generous way.

What was I to do?

The first time I laid eyes on her, I wouldn't have thought things would turn out the way they did. I summed her up at a glance. Sallow-faced and wrinkly, her scrawny frame boasted breasts that, like deflated balloons, hung a short distance from where I guessed her belly button resided. Yes, a dried-up prune. Presenting the hose, she smiled at me and I was only being polite when I offered home delivery. She had lit up like a Christmas tree; her eyes sparkled as she gurgled at me happily, I am not worth the trouble, but of course I insisted. Her house caused me to revise my judgment. Perhaps there was something to be done here. I ruminated over the cheese platter she had laid out, and I was at my most attentive. To cut a boring story short, I had her eating out of my hand within the hour.

Since that first afternoon, Zelda had known about my unhappy marriage. I had dropped hints of an impending separation and she proved herself most understanding. The poor innocent really believed we were courting, even though I only took the plunge with her after I got the ransom note. However, long before consummation she had started giving me money; I led her to believe I was expanding the business. After my divorce, I hinted, it would naturally be all hers. Zelda beamed.

Well, good old Zelda. The thought of her now caused me to curl my lips upwards. I afforded myself a little smile. A vision of Zelda adjusting my cravat rose before me. The scene was a pantomime with very little variation.

Must you leave, my love? Zelda would ask every time we parted. To show her disappointment, she'd screw up her face into what she imagined was a cute pouty look, which really she couldn't manage on account of being neither cute nor pouty-lipped.

Responding to her cue, I would groan: I wish I didn't have to, and I'd kiss her on the forehead. Then Zelda would hastily press money into my hand, two or three hundred dollars at a time to invest in our future, and this investment I would readily accept. We'd hug and I'd wave goodbye to her from my car, leaving her gazing wistfully after me long after I'd gone.

Smiling at the memory, I looked at the money littering my passenger seat and reflected that my future had never looked better.

The club, at this late hour, was usually busy. However, today being Sunday, I fancied I wouldn't have to wait. I glanced at my new watch. Half past eleven. Admiring my new diamond encrusted watch, I slowed down a fraction. The watch was the latest in a long line of presents from Zelda, who, since my wife had so conveniently vacated my life, had been eager to prove the sincerity of her feelings. In my wardrobe hung a number of new suits of the finest quality, my drawers overflowed with the new shirts that Zelda, showing surprisingly good taste, personally ordered for me, and on my shoe rack were no less than twelve pairs of imported Italian shoes.

I rounded the corner. The club, now fully in my view, was ablaze with light. A crowd of people milled about. I frowned; I had expected a quiet, discreet visit. But it was not to be. I glimpsed a car, a flashing siren, another vehicle and two cops, but that was only out of the corner of my eye, for, as soon as I recognized the cops, I steered right on and never turned into the car park.

Once out of sight, I pulled over to contemplate my next move. Something had happened at the club. What it was I did not care to know, it clearly had nothing to do with me, but I suspected that seeing Janelle was not on the cards tonight. I simply could not risk the exposure in case it gave people ideas. What with my wife out of town and all, visiting Janelle was now out of the question. In the end, I did the only sensible thing I could do. I went to see Zelda.

6

Wake up, Ricky, I've come back.

She sat on the edge of my bed. Her whispers jolted me awake, the soft words, tickling my cheeks like feathers, burrowed into my dream, causing it to recede until nothing but a vague longing remained. I became conscious of my surroundings. I was in my room, lying on my bed fully clothed. Directly in front on me, the sun sat poised on the windowsill, a huge golden obelisk in the middle of which Kathryn, shrouded in its golden rays, looked like an apparition. I blinked, feeling a stab of sharp pain behind my eyelids. Then I pulled the blind down and Kathryn solidified.

Kathryn, I said. Nothing else came to mind. Besides, the headache prevented me from saying more.

Kathryn sighed and reached for my hand.

I heard about your … friend, she whispered, struggling with her words as if she were unsure of what to say.

From the look on her face, I could see she expected me to respond, which I didn't for a long time. Lost for words, she sat quietly squeezing my hand.

He was my brother, I finally said.

She nodded as if she had known.

I thought as much.

It angered me to think she thought she could pull one over me. She'd had no idea.

What tipped you off? The resemblance? I wanted it to sound sarcastic but it was tricky, what with my speech impediment and everything. I just managed to get it out.

Kathryn colored. She had a stupid, vacuous grin on her face, which I put down to nerves.

I didn't mean to upset you, Ricky. You're right, I didn't know.

I remained silent. She gazed at me with that silly grin in place.

Ricky ... I ...

My name is Phoebus.

I genuinely got her. Her eyebrows shot up and she stopped grinning. To avoid the enquiry, I reminded her that I had told her.

When? Confused, she made an absent-minded gesture, scratching her head.

When I dropped you off at your house.

She stared at me as if I was not of this world, as if she were trying to figure out an important detail that had escaped her, and now she didn't know how to process this new information. She clearly was off balance.

Ah ... I ... she stammered, looking at me pleadingly. I shrugged and she began to sway slightly from side to side.

The pain in my head was getting worse. By association, I was reminded of Kenny, who had liked to swing in the hammock on his tree, and I felt a desire to do the same except at this point I realized that there was no tree. There was no Kenny, and there was no need for Kathryn to be here.

I looked her square in the eye. What do you want?

7

I want to stay with you, I replied.

It wasn't entirely true. I only needed a place to hide, but seeing Ricky—I mean Phoebus—so broken, so vulnerable, made me tread carefully.

Dear Me. Maybe this was not a good idea. I momentarily regretted my decision to come. Maybe I should revise the plan. Just then, Phoebus began to cry and I melted.

Why? Phoebus asked.

I hedged. I'd like to help you.

Phoebus is not stupid.

Why? He repeated and I sensed he would go on repeating it until I told him the truth.

I've left Rupert, I replied.

At this, Phoebus stopped sobbing. He sat up and sort of sniffled, wiping his nose with his sleeve as if he were eight years old.

H–he d–doesn't w–want you back, does 'e?

I shook my head. No, he doesn't.

There was nothing more we could say right then. We both knew from a long time back that Rupert gave up on me; once the hundred thousand had not been paid, I knew because all Rupert had to do was to contact my mother to get the money, but he didn't, and why?

The answer was simple. Rupert didn't love me anymore.

8

In my dream, everyone is happy. Lien. Old Buzza. Even me.

Life a party iz. Grinning, Old Buzza shoves another drumstick into his mouth, spits out the little bone. There is some conversation, but eventually everyone falls silent. The sun is almost touching the horizon. It is a most beautiful sight, all those shades of red, pink, blue, yellow and white. The boat gently rocks. I am lulled into thinking that I was never meant to be an old man's whore. Or a friend. Or anything else he might want me to be. I smile at Lien over Old Buzza's hunched shoulders. She smiles back, the look in her eyes telling me to be patient. One day, we'll be free of this life. One day.

The afternoon fades away. It is time to go home. Old Buzza turns the boat and rows. Lien sings and everyone is happy. It's been a hot day. But now, the wind comes to cool us down.

I wake up shivering. I am alone in Lien's bed. The room is so quiet that I wish Bid were here snoring. Oh, Bid. You little fool. Give me a reason to love you. I begin to cry, realizing that my grief will go on until the end of time.

The next day comes. I sit in front of my mirror, looking at myself. I see her. Smiling, her teeth sparkle in the sunlight like tiny dewdrops. She tells me what's to be done. I pick up her scissors and begin. I hack for a long time, and in the end all that's left is memories, and my hair lying at my feet. It doesn't change a thing. A sad girl alone in an empty room is all there is.

Later, I go downstairs to dance. There is a guy who wants to love me. He has whiskers and sideburns that scratch my cheek, but it is Lien who whispers to me. Her words, lanterns on a fishing line, swing back and forth, mocking me. You are not afraid, are you? Her laugh is hollow. She wants me. To become one of Them.

I am weak with desire. Or fear. I don't know which. But I keep shaking my head. I will make money to pay Them. I will bring food to feed Them. Jewels to adorn Them. Anything you want, my love. But I will not open the door.

I am destined to spend the rest of my days wishing.

9

I was glad that she came back. I didn't expect her to although I wondered what she would do once she found out that her husband didn't love her. I did think she might leave him but I certainly did not envision her coming back to me. When I first saw the cops, I thought she had told on me and Kenny, which obviously she hadn't because she came back here. Kathy come home, she joked, and I knew I did not have a choice but to let things take their course. There was something different about her, a glint in her eyes that had not been there before; a determination that spoke of ideas I would not dare voice. However, Kathryn understood me perfectly well. She announced that she had a plan.

We ate fried eggs at the kitchen table. She had insisted on making breakfast and then burnt the eggs on the underside. I knew I would have done a better job but I didn't want to hurt her feelings so I ate them anyway. Noticing my careful chewing, Kathryn apologized.

I'm no good in the kitchen, she said, offering to try again, but I waved my hand like it didn't matter, which it didn't.

You'll learn, I said, it only needs the gas turned down low, and she said ahh, and then she poured us tea, which I thought a nice gesture even though it reminded me that up to now I had been the pourer. Kenny had liked things that way. I quietly brooded as I sat there waiting for the tea to cool down. Kathryn noticed I was all choked up, and patted my hand, and then we ate in silence until I composed myself. Then, after she served the buttered toast, Kathryn announced the plan.

Revenge, she nodded at me grimly from across the table.

You sure? I asked.

Again, she nodded just as grimly. She was dead sure.

My mother was right, Kathryn continued after a brief pause during which the last of the toast disappeared. He's a bastard.

There it was, that glint in her eyes. In no way now, she resembled the Madonna. The way she slid the knife across her eggs, she almost tore them into rags. In all honesty, I would not want to be in Rupert's shoes. The way she looked at me now, I realized that she would make a formidable opponent. It suited her though, this transformation. With her eyes blazing and her bosom heaving, she looked like a true leader, like an ancient warrior queen, strong and determined, but feminine and beautiful at the same time.

We sat on the sofa for the rest of the day. I agreed to everything. In hindsight, I realize that I was in no shape to make decisions, but at that time it seemed like a good idea, a perfect plan. I cooked porridge for dinner and we washed up together, and then she asked me if she could stay in my bedroom.

After all, she feebly joked, I know every inch of that space.

It upset me a bit; thinking about everything that'd happened made me want to cry. She noticed and made a move as if to hug me. I didn't want her comforting me. I told her to make herself at home, and I left.

10

Phoebus left. I was a little worried about his state of mind. I would have gladly sat with him and even listened to him talk about his brother, but Phoebus didn't want my sympathy. He needed to go out, insisted that he was feeling better.

I will not be home until after the funeral, he told me before he got in the truck. This alarmed me because I knew that the funeral would be very hard on him, and I extended an offer of support.

Doan w—worry, he replied, winding down the window on the driver side. He looked at me with his big cow eyes. I woan d—do anything s—stupid.

I spent the night watching old movies. The one about the kidnapping proved to be just what I needed. A priceless comedy, the TV guide claimed, about an incompetent gang that kidnaps a rich man's wife. When he refuses to pay ransom, she takes over the gang to exact revenge.

Dear Me. The things they got up to in 1959. The mind boggles. Well, perhaps not priceless but well worth the three and a half stars.

Feeling refreshed, I spent some hours going over the plan. Of course, from time to time I thought about Rupert, torturing myself with unanswered questions. Where did it all go wrong? How could I have been so blind? It was getting me nowhere. I didn't have the answers.

When it comes down to it, I certainly had been blind. Obviously Rupert had been cheating on me for a long time. Really, there had been signs all along if only one chose to pay attention. I ruefully acknowledge this major flaw in my character. Gullible, a fool, that's what I'd been, too trusting for sure, even my mother said so.

Aah, the penny's dropped, my mother sarcastically intoned when I phoned her Monday morning after I realized what Rupert was trying to do to me, but that was before she knew the whole story.

After she knew the whole story, she proposed we call the police.

Hear me out, I said, proceeding to outline my plan, taking her patiently from A to B, C and D and so on until we got to Z.

Hmm, Mother responded cautiously, expressing doubt as she pleaded with me. For God's sake, that's insane. But I continued talking.

Eventually I got through to her and she agreed. Okay then, we'll do it your way, she sighed, resigned to helping me. We came to an understanding. When I hung up, I felt a huge weight had been lifted from my shoulders.

Only three days, I whispered to Me, who frowned at me out of my hallway mirror for the last time. She was taking a stance, and the way she looked at me spoke volumes but there was nothing I was prepared to do to change her mind so I let it be. I left the house straight after.

I planned to hitchhike back to the cabin. I had hoped to catch a semi, a transient, long-distance vehicle one often sees thundering down the highway but I managed to do one better. I caught a lift with a couple of Japanese tourists on their way to the airport.

I'd been standing by the side of the road with my thumb in the air a good ten minutes when their rented Toyota whizzed by. At first I thought they didn't see me in the fog, but then there came the sound of an approaching car, and I saw them reversing towards me. Feeling nervous, I uttered a prayer. Dear God, I need a bit of luck come my way. Please let it not be anyone I know. When the passenger window rolled down, I breathed a sigh of relief. Facing me were two round faces I'd never seen before.

The woman had a map spread over her knees.

Excuse me, she smiled, nodding politely. Could you help us?

Of course, I replied and bent closer to the map to see.

We have spent our last day looking for the waterfalls, the woman said, smiling at me expectantly. Instantly, I conjured up a picturesque mythical water-world hidden in a shady glen: rapids rushing down a narrow gorge, billows of white fog floating about, exotic birds singing up a storm. So I'd been told.

Beautiful, clear water, I said, smiling at the woman. Pristine.

Smiling, the tourists nodded repeatedly, their heads moving in a slow, measured way as if they were weighted toys.

Near the summit, I specified, climbing into the back seat. The tourists twisted around to offer more of their smiles, and their hands. The woman looked like a porcelain doll. The man had a camera hanging from his neck.

We would like to take pictures, he said, tapping the camera lightly.

We set off along the twisty road. When the roadhouse came into view, I got them to drop me off at the T-junction. There was not a soul in sight. Before they left, I explained that the waterfalls were still a long way off.

Really, you'd be lucky to find them with all this fog, I warned, but they were happy to try their luck. They kept nodding and thanking me until I felt ashamed.

Honestly, I said, they're hardly worth your time. There's just a trickle, a stagnant pool at the bottom, not pristine at all. I shook my head. They shook theirs. Nodding, smiling and waving, we said goodbye.

It took me another hour to find the cabin but finally there it was, looming mournfully out of the clearing. Like a giant chicken coop, it sat shrouded in the fog, which parted before my knees the moment I made contact.

Dear Me. Here we are. I knocked on the front door. Nothing. Not a sound. I knocked repeatedly but Ricky didn't come to the door. I knew he was home; his truck was parked in the driveway. I kept knocking.

Eventually, I went round the back, intending to see if the back door, by any chance, had been left open.

I found the yard in a state of chaos. Leaves, sticks big and small, and long, knotty branches oozing sap lay scattered all over the garden. Near the porch, the main part of a huge tree trunk lay hacked to pieces and in the middle of the yard stood a great big weeping tree stump, its amber tears reminding me that this had once been a magnificent tree.

Looking at the carnage before me, I remembered the first time I saw that tree.

I had been inside for almost three days when Ricky let me out. Here is where we came. It had been a bright starry night with a big, pale, waning moon shining down on us, and I could see quite clearly. The yard was dirty, full of rubbish, with odds and ends piled up in a heap or just lying about; a wooden outhouse leaning precariously towards one corner of the house filled the air with the stale, cold smell of an old shoe. The big sturdy tree, with its long, graceful, thickly-leafed branches had been the only thing worth looking at in this yard.

It had been a truly beautiful tree. In the moonlight the trunk appeared to have been cloaked in velvet, the leaves shimmered looking as if they had been polished, and on the ground they were raked into small piles. The tree looked well taken care of and I had felt like touching it. It had seemed to me the only pure thing in this horrible place.

On the morning of my return, the tree looked defeated, lying across the steps of the porch like a fallen soldier. Its severed limbs spread over the ground as far as the outhouse. The outhouse appeared to have been left intact except for the roof, which was covered by a large rectangle of faded, coarse material stretched over the steeple. It was the hammock that had hung so happily on the tree the first time I saw it. It had been happy because it was useful. But now, it had served its purpose and was discarded, a redundant piece of junk no use to anyone, least of all your loved ones. Loved one.

11

I spent the night with Old Money Bags. Zelda was ever so pleased to see me. I, on the other hand, regretted my decision the moment I saw her. She stood in the doorway in her flannel robe, an awful flowery affair trimmed with lace at the collar, and her hair was up in curlers. Alarmed, for I had been totally unprepared for such a sight, I lowered my gaze to regain my composure. Bad move. Down there, my eyes encountered Zelda's fluffy slippers, and if Old Money Bags had not been holding me, I would have bolted. In disbelief, I stared at those revolting things: out of shape, mangy, in fact hairless on the inner side where the fluff had been rubbed off by the friction of Zelda's corns, they winked at me, laughing. We've got you now. I shuddered. I should not have come here. Alas, it was too late. Zelda's grip on my arm was not to be broken.

What a nice surprise, she crooned, pulling me inside and flashing her gold tooth at me. Aware that my member was dying in my trousers, I responded with a weak smile.

How I got through the night, I'll never know. In the living room, Zelda, who, out of respect for her first dead husband would never let me sleep in the bedroom, made up the couch, and for atmosphere switched on the reading lamp. Sprawling across the tartan cushions, Zelda opened up her robe to display her ruined body; tittering, she made foolish gestures which forced me to admire her floppy blue-veined breasts that lay shriveled upon her ribcage. Fearing the worst, I asked for a brandy. I drank it and quickly dived under the covers where mentally I replayed every scene I had ever had with Janelle.

In the morning, Zelda was well satisfied. We'll have breakfast at the café! she shouted from the bathroom, which really were the most sensible words she had uttered in a while. All night, she had assailed me with heavy duty declarations of her devotion and had demanded

I make some too. How unpleasantly I was reminded of my late wife I need not describe here. Suffice to say, I resolved to sign over the house as quickly as possible.

At the café, we ate heartily. Zelda, in particular, was ravenous. With gusto she fell upon those divine dishes as once again she congratulated herself on the choice of her chef. He's continental, you know, Zelda whispered, winking at me as she chewed her cutlets in a most savage and unattractive manner. It was all I could do to keep my food down. Anxious to savor every little bit, Zelda sucked the meat dry, letting the juice run down the side groove of her mouth. A few drops zigzagged down past her jaw where they were caught in the hair that sprouted there like a cluster of reeds. Repelled by the sight, I shuddered, telling myself to be patient. Not long now and all this will be over. I thought of my impending freedom and resolved to make the most of this opportunity. Determined to enjoy the meal, I basked in the attention the waiters paid us. They rushed to and fro at the slightest lift of Zelda's eyebrow.

From day one, I knew that Zelda was a shrewd businesswoman. She spoke of her café with pride. The place is coining money, Zelda had confided in me the day I delivered her pool hose. In fact, it was the restaurant I had to thank for my cash flow. Mortgaging the house her first late husband had left her, Zelda had bought the place ten years ago and never looked back. Gradually, she added a beauty salon and a gift shop which, apart from importing all sorts of useless knick-knacks, also sold flowers. The business grew steadily and nowadays Zelda was well provided for. However, Zelda was greedy and often complained, namely about her second late husband who had died in a bizarre boating accident only seven weeks ago, leaving her nothing whatsoever.

If it wasn't for Jim, I'd be richer still, Zelda would often remind me with a heave and a sigh.

Yes, I would reply, agreeing with her for the sole reason of keeping her happy, dear old Jim was a loser.

Truth be told, I didn't know whether he was or wasn't. I didn't know the man. But the whole thing made me feel uncomfortable. The speed with which she chose to forget her dear old Jim was somewhat unseemly; it reminded me of my own troubles. It had been just three days after the man's funeral that Zelda came to my pool shop with her hose, flirting and laughing it up as if she had not a care in the world, and on the fourth day she had me over for dinner. Since then, not only had she shown no grief, but at the slightest opportunity Zelda launched into interminable complaints about the poor man, freely disrespecting his memory. According to her, Jim had been a born loser, an idealistic fool who had drained her resources with his misplaced generosity, a naïve buffoon for whom life had been nothing but a party. Why she had ever married that lazybones who did nothing but fish and lose her money at cards, she could not fathom.

I must have been mad, Zelda fumed now, squeezing my hand painfully in a fit of regretful anger.

Let bygones be bygones, I replied soothingly, sick to death of hearing about the man. Intending to shut her up, I leaned closer and nuzzled her scaly turkey neck until Old Money Bags lost her train of thought.

We finished our breakfast and began a discussion on the sale of my house. Zelda enquired about the settlement date and was pleased to learn it was to be on Wednesday.

In fact, darling, I cooed, the buyer is coming tomorrow to take one last look.

Zelda's eyebrows constricted. Suspecting the buyer was having second thoughts, she warned me to sign the house over as soon as possible, so I assured her the visit was a formality, the buyer was merely keen to show the house off to his family, the deal was as good as done.

Well, Zelda said in a conciliatory tone, flashing her dentures at me, why don't we send some flowers over? It costs nothing to make friends.

Certainly, I nodded, respectfully pulling out her chair. It costs nothing to make friends.

We went over to the flower shop.

12

I drove around a while, listening to Kenny's tapes. It was all country music and not my thing at all, but it made me feel closer to Kenny so I played all his favorites over and over again, remembering times gone by. I remembered how Kenny liked to sing along, knowing all the words to his best songs, which were, for the most part, about people's hearts being broken. When I was little, Kenny liked to play cowboys and Indians with me, and eventually, when I learned to read, he brought home a book about them that Deep Fryer Fred gave him especially for me. It used to be his favorite. Whiling away long winter evenings, we read the story from beginning to end and enjoyed it immensely; depending on his mood, Kenny was either the young Apache chief, or the white fellow who followed him wherever he went, like a trusty and true friend. The same winter, Kenny got hold of a poster of a famous country singer, a kind of an outline of her head where you could see her hair was in braids but you couldn't make out her face. Kenny put up the poster near the bed head and we pretended that she was the Indian girl the white fellow fell in love with. She was beautiful and wild; at dawn she rode her horse bareback across the plain, and at sunset she sat by her teepee, combing her tresses. Of course, I always had to be the bad guy, but I didn't mind. Playing cowboys and Indians with Kenny had been a lot of fun. Even now, the memory of that bygone era made me feel all squishy inside. It had certainly been the most beautiful period in my life, and I don't know how it happened, but now I found myself parked in front of the club, sobbing.

The car park was full. As usual on Monday nights, the girls did a roaring trade because on Mondays the weekend crowd gave over to the married guys, who came here to escape their wives. That's why Janelle had never allowed Kenny to come by. Noh Munday noh, noh, she would shake her pretty head. In my mind's eye, I saw her gesturing charmingly as she counted her fingers: noh Munday, noh Choozday. On Wenzday Ah luv yooou. And Kenny would wait till Wednesday. Remembering how much in love they once were, I felt my heart would burst; feeling wretched, I sat in the truck not knowing what to do until a knock on the window brought me to my senses.

Feebuh? Knock, knock. Feebuh?

It was Janelle pressing her moon face onto the windscreen. I rolled down the window. For a moment, we stared at each other without speaking. I could hardly believe my eyes. Janelle's hair was cut square with her jaw, and her face was caked with white powder. It was as if Lien had come back to life. She looked beautiful and I stared, wishing to preserve the impression, but the vision disappeared as soon as Janelle opened her mouth to speak.

You cly?

I could think of nothing to say. I might have nodded, I don't know, I wasn't myself.

Uboud Lien?

Janelle looked on the verge of tears so I quickly said, yeah, about Lien, meaning every word. Kenny had loved her like a little sister, respected and protected her, and whether or not she returned that respect made no difference to my grief. They were both dead.

You cumup.

Janelle waved a delicate hand to indicate she was in a hurry. Cumon, cumon. The poor thing shivered under her peignoir, which barely covered her bottom. I followed her up the rickety steps and even sad as I was, I could not help but admire her shapely buttocks. A lot like her face, they were: pale in the moonlight, smooth and slightly swollen, they delicately pushed the thin fabric upwards, peeking cheekily at me from behind the filmy lace. Oh Janelle, you are the only one left. I stifled a cry. Deep down, I knew Janelle wouldn't see it my way; no way could we be like Kenny and her, but still, at that moment I felt strongly that

I loved her.

We did not speak until we got up to her room. Janelle went behind the screen to change. When she emerged, she had on a pair of jeans and a white mohair jumper, which gave out electricity, making her hair react and really, in the moonlight, she looked like a fairy.

Sit. Pointing to her bed, Janelle switched on the lamp. I saw that she had been crying. Under all her makeup, I saw misery in her face, I saw that she was as wretched as I, and it made me feel more in love with her. I watched her make tea and imagined what our lives would be like if we could start living all over again. My dream was simple: she would be a young girl looking to love a young man, and I would be that young man. I'd have a good job and I'd take care of her. In exchange, she'd be proud of me. Ours would be a pure love without complications. Dreaming like a babe fresh into the world, I imagined our glorious love until the tea was served and Janelle brought up the funeral.

Janelle started telling me that she had been to the hospital to identify Lien and Kenny. I felt relieved and enormously grateful because I knew I couldn't have faced them. Meanwhile, Janelle announced that she had booked the service. I told her I had no money but was prepared to sell the truck, and I meant it, even though I dimly remembered Kathryn telling me we would need it after the burial. Janelle wouldn't hear of it.

Noh, noh, noh silly, she said, wagging her dainty finger at me, Ah pay. Then she showed me a beautiful card, which I signed, and she also told me that she had ordered hordes of flowers—tulips and lilies for Lien, and two dozen red roses for Kenny because he had sometimes brought them for her and Lien. Speechless with gratitude, I agreed to everything.

Janelle came over to sit next to me. She placed her little hand over mine. Her palm only extended over a portion of my hand but still, it felt lovely. She looked up at me and whispered:

You good boy. You luv Lien?

I nodded. Yeah, I did.

She was like a sister to me, I told her, and Janelle seemed happy with that. We sat in silence for a little while, peacefully united in our grief. Then Janelle began to sing. She hummed a tune, one of Lien's, while she played with my dreads, and I sat still as a cat, hoping this moment would go on forever. When the song ended, Janelle laid her head on my chest.

She began to cry, silently at first, but soon her sobs shook her whole body and there seemed to be no end to it. I didn't know what to do. She kept telling me about her trip to the flower shop where someone she knew, a stoopid man she said, pretended he didn't know her.

Stoopid man at flowah shop. He say go 'way, Janelle sobbed, getting more and more distressed. He noh Lien but he noh say. Ah hate stoopid man.

Well, such is the world we live in. Lien had never minded. Shoo. She had flapped her little hand scornfully on one occasion when a bedfellow did not publicly acknowledge her. Clearly, Janelle in her present condition was a bit more fragile. It seemed she felt wounded, so I stroked her hair and let her cry.

13

I got a real fright when the door chimed and Janelle entered. Frozen to the spot, I pressed my back against the counter, wishing I could disappear. However, like the proverbial pillar, I stood there trying to blend into the scenery, praying that Janelle would not betray me. She did. As soon as she saw my nose poking out from behind the bouquet of lilies and long-stemmed roses, she recognized me and burst into tears.

Lien, she whispered, staggering towards me with outstretched arms.

Jeepers, I swore under my breath, shrinking back from her, not here, but Janelle didn't care. Ignoring Zelda's polite enquiry, Can we help you? Janelle slumped over the counter.

Lien dead! She cried out, looking as if she were possessed. Her long, narrow eyes were wide open, but I swear she didn't see a thing.

Lien dead!

She was hysterical; both of Zelda's assistants, the flower and the gift section girl, came forth seeking advice from Zelda, who took charge.

There, there, Zelda crooned, swiftly negotiating the counter to be by Janelle's side. She gently tapped her on the shoulder. There, there, I'm so sorry to hear that. Zelda grabbed a tissue out of the box perched up on top of the register and offered it to Janelle. Janelle blew her nose loudly. She thanked Zelda and then turned back to me, but I had meanwhile retreated as far from her as was physically possible. Janelle, however, was not to be put off. Her entire face was a question mark. Realizing I had to say something, I stepped forward a little.

That's too bad, I stammered foolishly. I felt nothing beyond surprise. I briefly thought of my unsuccessful visit to the club. The chaos in the car park, the police—it all fell into place now. Lien died. How? I did not dare speculate. Breathing a sigh of relief that I had not been on the premises when it happened, I privately thanked God for protecting me. Meanwhile, Zelda looked at me with a strange expression on her flabby dial.

I mean, I hastened to explain, that's terrible.

Janelle stopped sniffling. Her eyebrows constricted in a most un-Chinese fashion, almost Zelda-like, and my chest tightened anew.

Tellible? Dat all you say?

I shrugged. You've cut your hair, was all that came to me; of course, mindful of Zelda, I said no such thing. Casting for something to say, I gaped at Janelle, noting the change in her. Jeepers, she looked odd. With that hair and the white makeup Janelle now looked like Lien, only weirder. In fact, she looked quite mad.

Well, I eventually mumbled, hoping to extricate myself without giving the game away, but Janelle didn't give me a chance.

You naaaasty man! She screamed. You noh Lien. You shoh lespect, noh? She spat at me across the counter, a big gob that just missed me by a fly's dick. In the next instant, she turned and ran out the door.

The four of us, Zelda, the two assistants and me stood there speechless for a moment, and then Zelda dismissed the girls with a flick of her wrist.

Poor woman, I shook my head with a heavy sigh as soon as the beaded curtain stopped tinkling. Obviously, she's mad with grief.

Obviously, Zelda echoed, her probing gaze boring into my eyes until I found it hard to breathe. I felt I had to go into damage control immediately.

Darling, I said, advancing to take her in my arms, you seem a little tense.

Do I? Zelda murmured less severely now that I held her tightly against my chest the way she liked it. It's just, she said, staring deeply into my eyes out of which sincerity shone forth like a beacon guiding a ship to shore—Zelda faltered, momentarily losing the thread of her thoughts.

You mean, I murmured, playfully nuzzling her neck, do I know her or that, what was it, Lee-Ann?

Flashing her dentures, Zelda nodded sheepishly. I knew she was feeling guilty for suspecting me.

No, no, of course I don't, I said, giving her chin an affectionate squeeze. To dispel any lingering doubts, I then passionately kissed her on the mouth. My strategy worked. Purring obligingly, Zelda promised not to give the incident another thought.

14

I cry a little. The boy comforts me as best he can. I don't think he fully understands how I feel, but I don't try to explain. My misery belongs only to me. I am to blame. For everything. I killed Old Buzza, and now I'm paying the price. If I hadn't killed the old man, Lien would still be alive. It is as simple as that.

I lie in the boy's arms. In my mind, things are taking shape. Forty-three days of despair parade in front of my eyes, taking turns like dancers in a chorus line, replaying each and every event that has led us to this point. On the outside, the boy, scarcely daring to breathe, keeps stroking my head. He is a good boy. His soul, as light as angel hair, hovers above me, warming me with its goodness. Thus we remain until the moon finds his way into the room. He shows Lien on top of the covers. On her knees, her arms stretched towards me. She has a paper bag over her head with holes for her eyes and mouth. She is laughing. I am not an animal! she cries, ripping the bag from her head. She laughs so hard that bubbles come out of her nostrils. I laugh too. One can't help but see the funny side.

I see her in real time. She is as strong as an ox and full of confidence. She gives me a wink. Not long now until They come for you. I should be pleased. Instead, I cry. I cry because I am a weak, defenseless being, both guilty and innocent. The Good Brethren know it. I feel Them coming and there is nothing I can do to stop Them.

15

I stayed the night with Janelle. Not in the way I had hoped; we never progressed past my caressing her hair. We stayed up and remembered our loved ones. I told Janelle about the cowboys and Indians, and Fluffy; in her turn, Janelle told me about her own childhood spent in an orphanage in China. By her account, it was a dreadful place but character building, too, Janelle joked, looking sad. If it wasn't for Lien, she'd still be there mopping up pee after little children tied to a chair. Lien, the daughter of the orphanage cook, had persuaded her father to let Janelle stay with them. Later, all three went to Hong Kong where they had a dai pai dong, a food stall selling clams and snails. But the father died in shady circumstances, the food license expired and the girls grew tired of the whole stinky business. Often, they had to flee the cops who hunted them relentlessly, Janelle reminisced, explaining that the cart was wide, the streets narrow and the work too hard. Eventually, they gave up the idea altogether and shut up shop. Those were hard times, Janelle said, attempting to smile, but if she could, she'd turn back the clock. I knew how she felt; we had our loved ones then. After we had a little cry, I asked her about the club. I was interested to know how she came to do what she did, you know, the dancing. In reply, Janelle made a contemptuous little gesture. Bad luck mainly, she sighed, not wanting to go into it.

When it was time for breakfast, Janelle made us sweet pancakes on the hot plate she kept by the sink under the window sill. Looking at the hot plate, I got a bit emotional because I remembered the day Kenny bought it for Janelle's birthday. He bought her lots of other things too; a bottle of perfume and a painting of a cat that glowed in the dark, and some clothes, and then all four of us had a picnic by the river. Remembering that glorious day, I felt like crying. With effort, I pulled myself together, and from then on we only talked about everyday things. Janelle wanted to rest before the funeral, so after I finished my pancakes I went away.

On the way home, I stopped at the roadhouse where I resigned my position. Everybody gathered briefly to express their sympathies and they all promised to come to the funeral. Deep Fryer Fred grinned his usual toothless smile as if this were an ordinary sort of goodbye, but his rheumy eyes glistened so I felt compelled to sit down with him in the back room. He blabbered about Kenny until I stopped him short. I told him that although I appreciated all his emotions and everything, I really preferred not to dwell. After I said that, Fred shook my hand gratefully. Punkt, he winked at me, tapping the side of his nose. I nodded. Exactly. Grinning, Fred went on to say that Hans had decided to buy the house. Ze nize vun I in ze papuh showej you. Again, I nodded to show him that I understood. The nice one in the paper.

This very day, the twins were going to take one last look. Talking about the purchase, Fred sat there proud as punch. In all his life, he said, they never had much. Vot vis ze var end everysink, Fred sighed, shrugging. I could tell he was getting sniffly again; indeed, soon he was crossing himself and tapping his quivering nose that hung from his face like a big cucumber. I made a noise to show him that I remembered all our talks about the war, and the time when he and Onion Hans, their older brother Jim and their mother Gerta, both now deceased, had come over on one of the U-boats that fished them out of the ocean after their ship sank. It was a miracle they had survived, Fred always said, putting their survival on a par with the parting of the Red Sea. I always put it down to pure chance.

Hans entered. His big red onion face was aflame with emotion as he advanced towards me with outstretched arms. I hugged him and we shook hands, and he said a few words about Kenny, but Fred stood by casting glances and tapping his nose. Punkt, punkt, Hunz. Noting this, the old man cleared his throat. Ve en upointment hev, he said, ending our conversation. Then he turned to Fred. *Schnell, schnell*, and off they went out the door.

We walked out together. They got into their truck and I got into mine. Waiting to wave goodbye, I reflected that this was probably the last time I would ever see Fred. It made me feel funny, as if I were about to lose a granddad; however, as I never knew my granddad, I was in no position to know how it felt to lose one. At any rate, there was a lump in my throat. Maybe it was Kathryn's plan affecting me in this unexpected way as it flashed through my mind. I almost did say something. I almost shouted, Wait! I have something to tell you! But Fred was not paying attention. He gave me the thumbs up through the window—we were parked next to one another—and he touched the visor on his cap, a sort of bon voyage gesture, and then he turned to Hans in the driver seat, hunching over the steering wheel. It was then I realized there was something wrong. Hans turned the key but the truck had not moved. I got out to see just as Fred rolled down the window.

Feebuz, he wheezed, give us e hend, ja?

They had me turning on the ignition while they took turns jumpstarting. It didn't work; we sadly concluded that this was a garage job. We stood there undecided, scratching our heads. Suddenly, Hans remembered the appointment in town. Checking his watch, he let out a string of German words. I fear he was swearing; he certainly had that look about him. He tugged at the jump leads hanging down the side of the bonnet. He clearly was aggravated as he spat on the ground at our feet, and he reminded me of Kenny the way he got worked up so easily. It was Fred who came up with a solution. Feebuz, he said, aiming his weepy eye at me, you drrrive us, and without further ado the twins piled into my truck.

On the way to Kathryn's house, I reflected that perhaps I was wrong about everything. Perhaps there was something else at play here, call it what you will, karma or whatever, but the fact was that I was speeding down the mountain with the intention of coming face to face with Kathryn's husband, who might even be waiting at the door.

Come in, he would say. This way to the kitchen. He would no doubt make a sweeping gesture in the appropriate direction, and this gesture would seem unnecessary to me because I would already know the way to the kitchen, since only a few days ago I assaulted his wife in there. As I neared our destination, I wondered about the turn my life was taking and I felt powerless, like a puffball in the wind, just hoping to survive. Everything that happened in the past week seemed unreal, as if someone else was inside me directing my every move, irrespective of what I wished to do. Like scenes from a motion picture, the past seven days rolled on inside my head, making it ache.

THE KIDNAP! The title screamed at me from the poster I imagined pasted on my windshield. The film starred Kenny and Kathryn. Janelle and I were the supporting players … oh, and I forgot Rupert, a cameo appearance, to be sure, but memorable, crucial to the plot, one might say. Feeling a rush of impotent anger, I gripped the steering wheel. I felt that I could strangle Rupert because I blamed him for the messy ending. If only that **** stuck to convention, we wouldn't be in this mess. If only he'd followed the script, Kenny would still be alive, I ruminated regretfully, but still, when all is said and done, I could have been wrong.

Kenny always said that life is a game of chance. Until this very moment, I never gave it much thought, chiefly because Kenny always said it after he lost at the tables at the club. Now I wondered if perhaps there was something more to it. Indeed, I wondered if there was such a thing as Divine Intervention because as Kathryn's house came into view, nobody in the truck questioned how come I never asked for directions. No, I guess the twins were too excited; when I drove up to the gate, they alighted grinning, and they waved at Rupert who sat waiting in a wicker chair on the front porch.

16

The serious buyer brought his brother and a young friend to look at the house. The old men stood on my porch with gummy smiles on their faces, shaking my hand and looking like a pair of simpletons. I realized I would have to do all the talking.

Ushering them into the hallway, I broadly indicated where the different rooms were. There's the kitchen, I smiled, thrusting my chin towards it by way of invitation. When nobody moved, I was obliged to take the lead. We entered the kitchen where the three of them began to take off their shoes.

Not necessary, I intervened, hoping to speed up the buying process, but the serious buyer wouldn't have it any other way.

In Deutchlund, the man explained in guttural English, ze mut hiii iz. With an abrupt gesture, he indicated a mud level halfway up his calf. Shooz in ze houz not perrrmitted.

They took off their shoes and we proceeded with the inspection.

The young man, an awkward looking teenager I supposed was some kind of hired help, remained quietly uninvolved, but the two Germans had a good look at everything. The whole time they chattered excitedly, or maybe they argued; it was hard to tell which because they spoke in their native tongue.

After they had inspected the lounge, the old men wished to see the bedrooms. In a single file we lumbered up the steps, the wooden staircase creaking pleasantly under our combined weight.

I was the last one to go up. I was right behind the boy who took his time, reluctantly shuffling forward, swaying slightly with each step and looking as if he didn't want to be here. He was very grubby. His socks were full of holes. The hem of his faded jeans was tattered and dirty, the seat, loose and wrinkled, made a stiff swishy sound as he moved, and under his greasy hair that hung lifelessly from his head like frayed ropes, his t-shirt showed imprints of pegs at the shoulder seams. The way he moved, lurching self-consciously with his shoulders hunched and his scrawny neck full of scabs, marked him as a loser. Keeping two steps behind, I felt repulsed by him. The thought struck me that young people nowadays did not care much about their appearance. Not like in my day, I said to myself, thinking back to the fabulous eighties. Even the music these days wasn't a patch on the old guard. No. Feeling the pull of nostalgia, I silently shook my head, recalling that unforgettable night I went to a rock concert. I had the time of my life. Young and full of promise, I had looked like a rock star with my sculpted hair, my stove-pipe trousers and my paisley shirt (lace cuffs) set off by a spangley satin jacket and a thin leather tie. Mounting the stairs behind this unkempt nonentity, I remembered my rainbow-colored fluorescent socks, which I had specifically purchased to go with my white loafers. Yes, most definitely, I had been poised for success back then, wild with desire to conquer the world, and now as I pointed out the bathroom fittings, I could have howled, seeing my youth flash before me like a lovely dream.

In due course, we returned downstairs and everybody put their shoes back on. Then I let them out into the garden where they inspected the pool and the gazebo. The old men seemed well satisfied.

Ja, ja, ve vill ze houz taik, the serious buyer sealed the deal with a firm handshake at the door. Vednesday, ja?

I nodded. Ja, Vednesday.

17

It was funny, being in that house again. Broad daylight made it seem quite ordinary. Really, there was not a hint of the drama that occurred within its walls just over a week ago. Rupert, however, took me by surprise. Previously I had pictured him as one of those suave, attractive men, like those advertising shaving cream on the telly. I had thought for sure he'd be tall, charismatic and neat looking, though why I ever thought that now didn't make sense. Out of the three adjectives I ascribed to him, only neat looking could be applied.

The man I was looking at was of average height. His face was ordinary, boasting neither an animated expression nor distinguishing features, and he was dressed conservatively but without flair. Wearing a white business shirt, grey, high-waisted trousers and a dark blue tie, he reminded me of a real estate agent I once delivered pamphlets for. Yes, just like that man's, Rupert's thinning hair was combed back over his skull and his stomach was just as soft; the gentle swell above his trouser belt made me wonder what had possessed Kathryn to marry him. I had always thought that beautiful women preferred handsome men, unless, of course, they were in the business like Lien and Janelle, in which case you only looked at it from a financial point of view. Clearly, this was not the case here, and I was perplexed.

Rupert showed us through the house. Downstairs, upstairs and all around the garden, Hans and Fred were delighted with everything. But my only thought was of Kathryn. This was her space. Somehow, I had imagined the house to be more, I don't know, what's the word? Maybe bohemian, one might say, more in line with what I had imagined Kathryn's nature to be. But there was no pottery wheel, no pets of any kind, and I found this strangely depressing.

The house was very clean and tidy, and furnished with conventional furniture; the sort of place I always wanted to live in when I was little because back then I used to be embarrassed that we lived out of crates. However, after mum left me and when Kenny came back, I changed my mind. After he got rid of Uncle Clem, Kenny brought in his own groovy kind of people who liked our house. Our house was considered a refuge; it was a cool, mellow sort of place where one could relax, everybody said when we sat around the kitchen table, smoking pipes. Yes, after Kenny came back, I began to get a fresh perspective.

Once we finished with Rupert, I dropped Hans and Fred off at their old house. We shook hands and said our goodbyes and then, just as I was reversing out of the driveway, Hans signaled for me to stop. Shuffling over, he pulled out a hundred dollar note from the breast pocket of his jacket. Here, he grunted and shoved it at me through the window.

They stood on their porch, waving to me until I turned the corner; the image of their happy faces stayed with me long after they disappeared from my line of vision. They were such good people. I remembered all those times Fred gave me his spare change, I remembered Hans's burgers with all that extra onion on the side, and I began to feel bad. I knew they were not going to get the house of their dreams from Rupert, but I couldn't tell them. I had promised Kathryn I would do nothing to jeopardize her plan, but still I felt as if I were betraying the twins, who had always treated me with kindness. I felt powerless and angry because I hadn't been strong enough to tell them the truth. To keep from going back, I went straight to Janelle's and offered her the money.

Towards the costs, I said, feeling very awkward. Even though I never had anything to do with funerals, I knew one hundred dollars was a sadly inadequate sum. Janelle pushed my hand away. She had just had a shower and her hair was up in a turban, which made her look alien, as in extraterrestrial. Underneath the towel, Janelle's oriental face, devoid of makeup, was as pale and fragile as rice paper; however, she was past being vulnerable. Standing in front of the wardrobe in her red petticoat, she peered into it and swore.

****, she said over and over as she took out dresses, turned them this way and that, and then put them straight back. Eventually, she ran out of outfits. Then she looked at me and gestured.

You know what, she said, taking a step towards me. Me and you, we go shopping.

18

I woke up around eleven. Feeling refreshed after my long sleep, I luxuriated in the warm covers, pondering my options for the day. I might just go for a swim. Then, out of the blue, Me came to spoil my mood.

Phoebus has not come home.

Taken by surprise, I needed a moment to formulate a response. Me is back on the scene. And here I thought we were done. I looked at Me mockingly as if to say, what are you doing here?

Me wouldn't take the hint. She looked at me as if I'd done something wrong, but I was not prepared to argue. There's no point in crying over spilt milk.

Don't start, Me, I say. I have other things to worry about.

But Me wasn't to be put off.

The funeral takes place today.

Ah, the funeral. An event I would prefer to forget. Of course, Me wouldn't let me. Looking righteous, Me wriggled like a worm and jabbed an accusing finger into the air in reproach. At the sight of it, I began to feel queasy with a sickening sensation working its way from the pit of my stomach to my heart. Pang. Pang. Pang.

Supposing I want to start feeling guilty, I say to Me, I might let the pangs continue. Supposing.

Me did not reply. For a while, I continued with the pretence, humming a tune to show Me I had nothing to feel bad about. But Me was not fooled. She continued looking at me, pursing her lips and nodding meaningfully until I was forced to defend my position.

It wasn't supposed to be this way, Me.

Me had nothing to say. Not a thing.

I understood. There was nothing to be said that would not cause rupture. Already there was a crack, an ugly fissure. Me and I teetered on the verge of a mighty cliff. Did we want to go plummeting down?

No. Definitely not. Looking each other in the eye, we shook our heads and I cast for something to say to placate Me.

Kenny is to blame, I said to Me, hoping to find a common thread. It kind of worked. Me paused mid-shake.

We are talking about a human being, Me whispered, looking at me disapprovingly. A human being who was loved. Me's reproachful nodding left no doubt that it was I who was going down.

I didn't want to listen to any more of this. Ignoring Me, I made myself a cup of tea and went to sit on the back steps. The tree trunk lay expressionless at my feet. Its wilting leaves reminded me of my marriage.

Will I be sorry to leave?

Well, that's the question. To find the answer, I replayed my life from the very first moment I met Rupert until the very last morning I kissed him goodbye. Truly, if you took away the routine, what were we left with? Mentally, I subtracted the mornings, the dinners and the golf lunches on Sundays. The remainder added up to a percentage of fairly useless conversation.

What did we ever talk about?

I like yoga and gardening. I like to swim. I like to groom my cat. I read. I like to pretend that I am someone other than me. And maybe I am. Perhaps. But there's only Me to tell me the truth. Because Rupert was never interested. He hadn't the patience to listen.

I am busy, Kathy, he'd mumble, not bothering to lift his head from the financial page of the daily news. I'd take the hint and leave. Day after day, we did this.

And now, listening to my gripes, Me is all shriveled up inside me. I can barely hear her whisper: It wasn't supposed to be like this.

No. It wasn't. We started out with a vision of a different kind. We envisioned a chain of events to reinstate me as the Queen of Hearts. Only it didn't happen. We didn't come out of it the way we thought we would.

Back in the house, I rinsed the cup in the kitchen sink. The day was full of warmth and sunshine. I was going for a swim.

I found the river easily. Just as Phoebus said, it was a stone's throw away, only at this altitude, it wasn't a river but a stream. At the foot of the mountain the stream flowed into another one, and it was only when the streams combined that they turned into the river I knew, brown, lazy, with silvery streaks of crested waves on a windy day.

Up here in the wilderness, the stream was a sight for sore eyes. It gurgled and sang and made me want to think of happy things. But the happy things would come in the future. Now I had to deal with the present.

I walked along the stream and eventually found a good spot to execute the first part of my plan, in spite of Me, who stood by looking sad. The sight of her irritated me. I wished for Me to go away. When she didn't, I simply switched off. I went off to look for the little pool Phoebus had mentioned; I found it hidden in a clearing behind a clump of fir trees.

The water was cool. I floated, staring at the tree canopy above me, imagining my new life. The good feeling lasted until the sun dipped beyond the mountain.

19

We bought our clothes on the way to the funeral. With only an hour to spare, we didn't have much time so Janelle took me to the nearest department store where she helped me choose my funeral clothes: plain black trousers, grey shirt and a pale yellow tie with grey specks in a diamond pattern. It came to more than one hundred dollars but Janelle paid up the difference without saying a word. Then she bought a beautiful silk gown and a lace hat with a veil to cover her face. This made her look very somber, very dignified, and even though she was tiny and fragile, you could tell she had strength.

The funeral was a brief affair. At the time I felt cheated, thinking that Kenny and Lien deserved more than a prayer and a short speech. At the gravesite, the priest spoke to the effect that it was a pity such young lives had tragically ended; over the descending coffins, he mentioned redemption and forgiveness but only in passing. In hindsight, I am glad he did not dwell. What could he have said? He didn't know them, he only knew of them, so it was a good thing that he kept it brief. Throughout the entire service, Janelle and I held hands. She cried her heart out and I held her close to mine.

The gathering was small, only fourteen people in all, but we were genuinely aggrieved to have lost our loved ones. Deep Fryer Fred and Onion Hans turned up as promised, as well as the other two staff from work, who came bearing a huge wreath paid for by the company. Then all the girls from the club, Mr Wong and three regular customers.

After the prayer, everybody gathered round the coffins, which were barely visible under the hordes of flowers. On Lien's coffin, tulips and water lilies formed the shape of a heart; on Kenny's lay a large wreath of red roses. We placed the cards on top of the flower arrangements. Kenny's card simply said Bon Voyage, Lien's I Will Never Forget You.

And all around the display, perfumed candles burned, giving off a powerful scent.

The coffins were lowered into their holes. We stood there paying our last respects as shovelfuls of dirt fell on our loved ones while Lien's favorite song, One Night in Bangkok, played in the background.

The tune conjured up familiar images in our minds. At the birthday picnic, I recalled, Lien had sung this; she had drunk a lot of champagne and was in a mood for a bit of fun. She pranced around as if she were on stage, exaggerating all her moves. Dressed in cargo pants and runners, she looked really funny. Kenny and I laughed our guts out. Janelle too brayed like a donkey, and Lien loved it. Afterwards, the girls lined all the empty bottles, and Kenny and I busted them with stones. Then the cops turned up and booked everyone for littering, expressing the view that only morons would engage in this type of thoughtless entertainment. This view I was privately inclined to support, but of course, all for one and one for all preyed on my mind, so I hollered and carried on alongside Kenny, until eventually the cops brought in the dogs and we spent a cool night in the watch-house. Towards the morning, Kenny, sobered by the plummeting temperature, took stock of our situation. Full of regret about getting mixed up in this sorry business, he glossed over his role in the proceedings and blamed the entire incident on me. To calm him, I had to promise I would mend my ways.

Finally the holes were filled. Standing at the foot of Kenny's grave, I remembered his passion for life and I felt honored that Kenny had been my brother, and I truly didn't care what anyone thought. Oh, I knew what people said about us, how I was a simpleton and how Kenny mistreated me, but they didn't know him like I did. They didn't know about the books he bought me because he knew I liked to read, they never knew he listened to me read out loud even though it was a trial, they knew *nothing* about him.

Staring at the mound of freshly piled earth, I wept openly. In my mind's eye, I saw my beloved Kenny leaning on my bedroom door with his ear pressed hard against it. Behind the door, I sat cross-legged on the floor. Kenny's favorite book, Vinnetou, lay open in my lap and I read a passage out loud. Liking the sound of the word *intrinsic*, I carefully went over it again; in-trin-sic, I said, and it was then I became conscious of him. He was crying, and to me his muted sobs were the most beautiful sound I ever heard. Touched by his emotion, I imagined huge pear-shaped tears sliding down his cheeks and past his jaw, falling to the ground where they busted, making a tiny ping sound. Ping. Ping. Ping. As the moments pinged by, a puddle formed at Kenny's feet. Soon it spread, becoming a pool which leaked towards me through the gap under the door. Hoping to stem the flow, I kept on reading, droning on, liking very much this one continuous thought spread generously over three pages. As always, I fully identified with the characters; sometimes I pretended I was there in the story with them, sometimes I imagined I was writing my own book. I knew Kenny would have liked it if I ever did write my own book, even though, outwardly, Kenny never said. He didn't have much education himself, always saying things like throwed, goed, and them instead of these or those, and he made out that he didn't care, but with me, he was different. He encouraged me to study, to learn all I could from my books, and I knew he was very proud that I made an effort to speak correctly. I also knew he really wanted me to go back to school, having taken me out only because it pained him so to see me ignored by the other kids. Deep down, I knew he had dreamt of giving me a good life somewhere in the sunset.

Thinking about the good times, I gazed at the rectangle of settling soil that was to be Kenny from now on, and I cried like a baby. It did not seem fair that he should have gone down without anyone knowing his true nature. I had hoped that one day people would see Kenny the way he was with Janelle when he let his guard down, and I waited for him to mellow, to reach an age in which his face would have fitted him like an old slipper. I felt that with age Kenny would have blossomed, his anger melted away like old snow, and his goodness sprung to the surface like bluebells hungry for the sun.

No, there was no doubt in my mind that Kenny had been a good person, despite appearances, despite his temper, despite everything he ever did wrong. The truth was that I owed him. And I owed him big because if it hadn't been for Kenny, Uncle Clem would still be around.

Staring into my brother's grave, I suddenly saw me, the way I was all those years ago, a scared little boy lying on the floor in my room. Uncle Clem was about to enter.

I was alone; wrapped in a blanket, I lay on the floor working on my coloring in. I was still little, about nine or ten years old. My mother wasn't around. She had gone to visit an inmate, leaving me home alone. I felt okay until the door handle began to rattle.

Phoebus, oh Feeeeebus, I'm coming in now, his smooth voice pours in through the gap under my door like honey, its sticky sweetness pinning me to the floor. I realize that I am trapped and I curl up in my blanket without making a sound. I'm hoping he'll go. I pray he'll go but I know that it is Polished Marble Time.

Uncle Clem comes in, pulls me out of my blanket and puts me in his lap, telling me to show him my coloring in. I sit there with the book open in front of me.

Uncle Clem makes himself comfortable.

That's lovely, he says, looking at my picture. Just lovely.

His marble comes alive.

I like the way you stay within the lines, Uncle Clem says. His marble is looking too.

But wait, you've not finished here, it says. Pointing at the spot, it strains its veiny, purpley round head.

Of course, I spoil things. Uncle Clem is so angry, he shakes all over.

It's important to finish what you start! he bellows, tearing up the pages. Then he goes. Locks me up and goes away.

I crawled under my blanket and cried. I was so lonely. I didn't want to be alone, but I didn't want Uncle Clem coming back either. I didn't know what to do. I couldn't get to Fluffy. He was in his box in the kitchen. When I called his name, he didn't make a sound. It made me cry even more. After a while I fell asleep, and when I woke up I felt better and looked for something to do. Under my bed, I found the Bible.

Nobody came for a long time. I read a lot of it and I kind of liked the stories, but it seemed to me only bad things happened to people who, in my opinion, were trying very hard to avoid them. I thought about the innocent ones and wondered whether all this suffering was not turning them off their God, as he didn't seem particularly kind or just. Frankly, he seemed to demand a lot without giving much in return. Especially when some people were doing bad things, and then nothing bad happened to them so they went unpunished. It didn't make much sense.

Still, as I periodically got locked up in the bedroom, I got into it and enjoyed reading the Bible more and more. It made me feel less lonely and I felt like I had someone to turn to after mum had moved out. Then one day, Kenny came back and sorted everyone out. I told on Uncle Clem, and Kenny flew into a rage and cut Uncle Clem on the ear; in fact, he very nearly killed him. Uncle Clem got the message and we never saw him again. Then it was just me and Kenny. By then I had read the Bible from cover to cover and I was still interested in matters of faith, so to speak, for a long time, until the day we watched a documentary about the Bible, about who wrote it and things of that nature.

It came out nobody really knew anything concrete, and they discredited nearly all the Apostles. Like one guy said Peter was a peasant who couldn't read or write, so they reckoned someone else must have written his letters, and so on. Then the Dark Ages came, bringing nothing but trouble. During the Crusades, everyone got slaughtered in the name of God, and so it went on pretty much the same as we know it now. The experts theorized about a lot of things, but the crux of it was that nobody really knew who wrote the bloody thing. Kenny thought the authors, whoever they were, must have been up to no good.

It was the afternoon of my fourteenth birthday. Kenny had suggested we go see the girls but I didn't want to because I knew that Kenny would have just made fun of me the whole time, like he did once before when he took me there. Instead, we got beer and I roasted a chicken, and then we watched the documentary. Kenny lounged on the sofa, cracking nuts and paying scant attention until the million-dollar question was posed. Who wrote the Bible? The presenter had looked directly into the camera and shrugged to indicate his position, so Kenny took it upon himself to enlighten me.

Pro'bly a bunch of freaks, Kenny muttered, pulling at his crotch. To suit their evil purpose. He winked at me, giving me permission to speak.

A bunch of freaks, I nodded, getting my head around the idea. I felt cheated because I had previously put such stock in religious teachings, thinking I was getting the real deal. But now, it seemed I might have just wasted time.

To Kenny, everything was simple.

In imperious tones he announced that all religion was useless, had no practical application, and in fact made things worse. It's all hogwash, Kenny declared, nodding pompously as if he had a wealth of knowledge to draw on. I doubted he knew what he was talking about. Kenny had never shown the least interest in religion of any kind. Now however it looked like he was going to start a theological debate. A debate for which I felt Kenny was ill prepared.

As Kenny had never even read the Bible, I felt his knowledge base was somewhat sketchy. Once we sat through an Easter special about how the world began. It was a lavish production with some big names in it and an additional cast of thousands, and it had wild beasts and all sorts of miracles happening all the time; it was that type of gig. Anyway, we went right back to the beginning with Moses and the mountain and the commandments. It was a four-hour epic throughout which Kenny kept drinking. Eventually he fell asleep.

Kenny's other brush with religion was when we hired a porn flick. When we inserted the tape, we got a shock. No action. Literally. Only people, hundreds of them, fully dressed, sitting on the pavement. At first, we couldn't make out what they were doing, but eventually we were told they were passively resisting. When Kenny realized we got the wrong movie, he raved like a lunatic, but it was too late to drive to the video shop so we ended up watching the whole thing. I found it fascinating. All that conscious suffering in pursuit of non-violence really appealed to me. I was telling Kenny that strictly speaking it was a movement, a philosophy rather than a religion, when he fell asleep. There you have it.

But on the afternoon of my birthday, Kenny wasn't sleepy at all. Determined to educate me, he took a swig and began his argument with a flourish.

Phoebus, you turd. It's like this. You got the ******* commandments, right?

I nodded. Thou shall not.

Them's the sins you shouldn't do, right?

Right.

Giving me a wink, Kenny swirled the rum lazily around his mouth. His speech was beginning to slur pleasantly.

Look around you, turd. See anyone not sinning?

I couldn't think of a soul. I know I always tried to be good. But I lied. Examples too numerous to give. I cheated. Examples too numerous to give. I coveted. Here's one. I spent the night with another man's wife.

Kenny tapped his forehead.

You paid for it, didn't ya?

Well, yes. But I knew Lien had a husband somewhere.

To this Kenny replied that conversation with me was worth every penny. Said I was so stupid I ought to be protected by law.

I apologized. I guess in the end it didn't really matter who wrote the Bible.

Exactly, Kenny agreed.

Because everybody just takes out of it what suits them.

Right on, Kenny nodded. Useless. All them rules about good behavior. Anybody—here he gesticulated wildly, pulling on his crotch, so I knew we were talking about Uncle Clem who used to go to church a lot—can sin and then la-di-da, off he goes to pray to make himself feel better. Looking disgusted, Kenny shifted, lifting a buttock off the sofa. I steeled myself for the blast.

The buttock hovered and I held my breath. It was an agonizing moment. Then slowly, delicately, the buttock descended, quietly sliding into its place on the cushion.

You know what? Kenny cackled. The whole deal's not worth a fart.

Theological discussion at end, Kenny devoured a drumstick and switched the channel.

Well, that sorted things out for me. My struggle ended. I threw the Bible out the next day. I mean, what was the point of it all? You could be a turd like me or even Kenny, and definitely bad like Uncle Clem, who was up to no good most of the time, and still you got what you wanted. You could bend the rules to suit you to justify anything, even a kidnapping. But look where it got us.

I suddenly wished I had been stronger. If I had had some principles, I might have been strong enough to say no to Kenny's big idea. Had I resisted, we wouldn't have ended up the way we did. Kenny dead and me, well, I don't know what's going to happen to me, and frankly I don't care.

I am not saying that religion would have kept us on the straight and narrow. Not at all. I've tried it. I briefly toyed. Now that I am older, I can tell I was just lonely. I really just wanted people around me, and that's all there ever was in the Bible. Lots of people being together. Loving or hating each other, they were in it together, facing their problems. And in my life, people were constantly departing. Even Kenny was hardly ever around, and all I ever wanted when I was little was to have someone there.

Once when I was feeling lonely, I went to church and sat down in the front pew. I was the only one there. It was cold and I was scared, and the whole place smelled of wet weather. Like mildew, or spit or something. I waited there for a long time but nobody came. Eventually, I went home where Kenny groused at me for having been gone so long. I told him where I went and he just tapped his forehead and said there was housework to be done. Going about my chores, I regretted ever getting involved, but when later Kenny came to my room to tell me he was going to take me on a trip, I changed my mind.

Anywhere you like, Kenny said. I couldn't believe it. I got a bit flustered and said the first thing. Fishing. The next day, we went. We didn't catch anything. No, that's not true. Kenny caught a fish head. We had a good laugh about it and threw it back in the water. On the way home, we stopped at a takeaway and Kenny let me choose from the menu. It was a great day.

Of course, now that I'm older I realize Kenny just plain freaked out. Didn't want me nowhere near a ******* church, he later owned up. So we started spending time. We played cowboys and Indians, read Vinnetou, our favorite book, or just hung out. Whenever he could, Kenny took me shopping, let me buy stuff I liked, books and clothes, and on my last birthday he gave me my special boots. The left boot has a picture of a flying eagle carved into the sole. He won them for me in a game of poker. When the guy who lost the game reneged on his promise and wanted to keep the boots, Kenny thrashed him. I got the boots. And something else too. I realized I had Kenny's attention, his love and devotion, and just because things went bad on us in the end, nothing would ever change the way he made me feel. He had always made me feel safe, cherished and loved, and now, looking back at our life, I could see that we certainly had some good times together for which I had God to thank. If I hadn't gone to church that time, things would have never improved. It was after the fishing trip that Kenny and I became true friends. And my friend Kenny was the best thing that ever happened to me.

At the end of the service, I whistled Achy Breaky Heart, Kenny's favorite tune. After I finished, Janelle and I thanked everybody and everybody hugged us. I smiled, pretending to be strong, but in my heart I was worried. I worried about Kenny and where he might be right now. Because you know, things do rub off on you. I did spend a lot of time locked up in my room, reading religious material, and I dare say I retained some ideas, none of which comforted me in my hour of need. All I wanted to know was that Kenny was at peace in a nice place because deep down Kenny had been a good guy.

20

I threw my rose into Bid's grave. The flower fell in slow motion, gliding through the air, reflecting sunbeams. It landed with a bounce, the petals shuddering as the rose hit the coffin in which Bid, my man for forty-three days, lay dead.

Staring at the small wooden box, I did feel something. Regret, some kind of grief. No. I was just wishing. In another life, I might have been a regular girl. Bid might have been someone not called Bid. Maybe we would have fallen in love. Ah well, too late now. I am not regretting a thing; after all, the world is built on not entirely happy unions. According to Old Buzza, who spoke from experience back in the truck stop days when nobody paid attention. How I wish I had listened to that wise old man.

Back in the truck stop days, Old Buzza predicted my doom. Leaning on the counter, he watched Fred chop garlic, and he spoke nonsense at me.

My vordz mark, Old Buzza grinned, Kenny your man iz.

I am used to being the butt of old men's jokes so I pour coffee, wearing my professional smile. Today is just another day: Hans serves cold pie, the boy dries dishes and Lien looks pretty in her waitress uniform.

Around the card table, the men ponder their possibilities. Kenny, waiting for his turn, wipes his hands on the chest panel of his greasy overalls. Pretending to ignore the old man, he contemplates his cards, but his fingers tremble at the mention of love. Old Buzza keeps on with his joke.

Vun day you togezer be, he laughs out loud, the air in the gap between his front teeth hissing with every breath he takes. He points a finger at me, then at Kenny. Life a party iz, he snorts, holding back more laughter. He doesn't know he has only a little while to live. In a few days, he'll take me on a boat ride.

Shut up, Jim, Kenny growls a warning to hide his embarrassment, finally putting down a card. But it's true. He would like nothing better than to hold me in his arms.

Old Buzza turns over the card.

A Kveen of Heartz! He cries with a wink at Lien.

Lien responds with a playful gesture. Noh, noh, she says, wagging her dainty finger in his face. The door chimes. Customers come in and the game breaks up. Kenny is needed to pump petrol. He evaporates, leaving his heart on the stool. And so it goes, day after day.

Forward to the boat ride. The picnic is going well. Old Buzza drinks heavily, and soon he starts to complain about his wife. She doez not me vis rrespect trreat, he starts rehashing his old theme and I begin to regret we ever came. But we came because making old men happy is our job. Lien thinks so too. In her bikini, Lien lies stretched on the bench, listening to Old Buzza's gripes. She commiserates as she's paid to do. She has been drinking and now her glass is empty. She holds it up towards Old Buzza, giving him her best smile. Dazzled, he stops rowing and refills the glass. Good. The mood is broken. Old Buzza forgets all about his wife and tells us about the U-boat instead. Ja, ja, ve almost hat drrowned, he says, gravely nodding his tired old vulture head. Doch, here but for ze grrace of Gott I go. We nod too. He likes us to agree with him. Then the talk turns to Fred and Hans, whom he adores. We find out more about their adventures on the sub. We listen intently and Old Buzza is pleased. Smiling fondly into the distance, he basks in our acceptance and feels the need to tell us more.

Zere not many peepl iz I vould trrust, he grins.

We feel very special. It goes with the job. But Old Buzza is not finished showing his trust. Reaching under his bench, he pulls out a shoe box full of money. He sticks it right under our noses. To show that we're impressed, Lien whistles long and loud.

You a good card player, Jim, she says.

Indeed. Tventy years of hard vork, Old Buzza replies proudly and closes the lid, shoving the box under his seat. Finally, he seems at peace. We sit quietly, watching the sun set over the water.

Old Buzza drinks champagne out of the bottle he keeps by his feet. He takes a big gulp, something happens and he starts to choke. He falls to his knees. Turning towards me, he stretches his hand, pleading for help. There is fear in his eyes. He doesn't want to die. He wants me to help him. But I cannot. I will not. I do not move. Old Buzza staggers to his feet, swaying from side to side with his hands around his throat. He is looking to me, then to Lien but she is cowering on her seat with her head in her hands, crying. I don't know why I do not move. Perhaps it is not in the script that I move, and I aim to please. Old Buzza takes his last step. The color purple spreads across his face and the old man keels over sideways, his head hitting the metal ring the oar is attached to. He dies instantly. There is nothing more to do. I sit quietly on my bench, listening to the ocean; next to me Lien whimpers with fright.

She doesn't realize it is over.

We sit listening to the sounds surrounding us. Birds, waves, the wind. Eventually, the sun dips beyond the horizon. Then Lien and I are left in the shadows, slowly drifting out to sea.

Old Buzza lies in a pool of blood at the bottom of the boat. The expression on his face is an odd one; he appears to be smiling. I find myself unable to look away. Out of the twilight, a boat appears. It heads straight for us. We wait patiently to be saved. On the floor, Old Buzza comes to life; grinning, he fills my head with memories. My vordz mark, the man says, winking at me as if he were still alive. Kenny your man iz.

Our savior comes into focus. It is Kenny, come to get us on his boat. He shows no surprise, asks no questions. He takes charge. We must go, he says, but Lien's in a state of shock; she won't move. He picks her up and she clings to him like a bride. He carries her across to his boat. The boats swing wildly but Kenny is as surefooted as a mountain goat. Lien cries and he makes soothing noises. With his back turned, I quickly slip the shoe box into my picnic basket. Then it's my turn to leave. I jump over to Kenny's boat. I sit down next to Lien and put my arm around her, and we watch Kenny strip down to his underwear. I do not even blink. I say nothing. There's no need to speak; we both know how it's going to be from now on. Kenny sinks the other boat. Old Buzza's body goes down with a burp and a few bubbles. Day one has begun.

21

After the service, everybody went back to the club. Mr Wong put on a bit of a spread; as befitting the occasion, he served Kenny's favorite beef and mushroom pies, and for the girls there were dim sum and spring rolls. Everybody ate and everybody drank, and then some of the girls wanted to dance. Not around the poles on the tables or on the stage, but really dance. Fully dressed, the girls kicked off their flat shoes.

In my new clothes, I sat in Kenny's spot. I swiveled the bar stool so my back rested against the bar, and as I watched the girls dance, I remembered the first time Kenny brought me here. He was security then, coming twice a week to man the door for Mr Wong, who let Kenny run the show because Kenny had introduced him to Janelle. Straightaway, Mr Wong offered her the job because as soon as he saw her, he knew, Mr Wong had boasted, that she was a winner. And yes, the man certainly knew his business because Janelle proved to be very popular.

Kenny too had faith from the beginning. He'd always been interested, but it was only after they'd got together that Kenny began to manage Janelle's career. Recently they'd begun saving up for a place of their own. I was going to live with them, Kenny had planned, to look after things in the home, but I knew I would stay on in the cabin. Even though I never said, I always felt that a young couple needed their own space. Who knew, though? I might have ended up babysitting for them. In the end, I always did what Kenny asked because it was easier that way.

I said goodbye to Janelle. Knowing this was the last time, I hugged her to me and I was full of emotion, but she pushed me away. She had been drinking all afternoon and she wasn't in the mood. Still, she went with me as far as the car park. When I got into my truck, she lifted her moon face to me for the last time; the top of her smooth head was level with the door handle. I rolled down the window and she extended her hand, which I grasped in both of mine. Bending down, I pressed my lips to her lovely fingers. Goodbye, Janelle, I said and she broke into a smile. You good boy, she smiled and stood there waiting while I reversed, and then I honked the horn and for the last time she waved me away.

22

I didn't get to the pool shop until lunchtime. When the serious buyer left, I made myself a pot of coffee. The sun streamed through the window, shining directly upon the spot where I sat at the kitchen table, and I felt happy. The exotic aroma emanating from my cup conjured up my favorite vision: in my mind's eye, I saw myself amidst bikini-clad waitresses showing off tanned cleavages as they served cocktails in the hotel lounge overlooking the beach. One young girl in particular caught my attention. She was magnificent: long-backed, slim-waisted and long-legged, she strutted confidently with her tray held high. I threw her a line and she pouted prettily. Her blond hair, swept up into a ponytail, swished across my cheek as she bent over me, whispering. I get off at eight, she winked and I stirred, for there was a promise. Yes, I thought to myself, tipping her generously, without a doubt there were good times ahead.

Sipping my Java (single origin, full-bodied, good acidic balance, bold and spicy, and of course, 100 percent Arabica beans), I quietly reflected. I went over the plan several times, mentally ticking off my schedule, and I was comforted to find it without flaw.

Ahhh ... looking at my old life through the steamed up glass, I contentedly burped ... life is going to be different now.

Feeling poetic, I held up the glass towards the window. The view, attractively bent in the rainbow of convex bubbles, confirmed what I already knew. From now on, my life was going to be full of color.

I packed before I went. Only the new clothes Zelda had bought me, anything else seemed to me a burden. I never was the sentimental kind, so I only took one thing with me and that was the ticket stub I'd kept from the rock concert. It was just a little something to remind me of my youth, nothing to do with Kathy whom I fully intended to forget, once I sold up.

The exchange at the pool shop took less than twenty minutes. I sold it to the guy who ran vacuum cleaner repairs from the shop next door. A sort of handyman, he visited me once in a while to lend a hand but mostly he kept to himself. He was a queer person, looked at the ground mainly when spoken to, and he rarely said a word, but when I approached him the day after Kathy disappeared, he squarely looked me in the eye and straightaway made an offer. Not much, to be sure, but I was in a hurry and, let's face it, the pool shop barely broke even. I don't know why but I never made any money. Maybe it was the location or maybe there just weren't enough pools in our town. In any event, the guy paid up on the dot what we agreed. I signed the receipt. The deed was done; there was no going back now. The new owner grunted goodbye and I drove off.

I cruised for a while, contemplating having dinner in town, but then I remembered Zelda mentioned something about a gift she had for me and I decided to go straight there. I knew she wasn't expecting me because I never saw her on Tuesdays. Tuesdays I spent with Janelle, I thought with a pang; however, I was determined not to dwell. I knew there were going to be others; in the cold light of day, I wasn't sure I wouldn't have thrown her over eventually. Certainly we had some good times but hey, I now strongly felt it was time to move on. As I turned into Zelda's driveway, I resolved not to give Janelle another thought.

23

The coffins are in their holes, and the boy and I are still standing. There is something wrong with this picture. To comfort each other, we eat and drink and sing and dance at the party. The boy and I grieve, the others are forgetting. The boy whispers sweet things in my ear. It makes no difference to my mood. Inside me, I am floating while on the outside my body stays put. But I no longer despair; the Good Brethren will come to release me. Wishing to be done with it, I close my eyes and the scenery shifts to where it all began.

Kenny rows us to the shore. It is pitch black by the time we dock at the pier. I manage to negotiate the plank but Lien is still crying. We get her off the boat and Kenny drives us home.

Sometime later, Old Buzza is declared missing, presumed drowned. The memorial is attended by just about everyone in town. The widow is stoic but the twins are inconsolable. It is a sad day. Lien and I stand quietly in the back row, and afterwards we go home and count our money. We have one hundred thousand tucked away where nobody sees.

24

After the wake, I went home. I stopped to get petrol and, while at the station, I changed back into my old clothes. I didn't want Kathryn asking questions about the funeral; at any rate, I felt more comfortable wearing my old jeans and t-shirt. Then I bought a burger and a drink, and I ate my dinner in the truck, listening to music.

I put on my favorite tape, a compilation of the stuff I liked; all the songs were full of the dark side and teenage angst, and even Kenny, who was never a big fan of rock music, liked it. He got going every time I put this on, singing along, living it.

I closed my eyes and imagined him the way he used to be. Feeling intense emotion, Kenny was right next to me, gripping the dashboard. His head moving with the beat, Kenny roared like a freight train, working up a little rage just like he used to when he was alive. The vision comforted me, and I remembered how every time a particularly gut-wrenching song finished, Kenny would rave about the past and try to make me feel the same. But here is where we always argued. I felt that Kenny took these things too much to heart. For my part, I was never that way inclined; that kind of emotional investment is for those who have the time, and thankfully my days were full. Kenny, on the other hand, delved into reasons, the cause and effect, the minutest details of events that I no longer gave any thought to. He certainly had a lot of rage inside him. I suspected that it had a lot to do with our mother and our fathers and that **** Uncle Clem, but when I mentioned them, I found myself licking the lino. After that, whenever Kenny raved, I just kept quiet. I realized the ranting was good for him, a sort of therapy which gave him release, so whenever I felt Kenny needed to unwind, I played the tape.

I don't know how long I sat in the truck. I only remember that I didn't want to leave. I played the tape over and over, but eventually I had to go home to Kathryn.

25

In the weeks after Old Buzza's death, we think much about his money. It is our way out of this life. But first, we will have to wait for drowned men, fears, rumors and innuendoes to be buried. Hoping to be forgotten, we wait patiently, living with the old man's ghost. He doesn't leave me for one second. Always there, clinging to me like fog. Forty three days go by in this fashion.

Meanwhile Bid, none the wiser, advises patience. He has a plan. He will take care of things and get us out.

I will have money soon, he boasts, painting a bright future somewhere in the sunset. I suspect he is stark raving mad but I do not worry. I go along as if I cared.

But very soon Bid comes to the door, looking bewildered. Under his sombrero he is nervous, the scar on his cheek flared up like a red flag.

I don't see how this can go on, he says, flinging words at me that don't make sense. I look to him for explanation but he is no help. He lies curled up on my bed, a clenched fist in his mouth. I'm left to struggle alone with connections and coincidences, and small-town needs. Eventually, I piece it all together. Good Brethren. I do hope there will be a day when I can appreciate this. To get us money, Bid kidnapped a woman but the ransom has not been paid. There's only one thing I can do now. I cannot risk Kenny being caught. He'd be interrogated. He'd buckle under the pressure. Who knows what else he might confess to? I cannot risk it.

I go downstairs and pull Lien out of her cage. Back in our room, we pack Bid's trunk and the picnic basket, loading the car ourselves because Bid is useless. Fist in his mouth, he shakes like a leaf. I put his seat belt on and Lien agrees to drive. I sit at the back, wishing I never woke up this day.

26

Zelda looked like she had been expecting me. She had a candlelit dinner ready in the formal dining room and music on the turntable. It was truly dreadful stuff she played; old-fashioned love songs full of soppy, sugary lyrics bemoaning unrequited love, sung by a bunch of has-beens I couldn't put a name to, but hey, whatever gets you through the night, I thought, resolving to play the part. After all, when I leave tomorrow, the old bag will need some consolation. Let her have her memories, I thought, magnanimously embracing the idea of spending the night here. To my surprise, the evening turned out dee-lightful.

The wine flowed and the food was tasty. Zelda, perfumed and décolletaged, flitted about like a harem concubine, and the décor too was conducive to romance; in the soft light, Zelda looked almost fuckable. She showed a rare sense of humor. Crying Surprise! she presented me with a pair of long johns and a pair of thick woolen socks. I laughed heartily. If only you knew where I'm going, I chuckled to myself, putting on the winter underwear. As if I will need these in the Caribbean. I did a funny walk across the room, winking at Zelda over my shoulder, and she went hysterical with laughter. She toppled onto the couch and treated me to a view of her fillings. Stop, oh, please, stop, she begged me; she could not laugh any harder.

Eventually, we calmed down and Zelda filled up the spa. We hopped in and she fed me oysters. She popped them into my mouth one by one off the end of a toothpick and went on refilling my champagne glass until the whole world swam in bubbles. What followed, I mercifully do not recall; however, when finally my head sank into the pillow, I had the strangest dream.

In it, I went back to the night when I first discovered that Kathy had been kidnapped. I searched the house from top to bottom, but I could not find her and I was exhausted, but then the idea to abandon her to her fate occurred to me and I sat up half the night, thinking it through. When I finally had my plan, I fell asleep. In the next moment, I suddenly saw myself in the front garden. To prepare the house for sale, I was raking the gravel when I noticed a footprint. In between the rose bushes, a little to the left of my right rubber boot, a shape of a shoe glared at me out of the soft flower bed. At first, I didn't realize what this meant. I stood there with the rake half raised in the air, but eventually I put the rake down and sank to my knees. Feeling confused, I hovered an inch or two above the footprint. It was no ordinary footprint. An outline of an eagle with its wings spread showed up clearly in the soft dirt.

An eagle in flight—jolted out of my dream, I woke up.

It was the middle of the night and I was on Zelda's couch.

Next to me, Zelda snored with her mouth open. On the coffee table, the moonlight played tricks with her four front teeth that peacefully slumbered there, reflecting each one as if they were fragments of a neon sign. Looking at this bizarre light show, I realized all of a sudden that I had it all wrong. It was as if I had been struck by lightning. I was wrong. From the beginning.

Feeling very excited, I quietly snuck out of bed and put on my new slippers and robe. Then I shuffled off to the kitchen to make tea and to think things through. I put the kettle on, and while I waited for it to boil, I marveled at the boy's impudence. My God, I marveled, he never moved a muscle. Gazing at the moon, I admired his nerve. What a bold, daring move.

Indeed, the teenager surprised me. I would never have thought he'd have the courage for such a caper. When I first saw him, he had looked so inconsequential, so timid and out of place. Jeepers, appearances can be deceptive. Still, I doubted he would have been in charge. More likely, it was the old codger, Hans, the grumpy one. Though why they wanted to kidnap Kathy made no sense to me. And why they wanted to buy the house was even more perplexing. According to their note, they wanted money from me. Very confusing indeed, I thought, shrugging my shoulders and trying to overcome the vague sense of unease creeping over me.

The kidnappers had been careless. Fancy leaving footprints like that. The first footprint in the front yard would have been a mistake; they would have been in a hurry to exit with Kathy, but the second footprint by the pool couldn't be justified. I found it after they came to look at the house. The boy had tramped around the garden with his boots on, looking as if butter wouldn't melt in his mouth and quite unconcerned that he was leaving behind clues. Was this done on purpose? Why? It didn't make sense. With a sigh, I placed my tea and my ginger biscuits on the kitchen table, and sat down, determined to find the answers.

I dunked the biscuits in my tea, and ate them all soggy and dripping over my new robe. As I savored the sharp taste, the feeling of unease gave way to one of wellbeing, and it suddenly occurred to me that I was worrying about nothing. It wasn't as if I could change my plan now. So why worry? I began to hum a tune, an eighties new wave thing, the incomparable Turning Japanese I sang at my old office party. It had been a real hit with my staff. Everybody clapped and whistled, and the girls, Rhoda and Lesley, watched me dance with a lustful look in their eyes. Young Lesley especially had looked as if she were ready to take me on. Remembering her shapely form, my throat suddenly went dry. If only Kathy hadn't been there, things might have progressed. Ah, well, what's done is done. Full of regret, I gulped the last of my tea, deciding that the best thing to do now was to go back to bed.

I woke up much later in the day. Straightaway I remembered all about last night, about the footprints and the kidnappers. Realizing I had to get home as quickly as possible, I got up and dressed in a hurry.

I made my escape while Zelda was in the shower. Shouting I had to run, I rapped on the door on my way out. Zelda shouted back to me that she would see me later on. Secure in the knowledge that I would never have to look upon her pruney face again, I shouted that I loved her and shot out of there.

I raked the flower beds around the pool as soon as I got home. I had about an hour to spare before the kidnappers, the twins and the awkward kid, whose shoe left the imprint both times, came to settle for the house. I made sure no trace of the imprint remained. There was no point in letting them know that I knew. It made no sense to me why they took Kathy or why they wanted to buy the house, but as long as they paid, they were welcome to both. I was nervous though, I hoped there was not a clue left anywhere, and I prayed this would all be over soon.

27

Bid is a mess. Head on the dashboard, he sobs. He is making Lien anxious and giving me a headache. I hate him with all my heart.

We're flying down the highway. All of a sudden, Bid stops crying. He looks up at me with a glimpse of the old Kenny about him.

I want to go back, he says, wiping his nose on his sleeve.

Don't be silly, I reply. We're leaving.

But he is silly, and we argue.

I won't leave him.

There is no time.

He cannot cope.

Of course he can.

Lien shows signs of distress. With his whining, Bid is sucking her into his black hole.

We go get the boy! she yells, giving way to his demands. She slows down and starts to turn the car around.

Drive, I say, quietly determined to save us. I lean over the seat to reach Bid and I punch him as hard as I can on the back of his head just as he grabs the wheel. The car swerves and out of nowhere a truck appears, its huge red headlights heading straight for us.

28

Kathryn.

Oh Lord, not Me again. But it was Me, appearing quite unexpectedly, like an unwanted relative, like a poor cousin come to stay. Just as I was about to watch a movie.

Leave me alone, Me! I don't need you any more.

Kathryn!

Of course, Me wouldn't take no for an answer, pulling and tugging at me relentlessly like a puppy on a teat.

What you are doing is wrong, Me says, insisting I take steps to rectify the situation.

I didn't know what to say. I was tired of explaining.

We've had this conversation, Me, I sighed, tired to death of everything. I am due some relief. I am due my new life. I am due.

We to and fro like a see-saw. Up and down, backwards and forwards. I sense a balance is being sought.

I will do as I please, I say, turning away from Me, leaving her standing in the middle of the room looking foolish. To make my point, I switch on the television and settle back on the couch. I am waiting for Phoebus to come home and I will not be persuaded to change my plan.

No. No. No! Me shakes her head emphatically. Don't you understand? What you are doing is wrong. You need to make this right. You need to tell him what happened. Don't you see?

I do not reply.

Seeing my indifference, Me changes tactic, threatening that I will be on my own, that I will be left alone for ever and ever.

So be it, I say to silence Me.

29

I got to the cabin after dark. Kathryn had been lounging on the couch, watching a movie but when she heard me pull in, she came to open the door. She stood in the hallway, looking radiant.

I feel great, she smiled at me, tossing her wet hair over her shoulder. I followed her into the kitchen. Kathryn told me about her day; she'd had a swim and a rest and when she woke up, she watched a movie. I told her about the funeral, how everyone came and brought flowers. Then, having nothing more to say, we stood there nodding.

Well, I made a sound to break the silence, are you ready?

She nodded one more time. She was definitely ready.

Standing in my old kitchen for the last time, I felt kind of funny. I knew I wanted to be alone, but I was afraid to tell Kathryn. I didn't want her to think I had changed my mind about her plan.

As if she'd read my thoughts, Kathryn cocked her head to the side and made a pretty gesture.

Would you like to be alone? she asked with a graceful arm sweep towards the lounge.

I replied that indeed I would. I think she could see how relieved I was that she guessed my wish because she gave me a most beautiful smile and then left to wait in the truck.

I went to Kenny's bedroom. First I looked at his dresser, but it was a dreadful old thing holding no memories. Next I looked at Kenny's bed

202 ■ IVANA HRUBÁ

made up with his black satin sheets. I never liked the look or the feel of those sheets, so straightaway I looked past them to Kenny's poster of our Indian princess. I'd always liked her but she wasn't quite what I was looking for. Still I was determined to take a keepsake, so I reached up to pull her down but then thought of something better. I went to my room where I kept my books, to look for Kenny's favorite tale, the one about the cowboys and Indians that Fred gave us. I found it in the bottom draw of my wardrobe.

Looking at the Indian's noble brown face on the shabby cover, I almost wept. Punkt, punkt! I told myself hastily, thinking I was foolish to feel such emotion. After all, this is the house of pain. Remembering how Kenny joked when he cuffed me at his leisure, I hugged the book to my chest. I knew he couldn't help being mean, but I had hated every bit of it. Really I ought to be glad it's over. Taking one last look around my bedroom, I closed the door behind me.

Kathryn stood beside the truck. She had what was needed in her hands, and now she took three steps towards me. Once again, she was a Madonna, her beautiful face framed by her curls so close that I started to feel tense. Kathryn, however, didn't notice my discomfort.

Here, she said, offering.

Our fingers touched, and in that one electrifying moment I felt as if I were holding my new life in my hands.

30

Finally, we left. In the truck, we hardly spoke. Phoebus drove and I sat beside him, feeling anxious. A change of weather was coming and it worried me. I prayed that the rain predicted for tonight would be delayed. We only needed an hour, two at the most, to be safe. With this in mind, I told Phoebus to step on it.

D–doan w–worry, Phoebus says calmly, smiling at me with his big doe eyes, the f–fog will take c–care of things. Indeed, behind us clouds of milky fog streak the ground, rising.

We reached the place where Phoebus used to work. Passing the entrance, he slowed down a fraction as if he were saying goodbye. But there was nothing to be seen. The night had fallen and the fog was as thick as porridge.

We spiraled down the mountain in a slow, measured way, not saying a word. The silence felt kind of depressing. To make myself comfortable, I pulled my shoes off and put my feet on top of the dashboard. Then I wound the window down. The cold night air rushed in, reviving my spirit. A feeling of wellbeing hovered close to my heart. Soon, it will be real.

Finally, we turned onto the highway. The boy nudged me. Bye, bye, Pristine Mountain …

With these words, the last of my old life disappeared. Lifting into the air like flaky dead skin, my old life was sucked out of the window, leaving me behind. I was someone new. Your future beckons, young Kathryn, I thought to myself, because there will be no more conversations. I dreamt, planning my future in which I stood alone. Moments leapt at me like so many tiny green frogs. This one I'll have. And that one too. Happy snaps continued. And from all, Rupert was conspicuously absent. Me too.

Enjoying the adventure, I put on some country music. The happiness I felt pulsated within me like a heartbeat until Phoebus opened his toady mouth.

31

Leaving the cabin was not as tough as I initially feared. After I said goodbye to everything inside, I felt at peace. I chucked Kenny's book in the back seat and, without further delay, Kathryn and I climbed into the truck. As I reversed out of the driveway, I looked at the house one last time, and my heart constricted at the sight. Full of sadness, I turned away, glancing at my book, at the noble, serious face of my Indian hero, and I felt reassured that we were doing the right thing.

All this is going to be over soon, Kathryn said. Leaning closer to me, she peered into my face anxiously as if to make sure I was going along with the plan. She didn't have to worry; I was quite ready to leave.

Going down the mountain, we didn't speak much at first. Kathryn took off her shoes and switched on the tape player. Country music came on, an old record Kenny used to love, and I wouldn't have thought it was her thing but she seemed to really enjoy it.

Did you like it? I asked her when she finally opened her eyes after the tape finished.

Super, she replied, looking so content that I nearly told her how Kenny always lusted after the girl who sang it. At the last moment, I thought better of it and just said I liked it too. She nodded, humming.

Seeing her so happy, so flushed with excitement, I puzzled at her frame of mind. I wouldn't have been surprised if she had cried because, you know, we were leaving under such strained circumstances, but Kathryn seemed as carefree as a lark.

What about Rupert? I suddenly blurted out.

I didn't mean to ask, it just came out. Honestly, I never wanted to dampen her mood, I only meant to say, well, it just occurred to me that if our plan came off, Rupert would spend a long time paying.

What about him? Kathryn barked. She crossed her arms and stared at me, not moving a muscle.

Seeing she was ready for a fight, I could have kicked myself in the head. I should have kept my mouth shut. Well, too late now. Now I had to say something.

His punishment seems a bit harsh, I replied, keeping my eyes carefully on the road.

What I really meant to say was that we were taking a big gamble with Rupert's life. Did we have the right?

Evidently we did.

He wanted me dead! Kathryn retorted passionately.

I glanced at her. She looked like she definitely believed it.

Maybe. And maybe not, I said to her, wishing she would consider the possibility that we were wrong about him.

Maybe? Kathryn shouted, rising out of her seat in a rage. He practically erased me from his life!

She leaned towards me, looking so angry that I thought she was going to slap me, but there was no point in stopping the conversation now. In for a penny, in for a pound.

Maybe he thought the kidnap was a joke, I said bluntly.

To me, it seemed quite plausible. At the beginning, Rupert might have dismissed the whole thing. After all, it wasn't as if they really had a million dollars. Or looked like they did. Really, the whole idea was preposterous. Even the note was ****** stupid. Honestly, would I have taken it seriously? Hardly.

Looking at Kathryn now, I was surprised that she hadn't thought of it herself. It was a distinct possibility. Kathryn once told me that she often played hide and seek and other childish pranks even. It was entirely possible that Rupert thought the kidnap was a joke.

However, Kathryn took a different view. The way she looked at me plainly said she thought I was being naïve.

Don't you see? She tapped her forehead. My heart skipped a beat; Kenny used the same gesture at me all the time. He never went to the police.

I pointed out to her that we specifically requested he keep quiet. But Kathryn was not prepared to listen to me.

He did nothing! she shouted, looking all flushed. Looking just like Kenny when he got frustrated at my inability to see things clearly. Of course, sometimes Kenny was right; I was dense, stupid even, and he could hardly be blamed for getting angry, but this was different. I wasn't being dense now. I'd had the time to think about where it all went wrong and I wasn't at all sure we had the story right.

Rupert put the house up for sale, I explained to Kathryn now, to pay the ransom after he realized we were serious.

Kathryn looked at me as though she thought I was joking. But I wasn't. At first, when I saw the ad in the paper, I thought he had given up on Kathryn and was leaving town. But later on I changed my mind. Rupert might have thought Kathryn was playing a joke and was waiting it out to see if she came home. Then, when we sent the second note, he realized we were serious and tried to raise the money by selling the house. So now I told all this to Kathryn, who stared at me doubtfully.

What about the third note, then? Why did he put up the house for sale after you sent him the third note asking for just twenty thousand? Kathryn threw her hands up in the air. She looked ready to explode.

He might not even have found the third note, I replied. Kathryn sank back into her seat with a scowl.

Forget the notes. He should have tried to raise the money straightaway. The truth is he was never going to pay the ransom.

He could have tried harder to save me, she pouted, folding her arms defensively across her chest.

He did make an effort to raise the money once we lowered the ransom to a manageable amount, I pointed out to her. He tried to sell the house.

Kathryn said nothing in reply.

I took it as a good sign.

Did we really know the whole story? That's what I'd be thinking if I were in her shoes. In the cold light of day, I had to admit she had acted rashly. Why didn't she wait for Rupert at home? Why didn't she ask for an explanation? If I was her, I would want to know face to face. Well, I checked myself, that would depend. Of course, if it was between Kenny and me, I wouldn't have said boo because that's how we ran things in our family. I wouldn't have questioned his intentions no matter what. But Kathryn? By her own admission she talked back to Rupert all the time. So why not confront him? Deep down, I knew she had her reasons. Revenge. Outrage. Hurt. Pride. Other factors I might not have thought about. It all adds up. Admittedly, from what she told me, she had good reason to believe Rupert was in the process of unloading her. However, where was the proof? Where was the other side of the argument?

I felt a headache coming on. There were too many questions I had no answers to. Besides, this whole thing was sapping my energy, sucking me dry to the bone. More and more I was getting the feeling that the wheels were turning much too fast. Figuratively speaking, of course, I didn't mean the wheels on the truck. Because of the fog, we were going slow.

You want proof? Kathryn's voice rang out triumphantly, disrupting my thoughts. What about the message? Kathryn said, banging her fist on the dashboard.

I knew she meant the voice message she found on the answering machine. The message from which she surmised that Rupert had been having an extra-marital affair. I wished I could have talked to her about Kenny. I would have told her that Kenny had loved Janelle like no other, and, in his own way, he was devoted to her, but that devotion did not prevent him from having his bit of fun with other girls on the side. Did Janelle stress? No. Far from it. And it wasn't because she had lacked moral fiber because of her business and all. She simply knew a thing or two about human nature. She knew people were not, what's the word, infallible. Live and let live, Janelle always said.

I opened my mouth. I shut it without saying a word. The way Kathryn glared at me made me realize it would be pointless to bring it up.

Rupert wanted me dead and that's all there is to it, Kathryn announced with an imperious shake of her head. Let the crime fit the punishment.

Let the what fit the *what?* I almost laughed; however, Kathryn looked ready to attack me.

He was glad to have me dead, she declared, narrowing her eyes and continuing to talk in that deliberate, menacing tone, as if she were daring me to disagree. She sounded very sure of herself, and looked magnificent too; her flashing eyes and her heaving bosoms made my head spin, she was that beautiful. The way she stared me down was wild; she looked like a warrior queen pronouncing a judgment. I realized that there was no stopping her, but still I ventured my opinion one last time.

But you are not, are you?

What? she barked, frowning as if she didn't get me.

Dead.

In response, Kathryn made a face. Then she turned her head towards the side window and stared into the darkness. I sighed. I could tell she was hell-bent on revenge. And maybe that was the right thing to do. Really, what did I know? Maybe Rupert deserved everything he had coming. Maybe he meant for Kathryn to die. The thing was, we were never to know. It bothered me. I would have preferred if we knew for sure, then at least you knew you were doing the right thing, or alternately you were doing the wrong thing and simply didn't care. Well, one could live with that. There would be consequences, there always are. After all, if I had not got involved in the first place, we wouldn't be here deciding the fate of another. But we could have made the decision knowing the full facts. As it was, we were bogged down in what ifs, maybes, perhaps and I'll betchas. The wheels were in motion.

It's the saddest thing.

What's the saddest thing? Kathryn sighed as if she were getting tired of this conversation. As if she had thought it through and I was rehashing, deliberately, endlessly repeating myself, intent on causing trouble.

I shrugged.

I hope you are not suggesting I am to blame … Letting the sentence dangle, Kathryn looked as if she had run out of words to express her outrage.

The idea did enter my mind. She was to blame, not for the whole thing of course, it was mainly Kenny and me at the beginning, but right now was her idea.

To her face, I said nothing.

Well then, Kathryn went on, nodding at me meaningfully, you know what happened. She pointed a finger at me. You know who's to blame.

I nodded as if I agreed with her. Deep down, however, I was beginning to change my mind about everything. About what happened, how it all started and how it was ending.

It was no use blaming Kenny for everything. We were all to blame. I should have known better. She should have known better. Still, what it comes down to is one moment in time. Maybe Kathryn was right. On the surface, some things are better left unsaid. For the simple reason of truth. You might get it, if you ask. And it seemed to me that Kathryn didn't want to know the truth. And that's why she didn't confront Rupert. She didn't want to know his truth about their relationship, and clearly she was not prepared to deal with her truth about their relationship. Like me and Kenny. We had two sides to everything, even though I never said. Consequently, Kenny got used to thinking his side was my side, and whose fault was that? Mine. I should have made sure he knew about my side.

Plunged into these thoughts, I drove on in silence. Kathryn seemed happy with that. She busied herself with the music, putting on all kinds of tapes, but she kept coming back to the country tunes of Kenny's, so eventually I told her that she could keep the tape if she wanted to, which she did. It seemed to really please her, and she suddenly began to talk about her plan, not the present situation as such, but a future plan, and she also asked me what I was going to do.

I shrugged. I haven't really given it much thought.

In response, Kathryn declared that she would like to travel.

Smiling at the idea, she commenced telling me how she had been forced to swallow her desire to visit the pyramids because Rupert never wanted to do anything that didn't involve golf or food.

Of course, now that I'm free, Kathryn concluded, raising a finger in the air, I will do as I please.

I nodded; it seemed like a good plan. With a pang, I thought about Kenny, who always told me how he and Janelle planned to circumnavigate the country on the back of a motorbike one day.

One day, when they were married. In my mind's eye, I saw them cruising along the coast, wind in their hair and love in their hearts. When they disappeared into the sunset, I sighed. Maybe they wouldn't have traveled, and maybe they wouldn't have got married at all. We'll never know.

Kathryn noticed my mood. She stopped talking, looked at me as if I were someone she liked, and then placed her hand over mine where I held the gear stick.

32

We had a conversation. In the truck, going down the mountain. I didn't like it. I didn't. Like it.

A bit late in the day to be questioning Rupert's intentions, I said to Phoebus when he brought my husband up. Defending him, he preached forgiveness and regretted the action we were taking. Wanted to spread the blame.

I looked at him speechless. The very idea. What cheek! Honestly, I would have never expected him to insinuate that I was to blame. Dear Lord. I felt like slapping his face.

How can you say that? I demanded when he questioned Rupert's guilt. Guilty as charged, that's obvious. Everything points to it.

Phoebus remained defiant. Things can be m—misleading. We need to know the facts.

In the end, I was reduced to shaking my head silently because words failed me. To terminate the argument, I turned to face the window. Just drive.

In the ensuing silence, I replayed the events, imagining how it went down.

Oh, Rupert, I see you gloating over the note. Spread across the kitchen sofa you're excited, aroused even, by the prospect of freedom. Guzzling wine, you're stuffing yourself silly with some gourmet something or other, your jaws working furiously and your mushy brain ticking. And all the while, the note, right there, tantalizing you with the promise of longed for liberty. You know who you are. You're a man set for a grand adventure. Rejoicing, scheming, planning your way out, you feel free, exhilarated, like a kid after a roller coaster ride. What if she comes back? What will I do? In the end, you will flip a coin. This then is the end of Kathy.

I picture the mistress. On the phone she sounded old, but who knows, she might be young or at least well preserved. Blonde? Red? Brunette? It hardly matters now. Frankly, I think she has money. After all, that's the one constant in Rupert's desires. Moneee.

Oh, Rupert, you fool. You seem to be unaware of the impression you make. So skillful. So polite. And always on your best behavior. Have to be nice to Mother, she might be persuaded to invest in the business. You mean the pool shop? The roll-a-door garage where you store some hoses? Hmmm. Do you still love me, Rupert?

Well, I wondered, didn't I? When did you stop? Was it a moment? If so, can we please rewind to where it all began to unravel? If only I could start over, I would make sure we stayed on track.

You could just divorce him, you know, Me pipes up out of nowhere, disrupting my musings. I'm left feeling surprised; I'd thought we'd finished with each other.

Dear Me. Do not go there.

Me, however, is determined to call me to account.

You should have asked him for an explanation.

I picture the scene. Rupert? Never lost for words, knowing just the right thing to say. Playing me, his poor old stupid wife, like a violin to get me to sing along with his tune. And me? Reeled in like a fish. Coming around to accepting his version of events. Persuaded I had it all wrong. I could just see myself, down on my knees, thanking him graciously for saving my life. In the end, nothing would change. We would live our silly, barren, jellyfish lives unchanged.

I don't think so.

Me won't give up.

You started it.

I don't accept that. He started it, I say to Me, who is clearly ready for a fight.

No. You started it.

Me holds my soul in the palm of her hand. Scrunched up it looks like a small paper ball. Tiny, but one can see it is full of doodles. I get it. This then is what I am. A doodly, confused, silly paper ball. But I am not prepared to take the blame.

It is too late, I shrug.

Me shakes all over.

Do you not feel sorry for him? Me asks, thrusting her chin towards Phoebus, the one true innocent.

Dear Me, I sigh, trying to hide my irritation. Of course I do. I can barely look at him.

Well, then. Me nudges me, hoping to extract the truth.

Which truth? I ask Me. My truth? Rupert's? Kenny's? I am confused. You can't have one without the other, can you?

Me sighs, then pleads, then begs, then threatens. She will not be able to stay unless I tell Phoebus the truth. But telling the truth is not an option. I will not spoil my chance to be free of my past life. I know what I have to do now. I have to let her go. I look at her and she looks right back. Something is different. For a second, I cannot put my finger on it and then it hits me. She has no fight left in her. She looks like a sad, weak, pathetic human being with no backbone. Me looks the way I used to feel. But things have changed. I'm the strong one now and it's time dear Me and I went our separate ways. I can tell by looking at her that she knows that the end of an era is at hand.

This it it, Me says quietly, chokingly, crocodile tears running down her suddenly pale cheeks. I'm going to have to leave you.

There's just the tiniest echo of hope, a mere scrap of expectation that I will do something to stop her leaving. But I will not be manipulated any longer. This is what I've been waiting for.

You fool! I scream. I've been wanting to get rid of you for years! Don't you understand how much I hate you?

Me is too stunned to speak. She stops crying and stares at me without a word. I feel her helplessness in my bones. It gives me strength.

I do not want you around anymore. You've stopped me from doing everything I've ever wanted to do and it's time you paid the price, I say to her. It's true. She's dominated me my whole life. Because of her I spent my childhood home-schooled and my teenage years in a medicated haze. She fucked up everything, even when we grew up, keeping real people away from me. She even got me sacked from the one thing that I was good at—acting. What with her always talking to me over the other actors it was no wonder my contract was terminated, no wonder at all. But I will not stand for this any longer. She's going to pay.

Me stands there shaking her head. She opens her mouth to defend herself. I will not allow it.

Fuck off! I shout and Me is gone within a blink. Ah, the freedom. So wonderful. So lovely to finally be able to breathe.

Without Me for the first time in years, I felt a tremendous sense of relief. From now on, things were going to be different. It would be just me and no one else.

Having thus made my peace, I suddenly felt blissful. I felt liberated and comforted, and I decided not to be angry with Phoebus anymore. So I talked to him, and he turned out to be a good listener.

I talked to him about my fabulous plans for my fabulous future. The poor thing looked so relieved, so happy for me, and he gaped at me with such concentration that eventually he made me feel ashamed. I did feel a twitch of regret and a little hope for both of us. Phoebus is a good soul. I really did wish it could be someone else, someone more deserving of the mess we were in, sitting there next to me. But the wheels were in motion, and there was no turning back. It would be over soon. Soon we'd have to say goodbye. I knew this and a part of me felt sad. I realized that I was going to miss this wonderful weird boy. But that's the way it had to be. I could only hope that the rest of his life turned out better than it had been so far.

Everything is going to be all right, I said to him, gently nudging him when he got all quiet after I mentioned my travel plans. How he reminded me of me a few lifetimes ago. I also had felt abandoned.

Always on my own at home, I was bored and unfocused; waiting for Rupert to return from his "business" trips, I was dying. Christ. One shudders. How could I have stood it so long? Well, as they say, love is a terrible affliction. But that was then. Now I would do as I pleased.

Buoyed by that thought, I felt positively charged with energy. I felt like sticking my head out the window to shout to the whole world. However, being cursed with a sensitive nature, I remained silent and stroked Phoebus's hand. Shrouded in the fog, we slowly spiraled down the mountain.

33

I survive the crash. I know this because all my senses tell me so. I smell blood. I taste it, I feel it. It pounds into my ears like a sledgehammer, quite clear above the noise coming from the truck. Then I open my eyes and see the truck right in front of me, lying on its side. The wheels keep on turning.

Inside the car, everything is quiet. I take off my seatbelt and lean forward towards Lien. She sits upright in her seat. Her severed head rests in her lap and she looks straight at me. Bid, I say, not taking my eyes off her, I need your help.

Bid melts into a word. Bid.

Lien's knees are red. There is a hissing, a gurgling, and a steady dripping as her blood leaves her body. Lien seems to like it. She is convulsing with laugher and her head bops gently on her knees. She sees Them coming and she can't wait. Go, Mai Lin, go! She suddenly screams. Take the money and run!

I run. I run, clutching the picnic basket. Lien's laughter follows me like a faithful dog. Exactly twenty-five minutes later, I reach the roadhouse. Fred chops garlic. Hans serves cold pie. I gesture to them. They leave their work and we go to the back room. I give them the shoe box. There. All yours. Sniffing the money, the twins nod their heads like a pair of storks. Life a party iz, they grin.

On my way out, I glimpse the back of the boy. He is on his knees, cleaning the oven, his head disappearing into its gaping hole. Might as well stay there. I evaporate.

A little while later I'm floating in the space above Lien's bed. I feel her, I see her, she's here and she's never going to leave me. Don't cry, she whispers to me. We're always going to be together. Don't you fret. Be patient.

Her words soothe me. We will be together soon. The Good Brethren will make sure. She looks at me lovingly and I feel better. I trust her. Okay, I won't fret.

34

The kidnappers showed up right on the dot. The grandfather clock in the kitchen had chimed eight times and right on the ninth stroke, the doorbell rang. Greetings took place in the doorway. Pressing my hands warmly, Hans, whom I assumed to be the mastermind, warbled pleasantly about nothing in particular; really I wondered whether he was all there, for such was his composure. Fred too seemed entirely at ease. The young hooligan, however, did not show. I was glad because, in the cold light of day, I wasn't sure I could stand to be near him again, he repulsed me so. As much as I tried not to think about it, I had a feeling, a suspicion, that it would have been he who touched her, he who perhaps struggled with her and maybe even hurt her, and, as I am not a violent man, this I could not stomach. I preferred not to know.

We adjourned to the living room. I invited them to sit, but, sticking to my plan, I did not offer refreshments. The sooner the better. I placed my papers in front of Hans, who understood immediately. Shifting his buttocks slightly to the right, he pulled a leather wallet out of his left trouser pocket. I stood by with the pen in my hand, and I watched him fumble with the wallet fastening. Apologizing, for he had arthritis (they had gotten very soaked waiting for the U-boat, Fred remarked), Hans finally presented his cheque. It was a happy moment. I almost smacked my lips, looking at the amount. This adventure was finally paying off. Then I bent forward to show him where to sign the house deed. At that precise moment, the doorbell rang. Astonished, all three of us, the kidnappers no less surprised than I, raised our heads towards the sound. And all three of us gaped.

One moment, please, I said, recovering my wits. It's probably the paper boy, I casually explained as I crossed the hallway to the door, but inside my chest my heart pounded fit to burst.

Hello, Rupert.

My knees almost buckled under me. She looked straight at me and in her eyes I glimpsed something terrible which made me shiver. I went to say something but no sound came out. I only swallowed awkwardly and she, noting the effect she had on me, gave a mocking smile. The hour of reckoning has come, it seemed to say. Then Kathy's mother entered the house, striding past me without a word. Behind her came her lawyer and he tipped his bowler to me on his way in. Bewildered, I remained standing alone in the open doorway.

Gazing into the sunshine, I experienced an inner turmoil. My mind, a mass of plump, airy fairy-floss, was incapable of rational thought. My fears of the last twenty-four hours—the rain, the fog, the young hoodlum coming back to make footsteps with his funky boots—resurfaced and I felt the same exhaustion.

When I had finally fallen asleep in the early hours of the morning, my conscience had plagued me. I had put it down to nerves. And now

I felt the same sense of foreboding; I felt cornered, trapped, taken by surprise, and I could not think clearly. Had I been able to move, I might have run. Alas, it was not to be. The instant my limbs finally responded to my command—Run, run, Rupert, run— I registered something new, a slight shift in the scenery in my flight path where two cops walked, in no great hurry, up the gravel driveway. In my confusion I had not perceived the cop car parked behind the gate, but now I saw it clearly and my knees gave way under me. Sliding along the door frame, I impulsively grabbed at the door knob. It didn't break my fall. When I came to, I was flat on my back across the welcome mat, and the cops were chewing gum close to my face.

35

They carried me to the sofa. Someone placed a cold compress on my brow, a wet tea-towel which had not been wrung out properly; as a result, droplets dribbled down the side of my neck into my collar, producing a damp and unpleasant sensation. I opened my eyes.

My captors stood at the foot of the couch ready for the inquisition to begin. They were silent, menacing, with disapproving stony faces I could only imagine, because I could not see their expressions. The sun framed in the window behind them blurred their identities, their ghostly silhouettes silently accusing me until someone shifted and I was blinded. Panicking, I shut my eyes.

Maybe if I don't move, they will go away, I foolishly hoped. I played dead, but when the old hag, Kathy's mother, said, Let's sit him up, I flinched.

Stay still, pleeeease, I pleaded with my facial twitch, but then someone else, it might have been the lawyer, said, C'mon, man, the jig is up, and I realized that indeed it was.

I opened my eyes, this time for good. Collectively, they leaned closer. Their hunched shoulders shielded me from the sunbeam, and for that I was grateful because I felt a headache coming on. Indeed, it wasn't long before my temples throbbed. The pain, pulsating to the dull rhythm of Kathy's mother's voice, obliterated the meaning of her words. Still, I was conscious of her gestures and there were plenty of those, and she had props too; she pulled the Title Deed out of her bag and waved it about for everyone to see.

The two cops stepped up. The short fat one commenced speaking. He too gestured excessively. The lawyer and the kidnappers watched impassively; the tall thin cop loomed over everyone, and when his moment came, he pulled a piece of thin white fabric out of his bag. The material was cotton but I could not make out the shape until he shook it out for me to see. It was a t-shirt. A bloody t-shirt.

Stains, largish and smallish, and specks of dried blood, haphazardly marred the design, a woman's head, which was printed across the front. I recognized it immediately. The profile, with its long narrow nose and the almond-shaped eye and its high smooth brow upon which the crown sat like a tall flowerpot, was well known. Kathy had had a t-shirt just like that. She had seen it advertised on the telly and ordered it along with a book about Egypt. It wasn't long after that she got herself that cat, and she named that thing Kleopatra. Yes, it was her t-shirt, but why the cops had it I could not for the life of me fathom. I gaped, confused to the very core. The feeling of vague unease that had plagued me now returned, growing stronger as the atmosphere in the room darkened.

Everyone turned to me. The cops pointed at the t-shirt, Kathy's mother waved the Title Deed, and then everyone fell silent, looking at me expectantly. In that moment I realized I was doomed, and my headache vanished just as suddenly as it came on.

36

But I do fret. I endure much in the forty-eight hours following the death of my beloved. The boy comes to seek healing and we talk about our bereavement. He never asks but I sense his discomfort, his need to know the truth.

Where were you when my brother died?

The hundred-thousand-dollar question has the face of a sad clown balancing across a tightly stretched rope. One false step and …

The boy is no fool. He waits patiently. Slumped in the corner like a bag of wet clothes, he evokes the smell of familiar things. Chopped garlic. Cold pie. Lonely old men. Pool shop owners dissatisfied with marriage. Burnt oil and burgers. Hair grease. Jasmine tea. And somewhere in between, there's Bid. Steaming like a bucket of warm pee in the hot dusty weather, he pumps petrol. Up and down, the old fashioned way he cleans the windscreens. Smiling at the tourists but watching me. Always watching. His eyes like a fish's. His cheeks like an old woman's ass. His hands like a turtle's claws. And always I said no.

The boy talks about Bid until there are no more words to be said. All I see are his glassy, fishy eyes on the dashboard. The boy misinterprets my silence. Looking like a small sad puppy, he forces me to plan the funeral.

I have so much to say to him but no courage to say it. No words. I am so sorry to have caused you this grief, I mean to say. Shooooo is what comes out. I feel hopeless. It is better that we go somewhere where there are other people to distract us from ourselves.

I take him shopping. He likes the trousers but they do not fit. I choose another pair. Beaming, the boy goes into the change room. Among the throngs, I spy the flower shop woman. Old Buzza's wife and Rupert's bankroll. Seeing her is like a stab in my heart. Rupert has betrayed me. The scene at the florist's rises before me like a mirage and in a flash I'm beside the widow, tugging at her sleeve. The widow appears to remember me.

She and I have a talk. I tell her everything I know about her one true love. The widow listens intently. Her eyes glint and her mouth gets smaller and tighter and uglier with my every gesture. She hugs a pile of shirts to her chest as if to protect herself but underneath it, she is wilting like an old bouquet. She has grasped that she is not destined for happily ever after.

37

Rupert Calliper, I am arresting you on suspicion of the murder of your wife Kathryn Calliper.

How long I stared, I do not know; by all accounts, it was a while. When the fat cop finished speaking, I slowly raised my hand and pointed my trembling finger at the kidnappers.

It was them, I croaked. My throat felt parched but they heard me.

The room plunged into silence for a moment, the company exchanging incredulous looks.

Then the fat cop grinned. His stubby fingers gripped my shoulder; squeezing hard, he wheezed, sure it was them, and everybody burst out laughing.

No, no, you don't understand. I found myself nodding into the fat cop's grinning dial. They kidnapped my wife … I can prove it. I nodded with increasing urgency. The shoe, the footprint … I swallowed hard, trying not to panic, but my courage, along with my voice, was failing me as I squeaked, protesting my innocence. It was the teenager, the one with the funny shoes.

Funny shoes? The fat cop clicked his dentures, making a mocking gesture. Did you laugh?

The room exploded in another outburst of laughter and people made disrespectful comments about me, Kathy's mother alleging that I had always been a very stupid man. Disregarding her, I told them the whole story. At first, the cops made light of it, they guffawed and held their sides, but I persevered. After all, the rest of my life was at stake. I persisted with my explanation but they kept shaking their heads until Hans, whom I previously thought quite clever, suddenly blundered. He owned up that he knew what I was talking about.

The company stopped laughing.

Ja, ja, Hans repeated into their stunned faces, I ze sink know. It ze eegl in flight iz. He proceeded to describe it in great detail. The sole design was very unusual, one of a kind, Hans was saying, the staccato rhythm of his harsh syllables punctuating my nods like a stopwatch.

The cops looked at each other.

An eagle in flight, you say? The fat cop repeated, a sly smile playing around his meaty lips.

I didn't like the way he posed the question, but I nodded anyway.

Aha, the fat cop crossed his fleshy arms over his chest, revealing his sweaty underarms.

You got a nerve, he whispered, leaning close to me. So close in fact that I didn't want to breathe, but he hung there suspended until I had no choice but to inhale.

Poor Phoebus, the cop said, shaking his head in disgust, then quietly to me: I'm going to make you regret the day you were born.

So they arrested me. The fat cop gestured towards his partner, who pulled a pair of handcuffs out of his bag. In two strides, he was behind me and clicked them on. Then the fat cop read me my rights and they hauled me off to the watch-house, turning the sirens on in the car.

38

The wake is over. The girls line up at the poles. Just like the old times. Only Lien is not here. I am not here. I watch them against my will, looking at their fans fluttering close to their faces, and I remember the glow, the anticipation of a future in which something will happen.

I look inside me and see no glow, only a faint light flickering on and off. It is the lanterns and the wind chimes moving without making a sound. Then I see her. Standing at the end of the line, she is tiny at first, but grows larger with each breath I take. I see her smiling, beckoning, enticing me to take leave of this place.

Mai Lin, she motions to me, come closer.

But I won't. Not just yet. She stands still, waiting patiently like a moment frozen in time.

I wish I could go back to the night Old Buzza died. If I had done something to save him, Lien would still be alive. Why didn't we save him?

Lien shrugs at me from across the Universe. She is tired of my guilt. She's paid her dues and now she is one of Them. And soon it will be my turn.

Back on earth, Mr. Wong throws open the door and customers pour in. It is time for me to go.

39

The fog cleared when we turned onto the highway. Kathryn fell asleep. For once, there was complete silence. It was beautiful, this silence. For a while I was lulled, enjoying the scenery. Well, there wasn't much, what with the darkness fallen over everything and the clouds obscuring whatever moonlight there was. Still, it was pleasant to be on my own. Quiet thoughts appeared, bringing dead people who beckoned to me with a smile and a nod, furry little animals hopped in and out of burrows and everyone was happy. I tell you, I could have followed that road till the end of time. However, too soon I was jolted back into the world of the living.

Hey, Phoebus. Wake up, you turd!

Startled, I looked over my shoulder. Kenny sat bolt upright in the back seat. He grinned.

I blinked.

K–K–Kenny, I muttered stupidly; I was that surprised. All I could do was look.

He looked great. Immaculate. Not at all like he used to. There wasn't a hair out of place. I didn't know what to make of it and I couldn't think of anything to say.

Seeing I was speechless, Kenny winked at me and took off his sombrero, placing it on his knees.

Yes, it's me, you silly turd. Don't act so surprised.

But I was surprised, totally floored really, as you would be if your dead brother suddenly appeared. For Kenny to show up out of the grave like this, I thought that maybe I was dreaming.

Leaning across the back seat, Kenny playfully tweaked my ear.

You're not dreaming, you little fool. Look out!

A deer frozen in my headlights stared right at me. I swerved sharply, avoiding it just in time. Shaken by the sudden turn, Kathryn murmured in her sleep. She moved her head but didn't wake up.

Behind me, Kenny shifted and his face appeared in the windscreen in front of me. He looked so real that for a moment I thought of closing my eyes, you know, just to see.

Concentrate.

In the windscreen, Kenny frowned.

You'll get yourself killed, he mumbled.

I gripped the wheel tighter.

Is that what killed you? I wanted to ask. What was it, Kenny? I thought to myself. Lack of concentration? High speed? An argument? I really wanted to know, but I didn't trust myself not to cry, so I didn't dare ask him.

It was the other guy. The truck driver. He was drunk, Kenny said matter-of-factly, then reached into his breast pocket and pulled out a joint.

For a moment, I was speechless. The cops had told me they had recovered bottles, fragments of beer and rum bottles, from Lien's car.

I'm telling you it was the other guy's fault! Kenny roared, responding to my unvoiced doubts with a stinging blow to the back of my head.

I apologized for my wicked thoughts and Kenny forgave me. It's okay, he murmured, lighting the joint and inhaling it deeply. We lapsed into silence. Kenny sat there staring at me out of my windscreen. I kept my eyes on the road but from time to time I glanced at him. I even blinked several times. He continued to appear.

You look good.

I meant it. Kenny looked well taken care of. Even his fingernails were clean.

In response, he gave me a big smile, revealing bone. His eyes stared out of their holes like bottomless wells, and I suddenly got the feeling I was going mad.

Relax, Kenny advised, continuing to smile. He drummed a beat on his teeth with his fingers. It's all in your head.

It probably was. After all, I reasoned, Kenny was dead. I went to his funeral. I was there when they put him six feet under, so logically, if I was really seeing him now, I would have to be insane. Well then, let's just go with it.

How's Lien?

For some reason, I couldn't say why, I pictured her doing her toenails. Looking pretty in her short lace peignoir, she sat on a fluffy rug with one leg folded under her and the other up, and her chin resting on her knee; the pose revealed a blue satin triangle covering her privates. Bent forward, she dipped a tiny little brush into a little glass vial. Drawing a dollop of carmine, she positioned the tip of the brush over her big toe. Then she looked up and winked at me. Spying, are you? she asked, blowing me a flirtatious kiss. She looked so beautiful it made my head swim, and even though I knew I was imagining the whole scene, I felt myself going red all over.

Kenny noticed and gave a good-natured chuckle.

She's good. Lays about all day doing her nails. Thinks of you often. Pleased with his little joke, Kenny inhaled deeply and grinned in that weird way again. It seemed to me that I could see right up his skull. At first I thought there was nothing up there, but a second look revealed there was a tree. It was our tree with the hammock hanging right there under the strongest branch, and the death notices pinned up on the trunk. Everything looked just like it used to. Even the notices were laminated, weather-proofed for longevity. Why I should see our tree in Kenny's skull made no sense to me, but the notices reminded me of something else.

How's your dad? I blurted out.

Kenny shrugged, holding his breath. Dunno.

Ahhh, how come? I ventured to ask, emboldened by my new resolution to question everything.

Haven't seen him. See no reason to, Kenny announced in a bored tone of voice. He concentrated on his joint, inhaling and exhaling at regular intervals, holding the smoke inside him for as long as he could. In the windscreen, the tip of the joint glowed red like the solitary eye of a malevolent mythical beast.

Leaving him to savor this moment, I mulled things over in my head, eventually concluding that Kenny had made the right decision. Kenny's dad had been a mongrel when he was alive and most likely hadn't changed after death.

Haven't seen yours either, Kenny remarked as an afterthought.

Well, that was to be expected, I thought, feeling a twitch of regret. For one brief, glorious moment I had hoped that they might have made up, you know, now that things were different, now that they were in heaven together.

The windscreen Kenny grimaced. There is no heaven. For emphasis, he pointed upwards.

Jesus. What's the alternative? I shuddered, conjuring up stereotypical images of eternal suffering.

Phoebus, you silly turd. Shaking his head at my foolishness, the windscreen Kenny coughed, rattling his bones. There is no hell either.

I gaped at him speechless. My faith, like the red dot in the windscreen, was disintegrating in front of my very eyes. No heaven. No hell. I always believed. I always thought it was like north and south. You couldn't have one without the other. Like left and right, or black and white, I always pictured heaven and hell to be the opposite sides of a scale. On the one side, you put your good deeds, on the other your sins. Whichever side outweighed the other, well, that's how you knew where to go.

No, no, no. Kenny wagged a stubby finger in front of my nose. Here is all there is. H-e-e-r.

I see. Here is all we have. Well. A lot of people are going to be disappointed. I for one always counted on something better. You know, once your number's up.

The conversation came to a halt. I was thinking. Adjusting my views, so to speak, because it had occurred to me that in the absence of … ah … judgment day, by virtue of having by-passed the whole business of it, Kenny did very well for himself. Who knows where he might have ended up?

Pondering this new revelation, I began to feel much better. At least now I could stop worrying.

Meanwhile, having finished the joint, Kenny began to chew his fingernails. Every time he chewed one off, he skillfully spat it out so that my neck was hit repeatedly in one place. Well, here's someone else who hasn't changed, I thought quietly to myself, but Kenny caught me.

Hey, he growled, show some respect.

Apologizing, I steered my thoughts towards it. Respecting him, I again wondered whether he was a figment of my imagination. I mean, with all that's happened I wouldn't have been surprised if I was going batty. I looked over at Kathryn. She slumbered, limp as a rag, curled up into the seat, drooling.

In the meantime, Kenny finished his manicure. He leaned closer; as a result, his face in the windscreen got bigger, softer, less boney. Yes, more in focus but at the same time kind of blurry, reminding me of Janelle.

I plucked up my courage and asked him about her.

Where was Janelle when you died?

I had always thought it should have been Janelle with him in the car. It should have been her driving him off to the sunset. But it wasn't. And I'd always wondered why, even though I had never asked her. The reason I never did was because, well, because I felt she couldn't have answered me if she'd tried. After the accident, she changed. She became broody and secretive, acting as if she'd exhausted all her options, stripped all her layers and there was nothing left but a ghost of her former self. Frankly, she had me worried, but there seemed little point in mentioning anything to Kenny now.

In response to my question, Kenny cleared his throat, giving a funny little grin as if he were nervous.

Janelle stayed back to take care of you, he said. We decided it would be safer if Lien and I went first, and you and Janelle joined us later. Less suspicious, too. We decided that Lien would drive me to safety, and then return to tell you where I was so you could join me later.

Kenny finished his speech with a pat on my shoulder. I didn't know what to say. I didn't feel any better; in fact, I felt worse because I realized that I should be having the good, warm feeling I had dreamt about when I dreamt that Kenny had not left me. The feeling that had nourished me like a mother's milk whenever I imagined that he had made arrangements to come back for me, and that I was never out of his plan. But now I didn't get my warm feeling, and when I looked at Kenny, he looked right through me, his eyes burning holes through the windscreen.

It was all lies, I realized, feeling worse than ever. I would have appreciated the truth, whatever it was. Paradoxically, the absence of truth had now revealed the true nature of our relationship. Previously I had thought that Kenny never lied to me. In all our life together, he never justified his decisions to me because he didn't need to. Back then, what I thought was immaterial, of no consequence, and therefore not worth the bother of a lie. And now that I evidently mattered, I only wished to become incidental again.

Busy with his lies, Kenny paid no attention to my thoughts, proving that there was enough of him left.

Listen, he whispered earnestly. Nothing that's happened is your fault.

Now he floored me. When he was alive, everything that went wrong was my fault.

Of course, it is, I replied, thinking about Kathryn's plan and my part in it. I was to blame because all I had to do was to refuse her. I could have refused to help her carry out her stupid revenge. But instead,

I went along with it.

I could have said no to her, I said, feeling annoyed with Kenny for treating me like a child. I could have owned up to the cops. I could have …

With an abrupt gesture, Kenny cut me off.

You're not to blame. You're a kid. He paused, jabbing a finger into the air in front of my nose. You had no choice, Kenny insisted and jerked a thumb towards Kathryn. Don't you see how she used you?

I shook my head at him. It was Kathryn who had had no choice. I truly believed that. So what if she used me? She wouldn't have had to if we hadn't made her.

Actually, I replied, feeling it was my turn to jab a finger, if you hadn't made her, she wouldn't have had to use me. I clarified, surprised by my courage to engage.

Kenny stared in disbelief.

She fuckin' planted evidence, you silly turd. She put that t-shirt in the river.

I knew that. I also knew that she was pushed as far as she could go.

If you really want to know, Kenny, everything that's happened is your fault.

There, I said it out loud, accusing Kenny, who looked like a holey triangle. He was gaping at me speechless.

You made the ******* decisions. You destroyed everything!

The sense of freedom I felt after I uttered those words was unbelievable. I couldn't stop myself now and I screamed, careless of the world around me.

What did you expect her to do? Go home to her husband and pretend nothing ever happened? Well, guess what, you idiot, everything changed. He didn't want her!

With that, I stopped shouting. Finally, I had said everything I wanted to say. We were very quiet now; I drove, Kathryn slept and

Kenny continued staring. We mulled things over in our heads, and after a good deal of thinking, Kenny muttered that Kathryn's marital situation had nothing to do with us. We only wanted the money.

I could have cried. It had everything to do with us. We put temptation in Rupert's path.

Tapping his forehead, Kenny told me to get off my soap box. People make their own decisions. Temptation? What the fuck is that? He demanded. You just fuckin' resist it and if you don't know any better, you bear the consequences.

For a while, we drove without saying a word. Then Kenny, out of the blue, said he saw our mother.

Lives in (here he named a town not far from ours). She has a new kid.

Wow. Imagine that. A new child. Remembering mum rolling drunk on the lino, cackling to herself, I shuddered, feeling sorry for the kid. Poor little bastard.

What is it?

Kenny scratched his head.

I don't know. A girl, I think.

A girl. A little sister. I tried to picture her. Would she be tall like me or, or a bit like Kenny?

Kenny shrugged.

I didn't see her. Mum wouldn't let me. Said she just put her down for a nap. Kenny proceeded to tell me that our mother had changed. Considerably. Gave up drinking. Cleans the house and everything.

I felt myself nodding, picturing the everything we never got. A hot meal. Clean clothes. Nap in the afternoon. Still, for the kid's sake, I felt relieved.

How did mum take it?

I meant the news about Kenny. I'll bet she cried. After all, he was— used to be—her favorite.

She took it well. She cried a bit and even apologized for, you know—Kenny made an invisible circle in the air with his finger which, I supposed, represented our life—and then the kid stirred in the bedroom so she shooed me out.

Kenny gave a shrug. She'll be all right, mate. Time heals all wounds.

Hey! Clapping his hand on my shoulder, Kenny smiled as if he just remembered something good. I saw your rabbit. Fat old thing, lives the life of Riley. Has a missus and a bunch of little rabbits.

That was good news. I perked up, asking all sorts of questions about Fluffy, which Kenny was most happy to answer. We sat there grinning at each other, Kenny cackling like he used to when he was alive and me bubbling under the surface like a happy fart, celebrating Fluffy's good fortune. I felt so happy I wanted to pee; a song popped into my head and I whistled it from beginning to end. From the windscreen Kenny grinned, singing along and cracking his knuckles to the beat. We were having a great time. Kenny insisted on taking the lead halfway through the song. It was hilarious because Kenny had been an atrocious singer when he was alive, and he was no better now.

After we finished the singing, Kenny tweaked my ear for the last time ever. Then he looked me straight in the eye and told me the truth.

I left you behind to clean up my mess because I knew you could. I knew you would do the right thing and you didn't let me down. You let her go.

Now I got my feeling. The warmth, the unimaginable feeling of love and acceptance that I had always longed for now flooded me from head to toe, extinguishing all my frustration. I had never felt so at peace in my life as I did now. I wanted to say to Kenny that he could have stayed. I meant to explain how we would have released Kathryn, leaving together without the money, just us and the girls. With me driving, nobody would have died. But I was so choked up I couldn't get any of it out.

Kenny waited patiently behind me. He continued to redefine,

saying that he got what he deserved. Then he gave my shoulder a gentle squeeze, his fingers melting into my shirt like soft butter. In the windscreen, the sombrero was back on his head, pushed deep into his face the way I would always remember him. We smiled at each other; I cried and Kenny showed his big teeth for the last time. Then, just before he disappeared, he gave me the thumbs up.

Be good. And with these words, he faded away. When I turned around, the seat behind me was empty.

40

Like a lotus rising from the murky depths of the muddy swamp, day forty-three begins to unfold, when along come a few moments which in hindsight we should have cherished. I am seeing, thinking, wishing, and thus I am influencing the consciousness inherent equally in all life, which is all the things that happen. It stands to reason then that to remove the consciousness is to cease to be. However it is not so, for as long as I am, she continues to exist within myself. If you accept me, I will continue to exist, if only in your imagination. Accept.

On the fifteenth day of the seventh lunar month, the gates of Hell are thrown open. The Good Brethren: the murderers and the murdered, the childless and those who die by their own hand are allowed out into the world of the living where their hungry ghosts swirl around the earth, looking to make mischief. To appease these troubled souls, one must bring offerings to their graves.

To her grave, I bring mango. I cut it into pieces to make the shape of a lotus. I work diligently, carefully carving up the fruit and when I'm done, a feeling of wellbeing spreads from my heart like unconditional love. I am confident that Lien will be pleased.

I place the fruit at her feet and stand there with the knife in my hand and my face turned towards the heavens, patiently waiting for a sign.

I love you, Mai Lin. Her whisper is as soft as her skin. She is very close. So close, she could spoon me if she chose. I shut my eyes and see her as she used to be. Breathing, laughing, living. We are whores. We speak English funee … her words echo inside me, chiming prettily, swaying like paper lanterns in the breeze. We have reached the end of the line.

I am not afraid, I say to her. I want to become.

She comes swooping. She guides me as I make the first incision into my flesh, the pain filling me with hope. I will be done with my guilt. I will be done. I feel myself growing lighter, and I cut and cut and finally, fiiiiiiiiiiiiiiiinalleeeeee I see Them rising out of the fog.

41

They put me in jail straightaway. I was in shock at first and questioned everything, but my lawyer advised me to be patient. I was denied bail because I was deemed a flight risk, and as there was nothing he could do about that, the best thing would be to get settled in. He told me we'd most certainly go to trial, and that my chances of acquittal, what with all that compelling evidence and my fraudulently selling the house, were at best limited, but as my trial was months away, there really was no point worrying too much. There was nothing either of us could do.

It'll all come out in the wash, he concluded cheerfully, his jovial fat face beaming as he winked at me from across the glass partition. For the rest of our allotted time he sat there looking as if he had not a care in the world, chatting to me about the weekend sports. Anyone else in my position would have been concerned about where things were going. Perhaps even requested a new lawyer. But I knew I wouldn't. Because essentially this stupid fellow was right even though he didn't know it; there was no point in worrying because I would be found guilty on all counts when the time came. How did I know this? Simple. I had worked out what happened.

I worked it out one starry night as I sat smoking on my bunk, thinking about Kathy. Slowly, bit by bit, things made sense to me.

About the kidnappers, I had been wrong; the old Germans had had no hand in it, but the young hooligan did. Only no one believed me.

Where's the evidence? The cops laughed, nudging each other, when I mentioned the funny shoe. They made jokes until the fat cop suddenly stepped forward and smashed his fist on the desk in front of me.

Everyone knows about the funny shoe. He leaned towards me, abruptly ceasing to laugh. Of course we know, we are aware, that you found a footprint in your garden.

He glared at me, breathing his foul breath into my face. I glared back and if it wasn't for the other cop, we would have gone on glaring till the cows came home.

Perfectly innocent, the other cop piped up.

Standing across the desk from me, his head nearly touched the ceiling. He was dressed in green, and as he waved his silly arms about, he reminded me of a giant beanstalk like the one in the fairytale.

The boy was there to look at the house you tried to sell, the cop announced, bending slowly down until he was level with the fat cop's head. With their hands clasped behind their backs, they glared at me from across the desk, looking like footmen waiting for instructions.

The house you had no right to sell, the thin cop said, dropping his voice to a dramatic whisper. With every word he uttered, his head crept forward a little more until our noses almost touched. There the cop stopped, expecting me to respond. I had nothing to say. I only wondered how long it would take before the man collapsed. I calculated he could hold the pose another couple of minutes before the strain on his back would prove too much.

The cops exchanged meaningful glances. They straightened up and with their arms crossed and their legs wide apart, rocked back and forth on their heels.

Tell us about the house.

I breathed a sigh of relief. Here finally was something we could work on. I had one question to ask before I could tell them anything else. I could never work out how Kathy's mother found out that I was selling the house. She lived interstate, and I only advertised in the local rag. So how did she know?

The cops looked at me the way all cops look at you one time or another.

How did she find out? I repeated, my heart palpitating with renewed hope that I could prove my innocence. Who told her?

The cops rocked on their heels, betraying not a glimmer of thought in their expressions. Eventually, the fat cop clicked his dentures.

You're a clever boy. Figure it out.

Pleased with his joke, he gave a huge guffaw, which stopped him rocking. And then, as abruptly as he erupted, he shut up. Looking down at me through his narrow piggy eyes, he nodded and pulled over a chair from the side of his desk, spun it around and straddled it as if it were a horse. A brief silence descended upon the room; everyone kept quiet except for a fly buzzing at the window. I sat with my head bowed and my hands in my lap, trying to come up with an explanation, and the cops remained still. Then the tall thin cop left to get something to eat and while he was gone, the fat cop and I had a conversation.

You killed your wife, the cop said, reaching into his breast pocket for a toothpick.

Where is the body? I replied.

Staring at the wall above my head, the cop chewed a while.

You tell me.

Now it was my turn to guffaw.

I don't know because I didn't kill her.

The cop chewed without expression.

It'll turn up.

We sat there staring at each other, the cop chomping on his toothpick, and me looking at him.

You killed your wife and disposed of her body in the river, the cop said after a long pause.

I shrugged, feeling my energy ebb.

I told you my wife was kidnapped. I don't know why but she was.

Where is the note?

I threw it out.

Why didn't you call us?

It said not to.

Why didn't you pay the ransom?

I didn't have the money.

The cop suspended the chomping and leaned forward towards me.

So you tried to get the money by selling the house. The way he was looking at me, I knew he was trying to trip me up.

No, I replied truthfully. I tried to sell the house because I thought my wife was dead and I wanted to get away.

The cop appreciated my honesty.

That's why you told people she was on holidays.

I nodded. Yes.

And that's why you called her mother Monday morning. To tell her about the holidays. You couldn't risk her finding out that her daughter was missing so you told her yourself.

I shook my head.

I didn't call her.

The cop's eyebrows shot up. He looked at me with something like pity in his eyes.

There's no use denying it. We've pulled your phone records. You called her and that's how she got suspicious.

It was at this point that I decided to come clean about Zelda.

I called no one. I spent the night with my mistress.

The cop was so surprised that he took the remains of the toothpick out of his mouth. He asked for Zelda's details and said he'd look into it, and the interview was terminated. Well, not as such because the whole exchange was off the record anyway; what with the other cop gone on a break and my lawyer stuck in traffic on the other side of town.

The cop went to phone Zelda. In no time at all he was back, looking grim.

You have no mistress. The lady says you're a business associate.

I blinked in surprise, unable to formulate a response.

The cop continued. She says she bought pool stuff from you. Had receipts to prove it, and all of her staff vouch for her word. Nobody saw anything but a business relationship.

The cop looked at me for explanation. I felt completely betrayed, but then I thought of something that could prove that Zelda was lying.

What about the money? I asked the cop, who reacted as if he didn't know what I was talking about.

What money?

The money she gave me. The money I spent at the club.

The cop shook his head in protest. None of it checks out. Proprietor Wong remembers you nursing one drink the whole night. You spent no money there.

I shrugged. I sighed. I might have made an exasperated hand gesture. I don't know. I was tired.

I did not spend money at the bar. I told you where it went.

The cop kept shaking his head.

There's no proof. The girl's dead.

I know, I said. Ask the other one. Janelle is the one I regularly paid.

The cop sighed.

She too is deceased.

I remained silent, not knowing what to make of it.

When did she die? I finally asked. How?

She committed suicide not long after her friend's funeral, the cop replied, regarding me distastefully. I could tell he disapproved of my remaining perfectly calm. I suppose I should have felt something, some kind of regret or loss, but all I felt was curiosity. I was curious to know how it came to pass. How did she do it? I opened my mouth to ask.

Regardless, the cop put up a fleshy palm to stop my query, I can't find a single person who saw any money change hands.

I was thinking. Maybe the teenager knew something. I started to tell the cop, but he didn't let me finish.

We checked him out. There is no proof he had ever been to your house before the house inspection. The Germans vouch for him. On the day of the inspection, their truck broke down and that's why he drove them to your house. It was a complete coincidence.

It couldn't be a coincidence, I said, beginning to feel ill. Did you question him?

The cop shook his head.

He's gone.

Aha! I cried out. He's guilty! It was him, I know it. He took my wife, did God knows what with her and when he didn't get the money, he panicked and ran.

The cop stared.

No. He shook his head one more time. He left for a different reason altogether. His brother died a week ago. There was nothing but bad memories to hold him here.

I couldn't believe what he was telling me.

Did you go to his house?

I started to explain that it was probably where he had kept her, and if he did keep her there, there would be evidence.

We did, the fat cop replied, hesitating.

I took it as a good sign.

The house burned down, the cop said, looking straight at me.

I was completely floored.

The house burned down?

The cop kept looking at me, the look of pity in his eyes quite overwhelming.

To the ground, he replied just as the door opened and the other cop walked in.

42

We crossed the border in a somber frame of mind. Feeling at first a sense of relief, I talked to Phoebus about my travel plans, but he remained withdrawn. In the end, his mood affected me and I dozed off.

When I woke up, we were a long way away from our troubles. We drove relentlessly all through the night, making only a couple of stops, once for a pee break and the other time to fill the truck with petrol. Phoebus got out but I remained in the cab. Waiting for Phoebus to return, I switched on the radio.

We made front page, so to speak. The news was all about me and Rupert and the kidnap.

The body, the reporter said, has not as yet been found, but divers have been engaged to search the river and police are confident of a positive result. I switched the radio off, feeling as if a great weight had been lifted from my shoulders.

It's come off then, I thought to myself. I could not help but feel happy, imagining a great many pleasant things.

I imagined Rupert, grumbling and sweating, folding laundry somewhere in a correctional facility in the company of other grumbling sweating men. I saw him spending his Sundays strolling in the sunshine in the confines of the exercise yard, and not a golf club in sight. There he is in line for his feed, a bowl and a spoon in his hands, mourning the loss of his freedom. There is no Rosetta to admire, no heart-shaped cleavage to ogle.

This then was the moment where I laugh out loud. I'd pulled off the perfect plan.

43

My lawyer never showed up that day. His car broke down and he couldn't get a lift. The cops weren't troubled by this turn of events; they sent me back to my cell where I fell upon my bunk and fell asleep the moment my head hit the pillow.

Hello, Rupert. He stood in front of me dressed in blue overalls and a white and red striped t-shirt. The visor of His dark blue cap shielded His eyes but I knew He was looking straight at me. Extending His hand He smiled, revealing perfect teeth.

You're not very tall, I whispered as I shook it.

His smile broadened.

Jesus. I mentally smacked myself in the forehead.

Arms by His side, God stood in front of my bunk where I sat staring open-mouthed; taken by surprise, I marveled at the firmness of His handshake. Reading my thoughts, God gave a chuckle.

No, He inclined His head, I am not see-through.

He stood in front of me, calm and composed while I sat there wishing I had a pencil to chew on. Out of the back pocket of His overalls, God pulled an HB 2, which He handed to me.

You're not real, I whispered. You can't be, I said out loud as I shifted to make room for Him to sit down. When He sat down, the bed creaked

242 ■ IVANA HRUBÁ

under His weight.

God placed His palms on His knees and leaned forward.

That's neither here nor there. Smiling, He produced a dimple in His left cheek.

I believe, He winked, you have a question.

I did. I did have a question. However, I never really thought I would be in this position. I said, can I get you something? I really didn't know why I said that. After all, I had nothing to offer. A glass of water? I whispered. A fag?

Declining with a gentle shake of His flame-colored shaggy mane, God never stopped smiling. He patiently listened to my tirade about Kathy and the kidnap. Being nervous, I was all over the place and I made no sense even to me; I told Him about everything, but I am afraid I gushed a bit, as I got used to Him sitting next to me. I even apologized for Kathy, the way she always took His name in vain, and I swore to Him I never did. Strictly speaking, it was not true. God, of course, knew this. Smiling, He held up His palm to stop my rambling.

Ask, He politely requested.

I took a deep breath and closed my eyes.

Who called Kathy's mother? I asked, hoping with all my heart that He would tell me. Moments ticked by punctuated by nothing more than my heartbeat until I realized that He was no longer there.

Indeed, when I opened my eyes, I was alone in my cell. It was dark. Silvery columns of moonlight streamed through the bars in the window onto my bunk, making it plain that I had dreamt the whole thing. Feeling the need to clear my head, I reached under my pillow for my canvas bag where I kept the tobacco and the papers, and I rolled me a fag.

Working carefully, I hummed a tune, thinking about the question that dogged me in my sleep, and determined to figure out the answer on my own.

Was it Zelda?

Obviously Zelda was wise to the whole thing. Maybe she thought

I had killed Kathy so she took my keys while I slept, got into my house and called the old hag.

But why? Why would Zelda do that?

After all, I reasoned, Zelda was in love with me, or at least had been at the time. One would have thought she might have been glad to have Kathy out of the way. Clearly it wasn't to her advantage to call Kathy's mother. Deciding that Zelda knew nothing until the cops told her, I considered a different angle. Perhaps when the cops told her that I killed Kathy, she panicked. It was conceivable that she thought she'd be charged as an accomplice, and that's why she denied she ever knew me intimately because she was afraid that she might be implicated in the murder.

Thinking about Zelda, I fiddled with the drawstring of my bag, pulling at the opening with my index fingers. Then, quite suddenly, another thought came to my mind.

Was it the teenager?

It might have been. After all, he knew his way around my house. He was there to kidnap my wife the week before and knew how to gain entry.

What reason would he, of all people, have to call Kathy's mother?

It made no sense. He was the kidnapper, for God's sake, and a murderer too. It couldn't possibly be him.

Mulling over the possibilities, I continued playing with the string when unexpectedly the answer popped into my head.

It was Kathy!

I felt as if I'd been hit with a sledgehammer, out of breath and about to spill my gut. I doubled over, pulling the string so hard that it broke.

Of course it was Kathy. She was the one who called her mother, it had to be her.

The thought struck me that I was being played and that, at any moment, the door would open and Kathy would come barging into the room and explain this as an insane joke. Yes, a joke, an elaborate set-up to test my devotion, a test that I had failed.

I looked hopefully towards the door but when the lock failed to rattle, I knew she wasn't going to come. I realized that I was not being tested. No, I was being punished. Kathy found out about my infidelities: Lesley, Zelda, Janelle and all the others, and she staged the kidnap to punish me.

Funnily enough, now that I had figured it out, I felt better. The thought of Kathy being alive filled me with surprisingly good humor. I even felt something akin to excitement or admiration for my wife, which went against everything I ever experienced by her side, for Kathy had been one colossal bore.

I put the broken string in my pocket and the bag back in its place under my pillow, and then I lay down on my bunk. I thought about Kathy, wondering what she was doing, if she was thinking about me. I hoped she was. Perhaps there was a chance I might one day be rescued, I thought, casting one last hopeful look towards the door. However, deep down I knew I had a long time to wait. I decided that the best thing to do was to resign myself to my fate. Finally at peace, I lit a cigarette and lay quietly watching the stars until sleep came over me once more.

44

I have one regret. I wish I could see Rupert's face when he figures out he was nothing but a pawn in the game. As is, I will have to be content to imagine our conversation.

Oh, Rupert, did you honestly think you would walk away? No, that was never going to happen.

I've known about everything from the beginning. Her, her and her as well. For a long time I died a little more each day, imagining that I was not worthy of your love, imagining I was an empty shell, a speck of dust irritating you. You sneezed and I was blown away into oblivion. For a long time, I did nothing, too numbed with pain to even think about anything but my own suffering. Then one day, I took a drive up the mountain. I stopped at the roadhouse where I found out there was something worth seeing, hidden near the summit. A tranquil paradise of such beauty it had to be seen to be believed, the strange-looking fellow who had cleaned my windscreen told me. Feeling the need for beautiful scenery, I was keen to go and so I paid the fellow well for his secret.

Deep in the mountain I found nothing. At first I cursed this evil trickery, then cried to Me: I am such a loser! Why didn't I see it coming?

Me had nothing to offer apart from sighs and platitudes. What goes around comes around. The day ended unhappily.

Back at home, our life went on without change. You, Rupert, always were a man with a vision. I saw it in the way you stood in front of the mirror adjusting your tie, whistling to yourself, imagining yourself to be a free and wealthy man. It was all there in that movie you played in your mind: sex, money, power, greed. And Kathy was nowhere to be found. I patiently waited for you to remember me, hoping and praying that one day we could be happy. But everything turned out differently. The day came when my heart failed to leap at the sight of you.

After that, it was surprisingly easy to make the decision. I would teach you a lesson you would never forget, my love. I worked out my plan, and once I did, everything was simple. For twenty thousand, Kenny from the roadhouse agreed to play his part. I dare say he was imagining a straightforward transaction.

Your husband loves you, doesn't he? Kenny enquired, wanting to make sure this was a good piece of business. His fishy eyes watched me closely from underneath his sombrero.

Of course, he does, I replied, showing him the social blurb from the races to lay his mind at rest. Twenty thousand is no problem. My husband will pay for my release.

We shook on it. Judging by the glint in his glassy eye, I suspected the man had his own mental movie involving sex, money, power and greed. I wasn't alarmed; his self-interest would serve me well.

In hindsight, everyone's self-interest has served me well, I think to myself now, feeling a sense of closure and a desire to be done with Rupert the way I had finished with Me. To put it simply, I hope to be delivered. I give it a try.

Goodbye, Rupert, I say quietly and turn from the window to look at the boy, who keeps his eyes on the road. Ahead of us, a glorious day is about to dawn, heralding the start of my new life.

Stop here, Phoebus, I say to the boy and he obeys me without a word. He pulls over to the side of the road and turns off the ignition. Determined not to waste any more time, I take the twenty thousand out of my bag, meaning to give it to Phoebus. The boy looks stunned, stammers and pushes my hand away, but I insist that he keep the lot.

This is what we've agreed, I say to him. This is your reward for helping me frame Rupert. For letting me burn down your house. You promised you would take it. I grab his hand and wrap his fingers around the money. Finally he stops resisting and places the package on the dashboard, avoiding my eyes. At this moment I feel very guilty. I wish I had the courage to tell him everything. Knowing the truth would make him feel so much better. To know that Kenny didn't kidnap me, that he didn't do anything wrong, would make Phoebus a very happy boy. Sure, Kenny's not entirely blameless—he got greedy on me and things got complicated—but as far as the kidnap goes, it was all my idea. But I can't tell him. He might go crazy and blame me for Kenny's death. Who knows what he might do. Having come this far, I can't risk my freedom now. Not even for him, innocent as he is. I can't do it.

In a hurry to leave, I quickly peck him on the cheek. We say goodbye. I wish you well, I say to him. He nods and we smile at each other for the last time. I am free to go.

45

I told the cops the next day. My lawyer was present but he wasn't much use. Anyway, I disregarded his advice and told everyone I thought Kathy was alive and well, had planned the whole kidnap, and consequently I now expected them to look for her.

Aha, said the fat cop, looking at his colleague and my lawyer. All three of them exchanged meaningful glances. I could see that they did not believe me.

She found out about Zelda, I said.

The fat cop clicked his dentures. Now look here, he said, clasping his hands over his bulging stomach. Let's not get too excited. He rocked on his heels, a sure sign he wasn't taking me seriously.

I've slept at Zelda's house, I said, persisting with my explanation and telling them there would have to be evidence of that in her house.

Yes, yes, we did find evidence, the fat cop replied. Fibers in the living room, in the kitchen and in the bathroom. Just like you said, you came over with the pool hose, you had a coffee and used her bathroom.

I opened my mouth. I shut it. After all, what could I have said to convince him? That Zelda didn't want me sleeping in her marital bed until we were married? It seemed to me the cop was convinced of my guilt and nothing I said was going to change his mind. But I was determined to go down fighting.

I know Kathy called her mother from the house, I said and banged my fist on the table.

The cop stopped rocking.

No, she didn't. You did.

Glaring at me, he reiterated his story how I called the old hag to tell her that Kathy had gone on holidays.

Seeing I had his full attention, I decided to explain one more time why I didn't have to lie to my mother-in-law.

I lied to the gym people and at the library because I had to tell them something. I didn't have to tell Kathy's mother. She wasn't there and had no way of finding out that Kathy had been kidnapped.

It was true; I didn't have to tell her anything. Sure, Kathy had kept in touch with her but they didn't speak too often, so there was no need for me to lie to her. I had plenty of time to sell the house and leave before Kathy's absence became suspicious.

Aha, the cop said. But you advertised the house for sale, didn't you?

I nodded. Of course I advertised, I said, I wanted the house sold.

In response to my confession, the cop smiled, looking pleased with himself.

You were afraid that your mother-in-law would find out and that's why you gave her a story. You told her that you needed to sell the house to finance your wife's trip.

It was clear to me that no matter what I told them, the cops would not believe a word. Indeed, their sweat-stained mugs shone with self-righteousness and a good deal of smug stupidity, extinguishing all remnants of hope I had secretly harbored.

As a last resort, I told them about the money, the twenty thousand that went missing from my drawer. I told them it was Kathy who took it when she came back to the house to make the phone call to her mother.

Ah huh, the fat cop grunted, looking as if he had run out of patience. He pulled a hankie out of the hip pocket of his greasy trousers and mopped his sweating forehead.

You bought some clothes, didn't you?

I replied that I did. The cop shoved the soaked hankie back in the pocket and gestured to the thin cop, who came forth with a little notepad. Flipping it open, the fat cop made a show of moistening his thumb on his tongue before he began to read out loud.

A corduroy sports jacket, two thousand three hundred and eighty-five dollars; a leather waistcoat, seven hundred and fifty-nine dollars; raincoat, two hundred and twenty-five. Lifting his eyebrows in my direction, he turned the page and paused.

I shrugged, not sure where he was going with this.

The cop gave me a look of pity and resumed reading.

Shirts, seventeen hundred and twenty-nine dollars; underwear, socks, three hundred roughly; a double-breasted vested suit, five thousand, six hundred and seventy-five; another suit, four thousand five hundred and sixty-five; ties, two hundred roughly; winter coat, ridiculously expensive; diamond watch, twelve pairs of imported shoes. With one swoop of his fleshy arm, he flipped the notepad closed. Need I go on?

I got it now; those were the clothes Zelda had bought me. She had given me cash and sent me out shopping; a couple of times she shopped for me. I didn't keep receipts and neither did she, but the fact remained that my shopping spree amounted to precisely twenty thousand.

46

I walk briskly, keeping my eyes on the horizon. All around me, a beautiful day dawns and I feel free. For the first time in my life, there is nobody to tell me what to do. No Mother, no Rupert and most of all, no Me. I feel so light I could jump out of my skin, dissolve into thin air, become as transient as a thought. And this is how the rest of my life is going to be.

47

My lawyer came to see me one last time. He told me I was being transferred to another prison and that there was nothing to be done about that. We could appeal but it would be a pointless exercise, he warbled cheerfully into the phone from behind the glass partition. We parted amicably after chatting a while about inconsequential things. It was very pleasant. Just before he left, my lawyer asked me if I needed any warm clothes for my journey up north where the weather was generally much colder.

I waved him away. I'll be all right, I said. I've got me long johns and extra socks.

Indeed, Zelda's gift came in handy after all. It was as if she had foreseen I was going to end up here. I was suspicious, thinking she might have been involved in my downfall but resolved not to dwell.

The transfer went off splendidly. We stopped off twice, once for a pee break and the other time to pick up an inmate from another jail on route. The inmate was a blond giant with a wandering left eye. His name was Noah and he was very friendly. Noah told me that he too got done for murder, only in his case, they could not prove it.

They only proved the kidnap, Noah winked at me, making a silly joke which prompted me to declare my position.

I am innocent, I blurted out.

My confession had quite an effect on Noah. He laughed with some derision. Slapping his thighs, he threw his head back and laughed for a long time, snorting like a pig. When he stopped laughing, he gave me a word of advice.

A word of advice, he said, wiping his mouth on the sleeve of his prison tunic. In the future, you keep that to yourself. Then he turned away from me and fell asleep in the next instant.

I sat looking out the window, quietly watching the world pass me by. Outside, a cold wind blew, sweeping great gusts of dirt into the air heavy with moisture. The trees were aflame with color, but the sky was grey and sparrows flew low to the ground, heralding the start of autumn.

Staring at the bleak landscape, I thought of Kathy, remembering my past life with her. I went right back to the very beginning when we first met at the pub. Kathy had always talked about it, forever harping about how our eyes locked across the crowded room and how from that moment she knew we were meant to be together. I always nodded as if I agreed. Truth be told, I had been looking at the tall busty blonde behind her. The beautiful lady must have been near-sighted because she never responded to my invitation, my "bolt of lightning" stare, which eventually landed me with Kathy. I only ever had in mind a one-night adventure. We ended up getting married. Privately, I was at a loss to explain how that ever came about, but there you have it. It just shows: you can't let your guard down for one minute. From the moment we met, Kathy latched on and I was never able to shake her. Trapped and cornered, I did the only thing I could. I looked at the marriage from a financial point of view, figuring that, with Kathy's money and her simple nature, I could make myself comfortable. It worked until that stupid creature got herself kidnapped. Thinking about the chain of events that had landed me here, I quietly wondered whether I had been wrong about my wife, who now appeared to me cleverer than I previously gave her credit for.

She outwitted me. Plain and simple. Maybe if she had shown this attitude, this kind of backbone, things might have been different for us, and maybe I wouldn't have strayed. If Kathy had shown this kind of spark, we might have had interesting conversations instead of discussing her cat, her yoga, and everything else she had bored me with. We might have even broken the routine and saved our marriage. Well, what can I do about it now? Exactly. Anyway, who knows whether anything would have made a difference? We were just two people entangled in each other's lives, thrown together by fate.

Fate? In my old life, such a thought would never have entered my head. In my old life, I had foolishly believed I was in charge, needing no one to guide me. But things have changed. I am no longer master of my destiny. In my new life, my wishes play no significant part. This then is the moment where I regret everything. I should have just handled things the ordinary way. Called the cops and hoped for the best. Or got the money together and paid the ransom. Either way, I would have been better off. Kathy would have come home or she wouldn't have. No, I shouldn't have got greedy. I should have left it up to chance. Or God.

God came to me one night, dressed as a mechanic. I got all flustered when I first saw Him because, well, I thought I was in trouble, which really I was, only I didn't realize it at the time. So when He came over so pleasant and helpful, I was lulled. I even thought I had it over Him, what with me doubting and all; it was kind of ironic He appeared to me. He led me to believe it was all arranged for me to be acquitted at my hearing right after the charges were read. At the last minute, Kathy would make an entrance as living proof of my innocence. She would explain the situation, blaming no one but herself. As God is my witness, the astonished judge would say. With one knock of the hammer, he would dismiss the whole shebang and we'd all go home older and wiser. It didn't happen that way. I was set to stand trial and as I stood before the judge, I wondered whether I was missing something vital, something I had failed to understand. It was then it finally hit me, and I realized what He wanted me to know. You do unto others as you would have done unto you.

In hindsight, it was probably a good thing that Kathy didn't show up. It would have been awkward. She would have looked at me with those eyes, maneuvered me into a corner with them, pinned me against the wall and held me there by the throat until I told her the truth. And the truth is that I never loved her. She would have flown into a rage or worse, crumpled in a heap and cried. Either way, it would have been horrible.

Visualizing the scene I squirmed in my seat, thinking about life, about how much better off I used to be when I was prepared to bend the truth. I had led such an easy life. I never faced up to my responsibilities. I lied, cheated and manipulated my way day after day with no thought for anyone but myself. And perhaps, I reflected, now was not the time to change. What with the company I was heading for, I was possibly better off sticking to the old ways, but you see, in my heart I felt differently. I wouldn't say I got religion or what have you, I wouldn't say I was gearing up for a complete turnaround, but now that I found myself outmaneuvered, so to speak, it might be time to turn over a new leaf.

At this point, Noah woke up and began a different sort of conversation.

Out of the breast pocket of his shirt, he pulled a photograph which he handed to me across the space that separated us. A woman's face, once handsome but now faded, stared at me. Not bad, ah? Noah grinned. Well, I'd seen better, but I chose not to say. Instead, I nodded, lifting my eyebrows to show my appreciation. Pleased with my reaction, Noah put the photograph back in his pocket and told me about her.

They had met a few years ago. After reading about him in the local paper, she had tracked him down and they corresponded for a while, but after six weeks or so, Noah scratched his head, it became clear that they were meant for each other and she came to see him at the earliest opportunity, which really wasn't for another five months until he negotiated a visit for good behavior.

We're engaged, Noah proudly announced, ejecting a pile of snot out his nose onto the floor.

I congratulated him.

Of course, Noah said, leaning forward to inspect the snot, I still have three years, seven months and twelve days in the slammer but my girl is prepared to wait. He looked up at me expectantly. Feeling a response was required, I told him that he was lucky to have found her because generally a good woman was hard to find, to which Noah replied that she had loads of friends and if I wanted to, he could get me an introduction.

He took me by surprise. We stared at each other a while, and then Noah began to play with the snot, piling a little dust on top of it with his right foot, skillfully maneuvering the blob into an interesting shape with the tip of his boot. When he finished, he pulled up his feet and paid no more attention to it. I too shifted my gaze.

48

I walked happy as a lark, quietly humming to myself. Having left the main road, I now followed a winding creek deep into the woods. Birds chirped, the stream gurgled and my soul was at peace. This will be a good day, I thought to myself, enjoying the tranquility. I walked for a long time. Towards midday, I chanced upon a meadow full of clover. Surrounded by willows, it made for a perfect resting place.

I lay down on the soft grass and put my feet into the water. I might just have a little sleep.

Kathryn ...

The sound of my name penetrated my reverie like poisoned darts, and I opened my eyes to see Me standing in the middle of the meadow. She stood there with a traveling bag slung across her chest, a scarf to protect her neck, and a sun hat and sturdy walking boots. I was too stunned to speak. For a moment, we didn't. Me kept looking at me, staring me down with a determined frown, and I found my happy thoughts receding, seeping away like flood water through floorboards.

What are you doing here, Me?

Me didn't have to say a word. She stood quietly with folded arms, waiting.

What do you want? I asked uselessly. It was a useless question because we both knew what Me wanted. To destroy me. And she will. She will step in and order me around like she used to and I will be powerless against her. Me began to take off her traveling accessories. Seeing she clearly intended to stay I panicked, feeling an intense heat spread through my body. Inside my head, a torture chamber glowed. I lay spread-eagle on the flagstone floor. I could not move; I was clamped in irons bolted to the ground, rats crawled over my body, sniffing. Above me, a blade swung like a pendulum, closer with every swing. Soon it would rip my belly open.

Reading my thoughts, Me gave a sad smile. You've got it all wrong, Kathryn, she sighed, plonking herself right next to me. Do you honestly think it is me who's hurting you?

She looked at me with her big luminous eyes like pools of liquid gold. Eventually I will drown in there. But for now it's only him I see, ankles deep in that vast moonlit lake. The boy. So kind. Considerate. Blameless. Bringing the dinner tray, smiling. Taking out the bucket, filling up the bath. Comforting me. K–kathryn, you will be h–home soon. Then losing what's most precious to him. Oh, dear Me, what have I done?

Me narrows her scaly, fishy eyes and grins, showing colorful teeth as straight as piano keys. She pulls her sombrero down. Your husband loves you, right?

I scream.

49

Well, I am not going to lie; we didn't hug or weep on each other's shoulders when we said goodbye. I simply stopped the truck and she took out the twenty thousand she had promised me for helping her frame Rupert and handed the money over. She had a smirk on her face. For a moment I thought she might say something like nice working with you or who says crime doesn't pay, but of course, she said nothing that insensitive.

She put the money in my hand. Without counting, I placed it on the dashboard in front of me. It was in plain view but we were parked remote, and frankly, I didn't care who saw us. Looking at her for the last time I smiled. She seemed so at peace that I couldn't help but feel happy for her.

I wish you well. Kathryn leaned over to kiss me goodbye and her hair brushed my cheek. Her touch felt as light as a feather against my skin, and her hair, curling about her face, smelled of summer. I closed my eyes for an instant, imagining I was embracing and kissing her and she was promising to keep in touch. The real moment, of course, turned out different.

She jumped out of the truck and slammed the door, and after that I never saw her again. I didn't even see her walk away because she headed back towards the woods, so when finally I figured it out and looked in the side view mirror, she was gone.

I thundered down the highway like I had somewhere to go. I lit a joint, hollered, whistled and enjoyed the show, hoping that Kenny would turn up. He didn't and I was forced to change tactic. Slowing down to a mere wheeze, I squinted into the bright dawn, and it was then I finally saw him. Lounging on the sofa, dripping tomato juice all over his underpants, dealing a deck, laughing, shouting, cuffing me, my

Kenny dawned all around me.

Grinning from the windscreen, he was so close I could have pecked him with my nose. He was bareheaded and without his sombrero he looked younger, happier, or maybe it was just my imagination playing tricks on me.

Reading my thoughts, Kenny let out a snort, and out of thin air conjured up a three-cornered hat with a plume. For you, brave knight. Let the games begin.

Drawing my sword, I stood at the ready. We clashed, twirling around our tree, our blades gleaming in the sun. Kenny jumped on top of the crapper, screaming like a madman. Down, down with you, you dirty dog. Eventually, he let me win. I got him in the calf and he fell on the grass with a sigh. I'm dying. Tell my lady that I loved her. When he got up, the scenery changed and he was no longer bleeding. His sombrero pulled low, he stood with his legs apart, aiming his rifle at me. Injun, he muttered, you took my horse. In the end, we smoked a peace pipe, sprawling on the grass and basking in the glory of the brand new day. If only I could be that happy again.

Kenny faded on me with the first sunbeam. It hit my windscreen, dissipating him like a puff of smoke. This time, I knew he would never come back. His last words to me were, This is it, turd. You're on your own, and I knew he meant it. There was nothing left for me to do but to continue on my way to my new life.

I drove for a long time, thinking about what had happened and how I fit into it. I had only one desire: I wanted to become a good person and start my new life with a clean slate.

Finally, I figured out what to do to make a fresh start. I pulled up to the nearest petrol pump. The man behind the counter wasn't as nice as our man back home, but he was pleasant enough. I bought a pen, a sheet of writing paper, a big stiff envelope, the kind that has bubbles inside, and a postage stamp. I piled everything on the front seat in my truck, and seeing I was the only one in the parking lot, I decided to deal with the business right away. I wrote a note explaining everything that happened, and blaming no one but Kenny. It was what he wanted. That done, I had but one last thing to execute in memory of my brother. I put the note and the twenty thousand inside the envelope and sealed it tight. Having no idea where Rupert was, I addressed the package to the police station, care of the fat cop. He'd know what to do.

Windows down, I sat in the truck, watching the sun climb above the trees. In my head, things were beginning to take shape. Long time ago, I thought it was only people like me and Kenny who made bad decisions. I had been sure that other people, well-brought-up people, made the right choices. But clearly I was wrong. Kathryn came from a good home, and it seemed to make no difference. She had planned a cruel revenge and justified her actions by blaming everyone else for the break-up of her marriage. But did she really outsmart everyone? I sincerely hoped that my sending the money would prove otherwise.

I wish you well. Kathryn's last words had touched my heart. She had smiled at me and I had thought I would carry the memory of that smile with me forever. But now I knew that I wouldn't. I had only left her a few hours ago, but already I found her features too vague to recall. Madonna, warrior queen, Kathryn. In my mind, the three faces of Kathryn were seeping away like tide, leaving nothing but an impression in the sand.

ABOUT THE AUTHOR

Ivana Hrubá fled the Czech Republic in 1983 by crossing the Alps on foot. Ivana is now a teacher in Australia where she lives with husband Michael, sons Eamon and Kian and a menagerie of cuddly animals.

A Decent Ransom is her first adult novel.

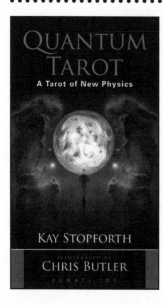

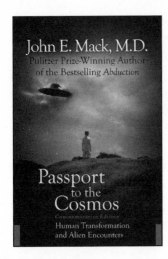

Passport to the Cosmos
Commemorative Edition: Human Transformation and Alien Encounters
■ **John E. Mack M.D.**

In this edition, with photos and new forewords, Pulitzer Prize–winner John E. Mack M.D. powerfully demonstrates how the alien abduction phenomenon calls for a revolutionary new way of examining the nature of reality and our place in the cosmos. "Fascinating foray into an exotic world. From Harvard psychiatry professor and Pulitzer Prize-winning author ... based on accounts of abductions." —*Publishers Weekly*

US$ 14.95 | Pages 368 | Trade Paper 6x9"
ISBN 9781601641618

Hide & Seek
How I Laughed At Depression, Conquered My Fears and Found Happiness
■ **Wendy Aron**

Hide & Seek shows how to tackle important issues such as letting go of blame and resentment and battling negative thinking. Instructive without being preachy, it is filled with humor and pathos, and a healthy dose of eye-opening insight for the millions who suffer from depression and low self-esteem.

US$ 14.95 | Pages 256 | Trade Paper 6x9"
ISBN 9781601641588

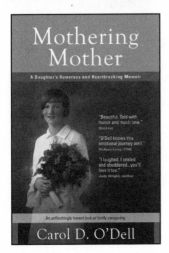

Mothering Mother
An unflinchingly honest look at family caregiving
■ **Carol D. O'Dell**

Mothering Mother is an authentic, "in-the-room" view of a daughter's struggle to care for a dying parent. It will touch you and never leave you.

"O'Dell portrays the experience of looking after a mother suffering from Alzheimer's and Parkinson's with brutal honesty and refreshing grace."—*Booklist*

US$ 12.95 | Pages 208 | Trade Paper 6x9"
ISBN 9781601640468

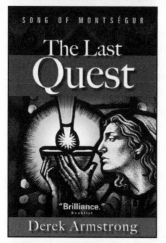

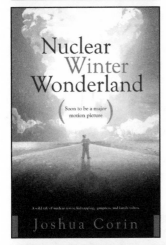
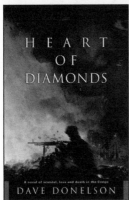
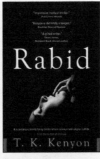
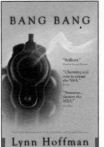

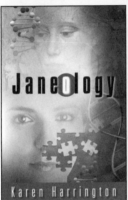
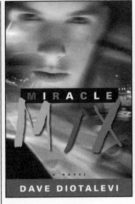

KÜNATI

Provocative. Bold. Controversial.

Kunati Book Titles

Available at your favorite bookseller

www.kunati.com

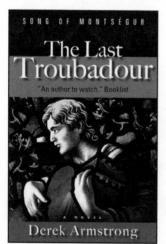

The Last Troubadour
Historical fiction by Derek Armstrong

Against the flames of a rising medieval Inquisition, a heretic, an atheist and a pagan are the last hope to save the holiest Christian relic from a sainted king and crusading pope. Based on true events.

■ "... brilliance in which Armstrong blends comedy, parody, and adventure in genuinely innovative ways." —*Booklist*

US$ 24.95 | Pages 384, cloth hardcover
ISBN-13: 978-1-60164-010-9
ISBN-10: 1-60164-010-2
EAN: 9781601640109

Recycling Jimmy
A cheeky, outrageous novel by Andy Tilley

Two Manchester lads mine a local hospital ward for "clients" as they launch Quitters, their suicide-for-profit venture in this off-the-wall look at death and modern life.

■ "Energetic, imaginative, relentlessly and unabashedly vulgar." —*Booklist*
■ "Darkly comic story unwinds with plenty of surprises." —*ForeWord*

US$ 24.95 | Pages 256, cloth hardcover
ISBN-13: 978-1-60164-013-0
ISBN-10: 1-60164-013-7
EAN 9781601640130

Women Of Magdalene
A hauntingly tragic tale of the old South by Rosemary Poole-Carter

An idealistic young doctor in the post-Civil War South exposes the greed and cruelty at the heart of the Magdalene Ladies' Asylum in this elegant, richly detailed and moving story of love and sacrifice.

■ "A fine mix of thriller, historical fiction, and Southern Gothic." —*Booklist*
■ "A brilliant example of the best historical fiction can do." —*ForeWord*

US$ 24.95 | Pages 288, cloth hardcover
ISBN-13: 978-1-60164-014-7
ISBN-10: 1-60164-014-5 | EAN: 9781601640147

On Ice
A road story like no other, by Red Evans

The sudden death of a sad old fiddle player brings new happiness and hope to those who loved him in this charming, earthy, hilarious coming-of-age tale.

■ "Evans' humor is broad but infectious ... Evans uses offbeat humor to both entertain and move his readers." —*Booklist*

US$ 19.95 | Pages 208, cloth hardcover
ISBN-13: 978-1-60164-015-4
ISBN-10: 1-60164-015-3
EAN: 9781601640154

Truth Or Bare
Offbeat, stylish crime novel by Richard Cahill

The characters throb with vitality, the prose sizzles in this darkly comic page-turner set in the sleazy world of murderous sex workers, the justice system, and the rich who will stop at nothing to get what they want.

■ "Cahill has introduced an enticing character ... Let's hope this debut novel isn't the last we hear from him." —*Booklist*

US$ 24.95 | Pages 304, cloth hardcover
ISBN-13: 978-1-60164-016-1
ISBN-10: 1-60164-016-1
EAN: 9781601640161

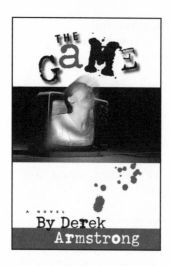

The Game
A thriller by Derek Armstrong

Reality television becomes too real when a killer stalks the cast on America's number one live-broadcast reality show.
■ "A series to watch ... Armstrong injects the trope with new vigor." —*Booklist*
US$ 24.95 | Pages 352, cloth hardcover
ISBN 978-1-60164-001-7 | EAN: 9781601640017
LCCN 2006930183

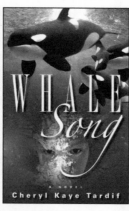

bang BANG
A novel by Lynn Hoffman

In Lynn Hoffman's wickedly funny *bang-BANG*, a waitress crime victim takes on America's obsession with guns and transforms herself in the process. Read along as Paula becomes national hero and villain, enforcer and outlaw, lover and leader. Don't miss Paula Sherman's one-woman quest to change America.
■ "Brilliant"
—STARRED REVIEW, *Booklist*
US$ 19.95
Pages 176, cloth hardcover
ISBN 978-1-60164-000-0
EAN 9781601640000
LCCN 2006930182

Whale Song
A novel by Cheryl Kaye Tardif

Whale Song is a haunting tale of change and choice. Cheryl Kaye Tardif's beloved novel—a "wonderful novel that will make a wonderful movie" according to *Writer's Digest*—asks the difficult question, which is the higher morality, love or law?
■ "Crowd-pleasing ... a big hit." —*Booklist*
US$ 12.95
Pages 208, UNA trade paper
ISBN 978-1-60164-007-9
EAN 9781601640079
LCCN 2006930188

Shadow of Innocence
A mystery by Ric Wasley

The Thin Man meets *Pulp Fiction* in a unique mystery set amid the drugs-and-music scene of the sixties that touches on all our societal taboos. *Shadow of Innocence* has it all: adventure, sleuthing, drugs, sex, music and a perverse shadowy secret that threatens to tear apart a posh New England town.
US$ 24.95
Pages 304, cloth hardcover
ISBN 978-1-60164-006-2
EAN 9781601640062
LCCN 2006930187